WASTELAND

Lynn Rush

*Donna —
it was great
meeting you
Lynn Rush*

Dana,
I was just
wanting you
know...

Crescent Moon Press

www.crescentmoonpress.com

Wasteland
Lynn Rush

ISBN: 978-1-937254-01-8
E-ISBN: 978-1-937254-00-1

© Copyright Lynn Rush 2011. All rights reserved
Cover Art: Jeannie Reusch
Editor: Steph Murray
Layout/Typesetting: jimandzetta.com

Crescent Moon Press
1385 Highway 35
Box 269
Middletown, NJ 07748

Ebooks/Books are not transferable. They cannot be sold, shared or given away as it is an infringement on the copyright of this work.

All Rights Are Reserved. No part of this book may be used or reproduced in any manner whatsoever without written permission, except in the case of brief quotations embodied in critical articles and reviews.

This book is a work of fiction. The names, characters, places and incidents are products of the writer's imagination or have been used fictitiously and are not to be construed as real. Any resemblance to persons, living or dead, actual events, locale or organizations is entirely coincidental.

Crescent Moon Press electronic publication/print publication: September 2011 www.crescentmoonpress.com

To God ~ Thank you for the gifts you've bestowed upon me, especially your grace.

To Charlie Boeyink ~ Thank you for loving me with your whole heart. You are more than I could have ever hoped for in a husband.

To Lynn Boeyink ~ I'm proud to share your name and call you Mom II. You're an inspiration.

I love you all.

ACKNOWLEDGEMENTS

This book wouldn't exist without the combined efforts of so many people. So thank you to the following: Cari Foulk, for her tireless encouragement; Steph Murray, my fantastic, knowledgeable editor; Ciara Knight, my wonderful critique partner who took the time to critique the entire novel for me early on; Kendall Grey & Rachel Firasek, who spend countless hours online with me, writing and editing; the FF&P critique group who are a constant source of support and encouragement; SavvyAuthors.com who provided the opportunity for me to meet my wonderful publisher; my family for offering me their unconditional love and support. A very special thank you to my best friend, Michele Trent, who was the one who encouraged me to "take the next step" on this journey to publication.

CHAPTER 1

Another two hundred and fifty years in solitary confinement might be worth the sacrifice if it meant spending five minutes alone with the beauty moving on the dance floor to this strange music.

"What are you staring at?" Gage's gravel-coated voice cut above the thumping bass.

I tore my gaze from the woman dancing and dropped it to the sweating glass of rum and Coke in my hand. "Nothing. Get away from me."

"Is that any way to treat your brother?"

An elbow dug into my side, clipping one of my ribs.

"I am *not* your brother." Two quick steps to the right, careful not to touch any of the humans milling about the bar, and I stood out of Gage's reach.

I surveyed the sea of thrashing bodies, searching for the woman I had no business finding. Overhead lights pulsed over the crowd. Inebriated movements morphed into a collection of uncoordinated jerks and twitches. Drunken couples groped one another in darkened corners. The stench of human sweat, ale, sour vomit and sweet drinks assaulted my senses.

So uncivilized.

My first night out of sensory deprivation, I shouldn't be in a place such as this. Too many temptations.

Scanning the crowd, I caught my gaunt reflection in the mirrored walls beside the DJ and looked away. I didn't need to be reminded of how two-hundred-and-forty-five years of isolation and endless darkness hollowed my full cheeks and morphed my silver eyes into a dull, lifeless gray.

Lifeless like me.

~ ☾ ~

A gigantic hand landed on my shoulder. "Come on, David." Even through the fabric of my cotton shirt the contact stung my skin, and I shrugged him off. "Don't."

Gage held his hands up in surrender. "Touchy, touchy. I haven't seen you in nearly two and a half centuries."

"You know I have been in confinement. Until about eight hours ago, I have not seen *anything* in almost two hundred and fifty years. Then Master pulls me out early and sends me *here*, my first night out."

Gage slid the loose strands of his strawberry blond hair behind his ear, his ebony eyes examining the crowd. "Yes, he does have an evil sense of humor."

"I am not laughing."

"I can tell it's a struggle for you, brother." He pointed toward my forehead. "I think a vein might burst soon."

I knocked his hand away. Despite being a six-hundred-year-old demon that didn't need to eat, Gage's six-foot-three frame didn't hide his padded stomach. Must have been indulging over the years.

At least a hundred bodies moved to the beat of the music on the crowded, half-circle dance floor. Most were scantily dressed women with long hair and shimmering skin. A waist-high mock-bar contained the flailing bodies to the designated area, and I propped my elbows on the wooden top, analyzing the crowd.

Gage laughed. "You're out five years early. Better than the full sentence, right?"

There she was again. Eyes closed, arms raised toward the ceiling, as if paying homage to the music gods, she swayed to the slow tempo. The ruby red, silk dress clung to the contours of her firm body. Her narrow hips swished doing a slow, erotic belly dance just for me. A thin layer of perspiration glistened on her skin, reflecting the flashing white, red, and neon green lights.

My breath hitched.

Beauty of such magnitude belonged in the Garden, not a place such as this. Long, stick-straight blond hair rippled down her back, bare, save the four thin straps securing her miniscule garment.

~ ☾ ~

"So, David, where is the Mark?" Gage's raspy voice snapped my concentration from memorizing the woman's delicate curves.

No use admiring something I could never have. Because if I did, I'd lose the little humanity the demon raging inside me hadn't yet sliced apart.

"I haven't seen the Mark yet." I looked away from the woman and forced myself to face Gage. "What are you doing here, anyway?"

"Checking up on you. Making sure you're doing what you're supposed to be doing."

Released from captivity mere hours and already Master had assigned me a shadow. He knew I hated being his runner, but to send a six hundred-year-old demon to keep the leash around my neck cinched. That was new.

"Why not the neophyte he usually sends to babysit?"

A growl emanated from Gage, and his jaw muscles twitched.

With the sting of my recent imprisonment still fresh, I would procure my Mark, young Jessica Hanks, and bring her to Master as contracted.

But I would take my time. So much had changed since my incarceration. Many things to learn.

I pushed away from the railing and wove past a group of three women, reminding myself to keep my eyes forward. No distractions. I'd been deprived of stimulation so long, a simple touch, especially a woman's, threatened to set off my demon. He'd already started clawing my chest to get out and devour the flesh these women so readily exposed.

I ground my molars, willing my demon to settle.

Clanking glass from behind me snared my attention. People congregated near the massive, wooden bar, whistling at the two men spinning bottles and tossing them in the air while they mixed drinks.

I turned back to the sea of people.

"A lot has changed during the time you've been in darkness, David." Gage waved his hand at the twitching herd. "Look at these women. They're half dressed, flaunting their bodies like whores."

~ ☾ ~

He stated the obvious. *Like I couldn't see all that lay before me.* My body throbbed with temptation. I sucked an iced cube from my drink to quench the fire building in my mouth.

The dark, claustrophobic room closed in on me. Probing lights seared my brain. Heat steamed the room, sweaty bodies prancing around the dance floor fanning the flame. I spied a vacant spot at the railing, and set my drink down on the shiny, wooden surface.

Gage slapped my back and stood beside me. "You *could* be tempted. I'm here to help."

"I'm sure that's all you're here for."

True, I'd never been to the state called Arizona. The state hadn't been unionized before my imprisonment. Gage might help me fit into this new world. I couldn't even figure out the cellular phone device I'd been given. Unbelievable how something so small did so much.

A dull throb made its way up the base of my skull. The bright lights sent a wave of nausea rolling over me.

"What do you know about your Mark?"

"Not a lot. Master sent me here, claiming she would be at this tavern. No picture. Nothing other than a name and an age. That isn't much to go on, Gage." I clasped a hand behind my neck and worked at the bulging knots.

My stomach roiled with hunger, but the loud music muffled its cries. Several more feasts, coupled with my demonic healing, and my human muscles would soon return to normal. Maybe then the aches and kinked muscles would work themselves out.

Gage gulped his drink and grimaced.

"What is so special about Jessica Hanks?"

He slammed his empty glass next to my elbow and drops of icy water splashed my bare arm. "That doesn't concern you. Does it?"

Hmmm. I struck a nerve.

I turned and scanned the crowd once more. The building trapped the stench of sweat and sugar between its cement walls. Bright lights and a subtle fog wove around the two-story interior. A loft overlooked the room, and people

~ ☾ ~

lounged on chairs and couches up there.

"Gage, we have no idea what she looks like. It shall take some time."

"The Seers saw the mark on her back. It will identify her easily enough the way these women dress these days."

"True." But having to look at all these beautiful women would test my resolve to keep my demon at bay.

"Not that I'm complaining, I rather enjoy the view." Gage glanced at me. "You could too if you would just relax and give in."

Surprising warmth grazed my right arm. Like lightning zapping my skin, I flinched. A short brunette stood mere inches away, her dark, sultry eyes fixed on me.

"I'm sorry." Her full, shiny lips curved into a crooked smile. "Didn't mean to scare you."

I dipped my head, acknowledging her apology and turned my back to her. The image of her ivory flesh bulging over the cloth of her plunging neckline burned into my brain, and I shut my eyes. The gesture did nothing to purge the image from my conscious.

My heart slammed against my ribs. My demon thundered, wanting out. *Take her.*

"Need a refill?" The woman's husky voice ignited a fire at the base of my spine.

Gage stood beside me, arms crossed over his chest, a grin filling his face. He would love for me to fold under the temptation of these women. To give in meant turning full demon.

I must stay strong.

A balmy hand rested on my forearm. I pivoted from her grip, sending a glare I hoped would discourage her, despite how much I fancied the feel of her soft skin.

The girl rolled her eyes. "Hey, I was just checking to see if you needed a refill." She palmed a round tray, on which sat a small pad of paper. She held a writing utensil in her other hand.

"Oh. You are the barmaid."

"Barmaid?" Another eye roll. "So, do you need a refill or what?" She pointed to the drink in my hand with her pen.

~ ☾ ~

Gage snickered. Her spicy perfume assaulted my nostrils and tickled the back of my throat. I bit back a cough. Between the flashing lights, ear-piercing music, and scantily dressed females dancing, I was close to becoming unhinged. Probably what Master wanted to happen.

"No. I am fine, thank you, ma'am." Two long strides carried me six feet from her. I squeezed the icy glass of liquor in my hand, hoping it would cool my skin.

Another stroke of warmth set me afire. I found myself near the entrance to the dancers, surrounded by soft, fair-skinned females, swaying their arms in my direction.

The glass slid from my hand and crashed to the hardwood floor but I never heard it land over the music. My breath came in short gasps as five women encircled me. My heart couldn't have pounded harder had I faced seven legions of demons in battle. Lights flashed in my eyes, and my vision tilted. Hyperventilation cinched my lungs.

"Hey, baby." A woman gyrated against my leg, her silky dress riding up her thighs.

Hands kneaded my backside. "Wanna dance?" another voice breathed.

Slender fingers grazed my chest. Despite the layer of protection my black, cotton t-shirt provided, the touch singed my skin like a branding iron. I snatched the frail wrist and pushed it away. My body stiffened. I leaned sideways to locate Gage. He stood next to the railing, his body convulsing with laughter. If I survived this sea of wicked temptation, I would kill him.

"Excuse me, please, madam," I said. "Pardon me."

My voice cracked like those kids in the prepubescent TV shows Master's minions made me watch on the plane ride from New York to learn the culture. I was four hundred years old. I didn't need this.

"Please. Let me through, ladies." I could have ground my molars to dust my jaw clenched so tight. My demon's nails sliced my chest from inside. Weak from my punishment, I wasn't sure how much longer I could hold him at bay.

The circle of women tightened. A curvy body flattened against my back, another to my side. Desire rippled through

~ ☾ ~

me, and my body quaked. Something rubbed against the front of my denim jeans. A hand with red-painted fingernails. I moved away, but the wall of blazing, supple bodies blocked my escape.

Curse Master for throwing me into this pit of temptation.

I held my hands up, scared to shove them too hard for fear I'd hurt them, but the demon inside me roared, pulverizing my insides in demand for his pleasures. I bit my cheek hard, the metallic taste of blood oozing into my mouth. I curled my fingers into my palms, preventing the black claws—*his* weapons—from bursting through my fingertips.

"All right, ladies, that's enough," a high-pitched voice said. I couldn't locate the source.

A female grabbed my hand and jerked me through the sea of soft temptation. The fingers clutching my forearm singed my skin as we broke through the human wall.

My gaze followed the hand grasping mine, and I found an arm of smooth, light skin that led to a shoulder over which a thin strap of cranberry-red indented the flesh. My eyes followed the crimson fabric to the ample curves of her breasts. I snapped my focus to her face and shook from her grasp.

The woman I'd watched dancing smiled at me.

Blond hair cascaded over her shoulders like a waterfall. Strands clung to her glistening chest where the dress met her cleavage.

I checked my forearm to make sure I hadn't been charred.

"You okay? I saw the Jezebels grab you." The soft voice flowing from her full lips rivaled a harp. Harmonic. Soothing.

I knew then I'd been in solitary much too long. "Ah, yes. Thank you, ma'am."

"Ma'am?" She raised a pale brow and inched closer. The scent of lilacs washed over me. "Are you for real?"

I shut my eyes and drew in a deep breath. "Pardon me." I glanced back at the pack of women. They'd found another man to accost, but his smile indicated he appreciated the body bumping. Not that I didn't, but the feel of their soft bodies crushed against mine was too—

"They do that all the time. They're regulars."

~ ☾ ~

I willed myself to stay focused on the woman's face. She stood five-foot-ten, shoulders back, so we nearly stood at eye level. Such bright, vibrant green emeralds returned my stare. "Regulars?"

"They are."

"They do that often?" I could not understand what would possess a group of females to act in such an unbecoming manner.

She tilted her head and inhaled. The gesture alone lured my gaze down. Her soft curves, confined by the scarlet fabric taunted me. The demon's searing hunger for her pierced my chest.

I had to get out of this place. To hell with finding Jessica Hanks. If I gave in to this sudden immersion, I'd never see light again. But if I gave in, I could ravage this woman standing inches from me.

No. I will not.

I'd fought the temptation to turn for four centuries. I wouldn't break now.

The music's tempo slowed and transformed into a different, flowing song. Of course the melody was foreign to me, but the crowd fell into a hypnotic sway. Reminded me of standing on a ship at sea. The woman had led me to the dance floor before I realized we'd moved.

Like a dream, a cloud of smoke enveloped us. The lady in red brushed against me, her body igniting a fire not stoked in a quarter millennia. Her hand rested on my chest, and she gazed at me with her sea-green gems.

Muscles along her jaw twitched. Her nostrils flared. "Who—?" She broke eye contact and cleared her throat.

Did she sense the demon scratching at my insides to get to her?

"We're almost dancing," she said.

My arms hung like weighted oars at my side, and I inspected the other couples to see what to do with them. Many men had their arms draped around the women's waists, some had hands on their backsides, slowly stroking.

Too much. "Excuse me. I must take my leave."

"You do look a little sick."

~ ☾ ~

"I detest crowds."

She removed her hand from my chest. "Then you came to the wrong place, didn't you?" She winked, flicked her long hair over her shoulder and strode to the bar, weaving through the mass of people like a ballerina.

She leaned over the counter and talked to the barkeep. A tall man came over and rested his palm on the small of her back. She flinched, then a smile creased her face, and she wrapped her arm around his neck. I almost felt her arms on me instead, and the thought left me gasping for air.

A large, longhaired man with onyx eyes appeared before me.

"Getting a nice look, buddy?"

"Excuse me?"

"Time for you to leave," he shouted over the music as he shoved my shoulder.

I already knew it was long past time to leave, but to be told by an overgrown, arrogant human? *I think not.* I batted his hand away and snatched his fingers. Knuckles popped beneath my grip. Veins in his neck bulged, and his eyes widened.

"You do not tell me when to leave." The demon scratched at the surface of my heart, begging to be unleashed on this imbecile.

"I know what you are."

I leaned close. The earthy, foul stench of ale laced his breath. "Oh yeah?"

"Demon," he said.

"Then you should know better than to come at me like this, *Human*." I released his hand and backed away. I couldn't afford a challenge right now. Not while working the woman's succulent lilac scent out of my system.

The human shook out his hand and stepped forward like he intended to challenge me. A snarl streamed from my mouth, and my nails elongated. I let the talons dig into my palms.

Better mine than his.

He pointed his finger at me. "Stay away from my sister or I'll end you."

~ ☾ ~

The tips of my fangs elongated, dipping into my bottom lip. He'd just challenged me, and I never backed down from one. But if I morphed, I would kill him. I would not make my Mark if I was discovered.

And that would land me into solitary *again*.

CHAPTER 2

I stormed out of the club unsure where I'd found the strength to back down from a challenge. Although nighttime, the thermal air provided little relief from the blistering-hot blood pulsing through my veins. Two thick-necked bouncers, one standing on either side of the door, watched me with narrowed eyes.

Two short men, holding the hands of equally short women, tugged their girls out of my path as I stomped past. My face must have reflected the agony festering. I stumbled onward, my army boots clapping against the concrete.

My chest constricted, I worked to keep the frenzied demon inside. His bays echoed within my skull. Dormant for so long, while in confinement, he urged for release. He longed for sex and death and havoc with such intensity, the emotions fermenting in my tired brain flamed my blood.

Ahead were the beginnings of darkness. The promise of reduced stimuli propelled me down the side of the club. An alley. Perfect. In this state I might not be able to control my other half if it emerged. I couldn't allow him out. I squatted against the brick wall. The smell of sour beer and soggy cigarette butts mingled with rotting garbage assaulted my senses.

Have to keep moving.

I hopped up, landing on unsteady legs. Darkness and quiet would help. Honking horns from the adjoining street, and the far-off wail of a siren had me hasten my pace in the direction of darkness. If Gage found me this close to transformation, he would provoke me further.

Like my last babysitter insisted on doing. He had soon experienced what happened when I was provoked.

~ ☾ ~

Deep inside, the beast within me awakened. Somehow, the man in the bar knew what I was, even though my brand was hidden beneath the fabric of my shirt. Not that a human would understand its meaning. The man wasn't demonic, but somehow he knew.

I hurried toward the darkness, chest heaving, focusing on my human side. Normally I wasn't so easily triggered, but the overwhelming wave of stimuli weakened my will. I sagged against the wall, jagged edges of brick digging into my flesh. The moon shone bright, but its light soothed my thrashing senses.

I breathed through my nose, then out my mouth. I let the darkness envelop me, hoping it'd calm the churning beast.

Soon, the agony piercing my heart subsided, and my human-half gained control. A flash of the lady-in-red's face had my pulse skyrocketing again. Soft skin and firm breasts pressed against my body, long cover of hair—everything an effective temptress would have.

Her lilac perfume filtered through my senses even here in a dank alleyway.

I slammed my hand against the wall, the pain refocusing me. "Damn Master for sending me here."

"He's already damned, David, as are you and I."

I straightened at Gage's voice and opened my eyes. The dim streetlights behind him hooded his features, rendering him nothing but a dark shadow blocking the entryway to the alley.

The demon shifted inside me, raking at my chest again. If he couldn't get sex, he would settle for a fight.

"Why fight it? You could have ripped that guy's head off in there. I could tell you wanted to." Gage moved closer.

I detected the challenge brewing in Gage's stare and tense jaw.

"Killing innocents in the middle of crowded dance clubs would not aid me on my mission." I rubbed my hand over my raw knuckles. The unyielding brick I'd pounded left my skin bloody.

Gage propped himself against the wall across from me and folded his thick arms over his chest. Besides his flabby

~ ☾ ~

stomach creasing his shirt, he'd remained fairly fit. His biceps tested the stretching limits of the short sleeves. Shaggy, strawberry blond hair drifted over his forehead, casting an ominous shadow over his already dubious eyes.

"True. Well, there's always later." Gage's laughter bounced off the towering walls.

I glanced down the other end of the alley. It intersected with a seven-foot tall brick wall, sealing the end.

"Be gone," I said.

I didn't dare tell Gage the man from the bar detected my demonic being. If he figured me out, and I was only *half* demon, he'd easily detect a full-blooded demon like Gage. But Gage would kill him without pause, as my demon half had urged me to do. I only killed if left no other option—*most* of the time.

I stood straight and moved around the menace staring me down. "I shall try for my Mark again tomorrow."

"You can't leave." Gage seized my arm.

"Don't touch me. I'm on sensory overload as it is."

His grip intensified.

I stared him in the eye—a direct challenge. He swung. I ducked and planted my palm on his chest. With a quick whirl, I drew my blade from my belt and aimed for his neck. Pinning his body against the wall with one hand pressed to his shoulder, I pricked the skin near his Adam's apple with the tip of the silver weapon. Darkness beaded and dribbled along the blade's edge.

"Haven't lost your touch, I see. Even after all these years, brother."

"Why do you test me? It will get you killed." I increased the pressure cinching his neck. "Your two hundred years seniority holds nothing against my strength."

He'd probably hoped my time in seclusion had weakened me enough so he could kill me. But nothing abated the demonic strength of the contract that turned me into what I was and bound me to Master. I often wished there was. Death would be better than this immortal, indentured life.

Fangs elongated and the tips of the vicious canines dented Gage's lip. His fair skin reddened, signaling the

~ ☾ ~

transformation taking hold. Full demons didn't have the control over the beast emerging like I did. It was their true nature, after all. The human form was only a mask.

He would be fully morphed in seconds.

"You kill me and it is back to seclusion for you." The acidic stench of Gage's fear coated his already foul breath.

"Might be worth it," I lied.

"I don't know *why* you're his favorite." He glared. The blackness of his pupils bled into the whites of his eyes. "You're just a half-breed."

Favorite? I pushed off him, allowing six feet between us. I would not kill Gage or anyone else if possible. My demon adored the carnage too much.

"Just step into it, David. Imagine the power you could have at your fingertips. The woman, in the red dress, you could have her body like I know you want to. Then it would be done. You would no longer be a half-breed. We would be true brothers."

Images of the woman flush against me burned my body to the core. I sensed the pleasure she would give me. Then I would be full demon. No remorse. No more struggling.

Thoughts rioted within the confines of my skull. I didn't want any of this. My fate had been decided by someone else. Before I had even been born.

I fired one last glare at my demon-brother and stomped further down the alley. At this moment, darkness was the safest place for me. Hell, I'd been in it for so long, it felt like home.

I threw a look over my shoulder and saw Gage turn the corner. *Good, I was sick of his ugly face.*

Like being yanked out of solitary, shoved on an airplane, then released into one of the sunniest places on the continental US wasn't enough, I was ordered to a bar packed with half-dressed women. It was a miracle I hadn't morphed into my demonic half and killed an innocent already.

That had to be Master's plan. Deprive me of everything, then throw me into *everything*, hoping I'd break and give into the darkness. He'd been tempting me for centuries.

"Hey, back off, buddy." A female voice reverberated off the

~ ☾ ~

surrounding brick walls.

I stopped to listen. I'd made it to the end of the alley and intended to hop the wall, but I couldn't with witnesses. I glanced behind me. Empty and dark.

"What's a cute thing like you doing out back here all by yourself?" a gruff, slurred voice asked. The ring of crackling glass filled the air.

I crept to the corner.

"Sir. You're obviously drunk. Would you like for me to call you a cab?" The woman's voice had gone from casual to strained.

I heard the squeak of a door opening, then a shuffle. My demon's blazing nails prickled at my heart in anticipation of action.

"*Let'ssss* call a cab. We can go to my place," the drunken man said.

I drifted closer to the corner. The bitter smell of alcohol stung my nostrils.

"That shall not be happening, good sir," the female said. "Come inside, and I will arrange a ride home for you."

Good sir? She speaks as if from my era.

More shuffling. The hairs on my arm stood in attention.

"Hands off. You are not allowed to touch me in such a manner. Get inside or—"

Claps echoed, and I stormed the corner.

The lady in red.

She cranked her elbow to the guy's forehead and buried her high-heeled shoe into his knee. His face bounced off the edge of the door, and he slumped to the ground, unconscious. Stance wide, knees bent, she stood over the motionless man, chest heaving.

Moonlight spilled its glowing rays over her like a spotlight. Lean muscles along her arms twitched.

She kicked his stomach. "You picked the wrong woman to—" Squinting her eyes, she jerked her attention in my direction. "Hello?"

I filled my lungs with fresh air, hoping to calm my churning insides. The light above the door she stood under couldn't compete with the darkness and the fifteen feet

~ ☾ ~

separating me from her. I knew my demon sight allowed me to see her easily, but she was human. She couldn't possibly see me.

"Hello?"

I stepped back.

She regarded the guy crumpled on the ground near the doorway and nudged his shoulder with her shoe. "You have a buddy out there?" Her forehead creased. "Who's there?"

"Ma'am, are you okay?" I managed to keep my voice from cracking with the rage fuming inside. For a man to treat a lady so horribly infuriated my human nature, which, in turn, inflamed the rage of my demon.

"Ma'am?" she whispered. "Wait. Are you the guy from in the club? Come into the light."

She released the door handle, but the man's foot stopped it from clicking shut. His body flinched at the impact. She tugged at the ends of her hair and faced the darkness.

The back wall cast a long shadow over me. Coupled with the darkness of the late hour, she should not be able to identify me.

"If you're okay, then. I'll be going." The grit of the asphalt crackled beneath my soles. I wouldn't be able to hop the wall as planned, but I needed to distance myself from her. The seductive energy rolling off her radiant skin teased my already tensed body. The subtle scent of sweat and lilacs was like a taste of sweet wine.

"Wait," she said.

Footfalls approached. A rumble escaped my throat, and I hustled around the corner to run the length of the dark alley to the sidewalk. Another figure, shadowed by darkness approached. Broad shoulders. The man who called the lady in red his sister. Whereas the seduction and pheromones rolled off the female, anger and protectiveness flooded from the man approaching.

If I stayed, I would surely fail to keep the demon at bay. I checked beside me and crouched. With one quick burst, I pounced to the top of the wall and disappeared into the shadows, keeping the humans in sight. Behind me lay an empty lot of dirt. I turned my focus back to the area behind

~ ☾ ~

WASTELAND

the club.

"Wait. Don't go." The woman approached the spot from where I'd just jumped. She must not have seen me leap onto the ledge of the wall.

So human.

Yet, she was strong in the way she handled herself with her attacker. And how she spoke. Old language, which I often used, prevented me from assimilating into this strange era. The darkness consumed her when she stepped out of the reach of the dull light. Her brother would soon come from the alley.

Her tall, slender body came into full view. The woman's skin glowed, despite the void of light. With the blond hair, she almost resembled an angel. I'd seen a handful through the years and with her beauty, she sure could pass for one.

"Beka. Is that you?" the man called out.

Beka. Beautiful name.

"Russell?"

He rounded the corner. "What are you doing out here in the dark?" He scanned the area, then gripped her shoulders. "Are you okay?"

She searched the shadows with wide eyes. "Did you see a man in the alley?"

"No. It's just me. I'm doing the rounds. What's wrong?" He guided her to the door, which lay propped open by the unconscious man's foot.

"I thought—" She glanced over her shoulder.

"What happened here? Who's that?" Russell knelt by the fallen man and pressed two fingers to his neck. "Are you okay, Beka? Did he hurt you?"

"I'm fine. Some drunk tried to—how do they say it—get up my skirt?"

"If you would stop wearing that unsuitable attire, maybe they wouldn't behave in such a manner."

She turned her back to her tall, brown haired brother and looked in my direction again. Her gaze swept over me, but she didn't appear to see me. Then her eyes narrowed. I froze, knees aching as I squatted. Maybe she was a supernatural and able to detect me. I sensed nothing of that nature, but

~ ☾ ~

despite the lack of light between us, her eyes penetrated the distance separating us. My heart lurched into my throat.

Beka.

A deep breath stretched the fabric taut over her firm breasts. The sight sparked a wild fire so fierce it nearly toppled me.

"What are you doing?" Russell nudged her shoulder.

"Nothing. I thought I saw someone." She turned away. "I think I'm hallucinating. I didn't have any alcohol tonight, but I feel like I am intoxicated." Her slender fingers disappeared in her long, blond hair, and she combed through the locks.

The air carried a hint of lilac, and I inhaled the essence deep into my senses.

"Tell me what happened back here," Russell asked.

"Please move that guy inside and call him a cab."

"You're too nice. I'd leave him here to deal with the elements."

"That is the difference between you and me, is it not?" She elbowed his gut, then grabbed the door handle. "And my clothes are not inappropriate, *brother*."

"I shall never get used to the clothing women wear in this century."

The door latched shut and silence ruled the alley. Beka and Russell were not human after all. No wonder Russell was able to detect my demonic half. I didn't sense an angelic presence, and I didn't recognize them as demons, either. Russell identified my evil so they must be Hunters. Possibly Guardians.

Either way, this complicated things.

I stretched from my crouched position and shook out my numb legs. Dark and quiet. Exactly what I needed. The back door to the bar snared my attention again, and I visualized Beka standing there.

She must be a test. A trap. Something Master had placed in this mission to make me fall. But she wasn't even human.

Time to figure out what mess Master threw me into.

~ ☾ ~

CHAPTER 3

"Why did you not locate Jessica Hanks last night?" Master's raspy voice crackled through the cell phone.

"Sorry, sir. I shall try again tonight. Are you certain she is at Club Noir?" I slouched onto the hotel desk chair, the cool, wooden back chilled my bare skin.

"Nothing is certain, son." His voice rumbled. "But you are my runner, and you are to retrieve that which I instruct you to."

I hated when he called me son. I didn't want him as my father, yet, technically, he was since he owned my soul.

Damn you, Mother.

"I will do as you command. Is there any more information about her? All I know is that she's fifteen, an orphan, and bears The Mark of Elpida on the small of her back."

"That is all that has been revealed to the Seers. You will have to find your Mark with that information."

I rested my elbow on the desktop and swiped the square sensor pad on the laptop computer I was given. Amazing device, much like the cellular phone. "I was shown how to use the Internet and searched popular websites called Facebook and Twitter but have brought up nothing useful."

"Do not waste your time with such electronics. Use your instincts. They will not fail you."

"Yes, sir." I ran my hands over my chest, which, after seven more feasts, had begun to fill out again. Soon I would resemble the same twenty-two-year-old man I'd been frozen at four centuries ago.

"Gage will stay with you to help you assimilate to the twenty-first century. You've been gone a long time, son."

"Indeed." He should know. *He* put me in confinement, and

~ ☾ ~

it was beyond my control I did not obtain my last Mark.

"Do not make me incarcerate you again by failing to retrieve young Jessica, do you understand?"

An icy shiver slid down my spine. "Yes, sir."

A click, followed by two brief tones indicated the end of the call. I clicked the phone off and pivoted in the stiff chair. With a flick of my wrist, I tossed the device Gage had called an iPhone onto the bed across from where I sat. The thick, flower-printed blanket swallowed up the fascinating contraption.

I burrowed my toes into the plush carpet and tunneled my fingers through my hair.

Master never checked up on me while on assignment. The babysitters called in updates. His added interest and his assigning a six-hundred-year old demon as my shadow meant something. Had to. Jessica must be more than a routine soul harvest.

The flicker of the muted television broke through the darkness. I'd stared at the little box mounted on the wall all night, learning more about the pop culture of this decade. Frankly, I was intrigued. Society today tolerated much more than before my punishment.

My human side longed for a normal life, to experience the new world surrounding me, but my demonic contract denied that pleasure. Any failure on my part to secure the Mark identified by Master and his mystics was punished with confinement—*after* fifty years of flesh melting flames.

After a full twenty-four hours of eating, sleeping, and enjoying the use of my senses, I refused to go into absolute darkness again. No, I would get this Mark for Master and become acquainted with this strange era.

I rubbed the black crescent inked over my heart, Master's symbol of his ownership. Sold to him by my mother, contract signed in her blood. I ground my teeth at the thought. Trapped for eternity because of her.

I bolted off the chair, strode across the large hotel room to the window and heaved the curtains open. I blinked through the explosion of blue lights floating in my vision and took in the sights. Late afternoon sun bathed the quaint town with its

~ ☾ ~

piercing rays. At least Master let me live in luxury while on this assignment. From the top floor, south side of town, I had a complete picture of the city.

Signot, Arizona. Population five thousand.

I faced the quiet room. The food service tray, filled with empty plates sat at the foot of the bed. I patted my bulging stomach. The food had improved over the centuries. The bathroom door in the corner was cracked open, and I stared in awe at the luxury of the indoor plumbing. Hot water by command.

Very civilized.

I gripped my neck and kneaded the cramps. My bare back absorbed the sun's heat spilling through the window. Despite the comfortable wood-framed bed, which occupied much of the room, my muscles remained stiff. I closed my eyes, willing myself to relax. Beka's image flashed, demanding I open them wide again.

Her beauty led to pleasurable, yet torturous, dreams. Even now my body responded to the thoughts, immediately recalling how she felt so close to me at the club.

Agonizing reminders of what I would never have.

"David," Gage yelled through the door and pounded. "Let's go."

So much for my peace and quiet.

I snatched the cream t-shirt from the back of the desk chair. Guiding the cloth over my head, I slid it over my chest, covering Master's brand.

I have to find a way out of the contract. Somehow. Some way.

"David."

The bed sagged beneath my weight as I sat on the edge and laced up my combat boots. No need to hurry for Gage.

I brushed my hands down my chest, smoothing the soft, cotton shirt. According to the TV shows and movies I'd watched over the last twenty-four hours, the wardrobe provided by Master's staff enabled me to resemble a modern human male. I'd refused to cut my dark cover of hair and wear those strange shoes called flip-flops, though.

I stood and held out my arms in front of me. Even after

~ ☾ ~

sitting in complete darkness for so long, my skin was bronzed much like the desert dwellers of this town.
Strange.
I meandered to the door and leisurely opened it. Gage stood, palms resting on each side of the doorframe. The blood vessel on his left temple twitched, and his face held a red tint not quite as dark as his demonic skin.

His outfit resembled mine, yet his sable, short-sleeved cotton shirt had a gray print on the right sleeve. Faded blue jeans and flip-flops topped off his human disguise.

"Don't keep me waiting again, *half-breed.*"

I resisted the urge to laugh in his face. A fight would prove counterproductive, though a contest would ease the tension of my knotted muscles. The woman from the bar and then Master's phone call had unsettled me so deeply I needed an outlet. One that would sate my demon for a spell.

Gage released his grip on the doorframe and let me pass. Without a word, I barreled down the hallway. Closed doors lined the beige walls. The thick carpet dulled my heavy footfalls as I made my way to the open space in front of the elevators.

Still uncomfortable stepping into a box secured by mere cables eleven stories up, I veered in the direction of the stairwell. I needed the exercise anyway.

"I'm not taking the stairs," Gage said.

I stopped, hand resting on the door handle. "I'll meet you downstairs, then."

The corner of Gage's mouth cocked upward, and he pinned me with a stare. "Don't be a baby. Get in."

The metal handle groaned beneath my grip while I contemplated his directive. Damn him. He was right. If I was to assimilate, I should work to conquer the fear of confined spaces.

I joined him in the elevator. The doors rolled shut. Within seconds, the platform fell out from beneath me and my stomach roiled.

"So, since she is an orphan, I checked county records and conned one of the workers into letting me peruse some files," he said.

~ ☾ ~

The calming music piping through the ceiling was of no aid to my tense stomach. I stared at the blinking box that indicated which floor we'd passed. Level one couldn't come fast enough. "Conned?"

Gage's tongue swiped over his lips, and a wicked snicker leaked out. He resembled a miniature devil when he did that. Only missing the horns. He relished being a demon way too much.

"Just turned on my charm, took her out to a fancy dinner, then warmed up her bed real nice." He laughed. "She was putty after that. Too bad I found nothing on Jessica."

"Gage."

"Hey, anything to help a brother out." He turned and studied his reflection in the mirrored wall beside him. "Take the final step and you can do little things like that. Anything you want you can do."

"Back off. Four hundred years you've been telling me that crap."

"Just give in, David. You don't know what you're missing."

"No." The claustrophobic box stopped with a jerk. The doors rolled open, and I marched out with Gage close behind.

"Your momma was a whore, signing a contract for her first born just to get rich." Gage laughed. "And she died during childbirth. How fitting."

I gave the lobby a peek. Empty enough. With blurring speed, I backhanded Gage's face.

"Hey." His voice echoed off the vaulted ceilings and bounced off the tiled floors. He pinched his nose to stop the crimson flow. Tears welled, and he grumbled.

"Told you not to ever mention my mother." I strode to the valet and handed him my ticket. When he eyed Gage, I said, "He is fine. His disease is no longer contagious."

The overweight valet's mouth curved downward, and he shuffled back.

Gage moved in my path, one hand on his nose, but the other pointed, his finger aimed at my chest. I jerked it backward, crackling knuckles. His dark eyes flared with a challenge.

My demon stirred. "Are you sure you want to issue

~ ☾ ~

challenge to me, Gage?"

He held my gaze a long breath but diverted it to the slick, marble floor.

"Wise choice." I released his hand and sidestepped him, my heart strumming. What my mother chose to do wasn't up for discussion with anyone.

It hurt too much.

Ten minutes later, I maneuvered the SUV, into a parking lot four blocks from Club Noir. We made our way to the establishment, bathed in the golden rays of the setting sun. The feverish heat, however, had not receded with the sun. Trickles of sweat slithered down my spine and dampened my neck beneath my hair.

"You look more comfortable tonight than last." Gage stared straight ahead, his jaw tight as we walked past the empty stores near the club.

"I was not very productive yesterday, but Master's plan to tempt me didn't work. He'd rather me be demon fully or in solitary, wouldn't he?"

"Indeed."

"Why?"

"You cannot be killed. Yet you choose not to join him."

"My contract demands I be his runner. Collect his demons for him. Not join him."

"What you are doesn't make sense, but your mom made the deal with Lucifer himself. No one can override that. Not even Master."

No wonder Master threw me into solitary so quickly. I scare him. I didn't try to hold back a smile.

Gage pocketed his hands and threw a glance my way. "Is it terribly painful if you don't gather the Mark you're assigned to get?"

My spine straightened like a rod had been shoved down my back. "Put it this way, I'd rather be in solitary a millennia to avoid the burn." I pointed to the right. "Turn at this light?"

"Yes. You're learning the town."

"I went exploring during the day. It is very small, but relatively easy to navigate." We turned the corner, following the sidewalk past a dimly lit hardware store. Cars buzzed by,

~ ☾ ~

and we passed an elderly couple strolling down the sidewalk.

"I heard the first fifty years your flesh melted off, except for your brand, of course." Gage laughed.

I glared. "Glad to amuse you with my suffering."

"Your flesh truly burned off?"

"Not literally. But yes. It felt like it was ablaze."

"I was in France at the time, but I heard gruesome stories." He grimaced. "I didn't believe it at first. But with Master, you never know."

I huffed.

"And you didn't grab the demon because . . ."

"She was killed in a fire before I could get to her. It wasn't even my fault, but still, I didn't get the demon in to Master, so I paid the price."

Gage reached for my chest. I snatched his hand before he made contact. "Why do you insist on touching me?"

"I wasn't going to. I was just pointing to your chest, where your brand is."

"And." I shoved his hand to the side. "Your point?"

"I can't believe you've held out so long."

"There has to be some way to be freed of my contract." Now that I had my wits about me more this evening, I would find answers.

"Still on that pointless quest, are ya'? You know Master's aware of your sneaking around, don't you?"

"Again, your point is. . ."

"He just laughs. There is no hope for you, David. We're all damned. You in particular." He tossed me a sideways glance. "You should just accept your fate."

"Never."

~ ☾ ~

CHAPTER 4

At least tonight the women grinding to the music didn't trigger my beast so easily. I'd been out of the darkness long enough to tolerate the assault of stimuli on my senses better.

Although the fair-skinned females still brought my body to a scalding level more times than I would have liked, I remained focused, searching for the Mark of Elpida. I had to. Something deep inside me told me finding this Mark meant more than a soul for Master. Gage hovered, like the annoying peon henchman he was, but proved useful helping me assimilate as Master said he would.

I rested my elbows on the round table, staring at the sea of swaying people on the dance floor and ran my finger across the top of my cool glass. Most women wore shirts exposing their backs, but I had yet to see the Mark of Elpida.

"So, you enjoy babysitting?" I asked Gage.

He grunted, sat straight, and peered over my shoulder. "Hmmm. I think I see my next bathroom rendezvous."

"You're sick."

He ran his fingers through his hair and patted down the front of his t-shirt. "Horny is more like it. I'll go check and see if she's got a tattoo on her back or anywhere else." He gulped the last of his drink and stood, tucking in his shirt. "Enjoy your time of *solitude*, watching what you can't touch."

Gage paraded away, parting through a ring of three young females toward a tall, raven-haired woman who wore an equally dark leather outfit. A silver zipper ran from the point of her cleavage and followed a curvy path to the hem of her short skirt.

I studied the ice cubes floating in my caramel-colored drink. The table wobbled when I shifted my weight to the side

~ ☾ ~

and the candlelight flickered. I stuck my forefinger in the frigid drink and dunked the ice, fighting to hear my thoughts through the thumping bass pounding around me.

I should be searching for Jessica, but with Gage distracted, I'd rather sit for five minutes and not worry. Get lost in the music I was becoming familiar with.

"Want to dance?"

I turned and met the sultry-eyed stare of the blond beauty from the previous night. *Beka.* I clutched my glass and focused on my breathing to keep my heartbeat steady and the demon's claws at bay.

"It's not as busy as last night." She strode behind me and stood next to the table, leaving a subtle scent of lilac in her wake. She was so tall I had to look up, and I wasn't a short guy, even sitting. Her long, ivory legs ended in sparkling stiletto heels. Each muscle flexed as she shifted her weight to her right leg.

My body tensed. "No. It is not as busy." I focused on my glass, trying to wipe her short, skirt and snug tank top from my memory. Long, muscular arms and pale skin went on for miles. Master must have sent her to tempt me. To see if I would give in. He'd done it before.

From the corner of my eye, I saw her move. She eased into Gage's vacant seat and rested her elbows on the table. The ends of her shiny hair settled on the smooth surface. She clasped her fingers together and fixed her emerald gaze on me.

"You were in the alley last night." She angled forward, her plunging neckline exposing the top of her breasts.

I diverted my focus to my drink, wiping the sweat from the glass with my thumb. The pounding bass resonated through my mind, scattering my thoughts.

"I knew it. Where did you go? I tried to see you."

"You were safe, so I left."

She raked her teeth across her bottom lip and leaned forward but stopped. "I've never seen you in here before yesterday. New to town?"

I stared into her eyes. She inclined her head as if encouraging me to speak. The blood in my veins flowed

~ ☾ ~

hotter than the Mohave Desert sands. Her long, slender fingers circled the rim of the cup holding the flickering candle. *What would it be like to twine my fingers with hers? To feel them touching me as we—*

"Are you okay?"

I coughed through the bundle of nerves choking me. "Yes. I am new to town." I scooted my chair back. "I should be leaving now."

"Why? It's early."

"I'm sorry. I need to leave." Actually, I should stay since I hadn't located my Mark. I'd guessed the other women here weren't Jessica by their age alone. Not sure how a fifteen-year old girl got into a dance club such as this. But I followed Master's instructions, hoping to avoid the flesh-burning consequence of missing my Mark.

"At least dance with me before you leave," she said.

Temptress. A trap planted by Master, himself. I had to stay strong, yet I could *not* stop staring at that graceful female. Above the scent of sweet liquor and human sweat hanging thick in the establishment, a trace of her lilac scent wrapped around me. The demon demanded I draw her close and taste her lips. The sting of my fingernails biting into my palm dragged me back to the moment. I should learn more about her, so I knew my enemy.

So I told myself.

If Gage asked, I would tell him my suspicions of her. I dipped my head, agreeing to a dance. Her eyes went wide, and she stretched for my hand. I jerked it back and stood, gesturing for her to lead. She rose to her feet, her eyes meeting mine.

My pulse strummed in my head louder than the bass thumped. I wasn't sure I knew how to dance to this type of music, but I'd been watching people for over an hour. Hopefully something sunk in.

She led through the crowd with the grace of a swan. People often patted her shoulder and said hi while we made our way to a space for us to dance. She turned toward me, a smile filling her face. Her eyes shone beneath the probing lights, and her body began to sway to the music.

~ ☾ ~

I followed her motions, keeping two feet between us. Didn't matter, though, the sizzling heat radiating from this beauty had tripped every nerve in my body. It was Sunday night, so the diminished crowd made sense. Fewer people to bump into and aggravate my demon. Beka's gaze fastened on me and everything else faded from existence. Her eyes moved slowly, as if taking in every detail of my face, but paused at my mouth. She grazed her teeth over her bottom lip.

The demon stampeded within my chest, and I physically tensed to restrain him. Her gaze continued to sweep down my body before making eye contact with me again.

Within a minute of beginning our dance, the song blended into a slow harmony of subtle tones and pitches. Partners stepped close to one another. Two hands slid up my chest, encircled my shoulders and clasped behind my neck.

That elicited a shudder and a gasp.

"One more dance?" She focused on me, her lips puckered out. "That song was half-way through, so it doesn't count."

"I should g—"

"Just one."

She gathered me to her, flattening her breasts against my chest. So close she had to put one of her feet between mine so we could move. Her warmth seeped through her thin shirt into mine. Hunger for her forced the air from my lungs. The demon demanded to be let out.

"So, do you have a name?" Her minty breath washed over me, and I put my hands on her hips.

"What is yours?" I asked.

"Rebeka, but everyone calls me Beka."

"You frequent this establishment?"

Her inner thigh skimmed my leg as she leaned into me more. My hold on her hips tightened, keeping her core from mine. The prickle of my demon sliced at my heart, urging me to pull her close. My heart pounded and body tightened. I couldn't handle much more touching before I lost control.

"Yes I'm here often." She held my gaze. "Tell me your name."

"I am David."

We swayed in silence, her body dangerously close to mine,

~ ☾ ~

yet I absorbed every touch. I played with fire remaining in her embrace, but for unknown reasons, I dove in further.

"Where are you from, Beka?"

"Here. I was raised here. You?"

"Nowhere special. Passing through town."

Her gaze inched down. "Just passing through? How long will you be here?"

"Not sure yet."

Her teeth sank into her lip again.

I stiffened. That gesture with her mouth was too much. "I should be going now."

"Will you be back?" She loosened her grip.

Frigid air seeped between us, and I wanted to pull her close again. She felt like heaven against me. "I might be."

"Hope so." She winked.

My gaze swept over her body, taking in the soft, delicate skin held captive by her tank top. With each breath her chest swelled. We hadn't danced quickly, but she was winded.

A thin, black line of ink peeked out from behind her earlobe. The beginnings of a tattoo. Possibly marking her identity. Guardians bore a tattoo distinguishing them from humans. I drew in a breath, strengthening my resolve to remain in control, and cupped her cheek. She gasped and leaned into my hand like I'd hoped.

The fury of blazing heat streaming from her face in my grasp threatened to distract me. My pulse hammered. But I had to see the mark. A thin line followed the curve of her lobe and disappeared into the shadow behind her ear.

Her teeth grated her lip. Must be a nervous habit. But the action chipped at my resolve each time.

One quick taste.

I brought my other hand to her face, the side with the mark, and curled my fingers around her neck, moving my thumb behind her ear. Her hands cuffed my wrists, but not to push me away. Instead her stare bore into mine like a freight train. The flashing lights of the club bounced a coral, teal, and violet rainbow over her shimmering skin.

The people surrounding us blurred into oblivion, and the music faded into a storm of muffled pitches and tones.

~ ☾ ~

WASTELAND

I concentrated on her shining lips and took in the warmth of her body so close to mine. I wanted only the sense of touch to be awake while I reveled in the silky texture of her skin. For so long I'd touched nothing. If I was going to break my rules, I would enjoy it.

Her hands glided from my wrists down my forearms and up my biceps, sending a ripple of desire through my soul. I could resist no longer. I brushed my lips against hers and tasted melon. She heaved a sharp breath and clamped her fingers around my shoulders, holding me in place.

Scents of lilac permeated me. My heart hammered, and my demon pounded, wanting out.

Wanting her.

I turned my head, severing our connection. Too intense. *Must stay in control.* She let out a whimper. I pressed my mouth to her cheek and tilted her head.

I almost wished I hadn't.

She bore the mark of a Guardian, immortal protectors of the humans.

I drank Beka in for three long breaths, knowing it may be my last chance to hold her close. Because if Beka truly was guarding Jessica Hanks I would more than likely have to kill her to get my Mark.

~ ☾ ~

CHAPTER 5

"A Guardian?" I punched the light post on the corner of Fifth and Grand and pain radiated down my hand, into my wrist. "Beka's a Guardian?"

Across the street, on the opposite corner, a young kid with a buzz-cut strutted out the door of a small café and jammed a key into the door handle. White wires protruded from his ears, and his head bobbed to a beat I didn't hear.

I paced the sidewalk, waiting for the light to turn. Sweat streamed down my back. The malodor of exhaust hung thick as two cars idled. Master had thrown me into a den of Guardians. Jessica Hanks must be quite important to have *two* near-angels protecting her.

The light flashed neon green and I crossed the street. A distant car horn blared.

Guardians. Only killed by beheading. And I knew, because I'd beheaded many in my day. But Beka, how could I—if she found Jessica first, I would have to kill—

I kicked a crumpled can into the brush bordering the parking garage. "Shit!"

"Learning this century's foul language already, brother?" Gage asked.

"Quit calling me brother." I slid the back of my hand over my damp forehead. "Have fun with your *jade*?"

"She was exquisite. And oh, she didn't have the Mark of Elpida in case you're wondering. You have any luck?"

"No. I searched all I could. No young girls hanging around the bar either."

"There are living quarters above the bar. We will check those now."

I finally faced him. His disheveled hair stood on end,

~ ☾ ~

defying gravity. "You could have at least cleaned up a little, Gage."

"I saw you with her." Gage's eyes narrowed.

I crossed my arms over my chest and nailed him with a glare.

"Dancing with that woman. You toe a fine line, brother."

"How else can I check for tattoos if I do not get somewhat close? She'd been at the club twice now."

"She does not look fifteen."

"Difficult to tell these days. But, no, she is not the Mark." Just someone I would eventually have to kill to get to my Mark, I feared.

He shoved his hands through his messy hair. "Then that's one less female you have to feel up."

"I shall leave the *feeling up* to you. I will go search the apartment." I did an about-face. "Can't have two people lurking around."

"I will be close by."

"Of course. Tell Master I said hello when you call in your *report* like the good little boy you are."

I turned three streets before the bar and went two blocks past to get into the back alley from a different angle. Hugging the shadows cast by the tall, brick buildings, I made my way toward the club. The narrow passage behind the structures was a haven for dirt, loose papers, and a rancid-smelling garbage container.

Such filth, yet the absence of bright light helped me tame my raging demon. He wanted Beka. I couldn't blame him. For over four centuries, including two and a half in sensory deprivation, he'd been denied his carnal pleasures. And Beka's statuesque beauty and pureness billowed from her in tangible waves, of course my dark demon wanted to extinguish it. Defile her. Dominate her. *Kill her.*

In the alley behind the bar, a fire ladder hung high above the back door to the club. I slowed, held in a breath and let it flow out my mouth. The bass thumped through the thick walls. I sensed no other movements.

With one quick jump, I seized the cold metal and hoisted myself up. Once my feet touched the steps, I propelled

~ ☾ ~

skyward onto the metal staircase.

It creaked beneath my weight.

The first set of square windows above the club level was dark. I cupped my face against one. A desk with a computer propped on top flashed the Club Noir logo.

Offices.

A quick glance up showed me another row of windows. I worked my way upstairs.

"Be quiet, Russell. He is not." Beka's harmonic voice flowed out below me.

I froze, only fifteen feet above her. Hopefully the metal wouldn't creak again.

"He is. I can feel it." Russell stormed past her through the door from the club.

"I have the same senses you do, *brother*, he is not demon. He is human." Beka crossed her arms over her chest, sending some of her flesh spilling over the seam of her top. I had a clear view and had to work to keep myself from moving, fearing the metal would groan again.

Sweat trickled along my temple. *Stay focused.*

I folded my fingers into a fist, allowing my nails to elongate enough to break skin. A much needed distraction from the lure of Beka's beauty.

"I confronted him last night. Told him I knew he was demon. He didn't deny it. Beka, he's here for a reason. Has to be."

"You're wrong. You probably startled him by calling him a demon. He's so jumpy. Flinches every time I touch him."

"You are *not* to touch him." Russell pivoted and pointed his finger at her face. "You hear me?"

She slapped his hand away. "First of all, remember who you are speaking to. Second, you are wrong about him. You're just paranoid. This is a new city, we are not sure where our charge is yet, but we'll figure it out. We always do."

"You can't join with him. It is forbidden. You know you are to be—"

"There's something about him. Something special." She hugged her mid-section and turned her back on her brother. "I cannot explain this feeling. I've existed for so long, seen

~ ☾ ~

much. But I've never felt so drawn to a human."

"Drawn?" Russell shot his hands skyward, then buried them in his dark hair.

My stomach cramped, but he didn't see me. If I remembered correctly, the Guardians didn't have stellar night-vision.

"What do you know about drawn, Beka? You met him only yesterday." He moved in front of her.

I glanced up. One flight of stairs down to the window, another to the roof. I stayed frozen, gripping the railing. If they saw me, and figured out what—or who—I was after, I would have to kill them both. I didn't think myself capable of taking Beka's head. Russell's, on the other hand...

"Beka. Think rationally about this. You can't—"

The back door flew open and both jumped. "Russ. Better get in here. Some asshole's starting a fight."

Beka and Russell hurried into the club. The door slammed shut, and I relaxed. I might have to try out the whirlpool jets in the hotel tub tonight.

So. She felt drawn to me. I was honored to earn the attentions of such a fair lady. After only two meetings, she'd already worked her way into what was left of my human heart. If only I wasn't the antithesis of her existence.

I finally let my breath out and climbed the last set of stairs. I peered in. Even with my enhanced sight, all I saw was darkness—the panes had been covered with something I couldn't see through. I shuffled to the side and tried the next window. A living room with two plush, cloth chairs flanking a large, caramel colored leather couch.

Tinting on one set of windows but not the others might mean something was hiding or being hidden.

Fingers shoved under the window frame, I tugged. Locked. Same with the tinted window. I couldn't risk breaking them to enter and alert the Guardians to my presence. Or Gage's. I sprinted up the last of the stairs and hopped onto the roof. The gravel shifted beneath my weight as I circled, scanning the area.

The moonlight spilled over the neighboring business establishments and apartments. But they were deserted, save

~ ☾ ~

a few chairs. Sunning on rooftops must be something the humans did.

A door in the middle of the open rooftop was shut. Two plastic chairs sat near the ledge with a little table between and a long blanket spread over the rocky ground.

A telescope next to the ledge pointed skyward. I neared the picnic setting and squatted. I brought the corner of the blanket to my nose. Beka's lilac scent tickled my senses, triggering a firestorm in my stomach.

Her image danced in my mind. Her long, graceful neck. Full lips. Her inviting mouth.

I bound to my feet, shaking off the memory of her body against mine and moved to the door. One quick twist of the knob and the lock broke.

Creaking hinges rent the air and I froze, listening. Inside the stairwell an pool of darkness greeted me. No sounds and only the stale scent of cement and dust. Two flights down brought me to another door, more than likely the hallway to the apartment.

My ear to the door, I slowed my breathing and my body—still as if dead. Another demon trait.

No signs of any movement or people.

I slowly turned the knob and the door cracked open. One closed door between me and the exit at the far end of the hallways. Had to be how they entered the apartment from the ground level. I checked my watch. Nearly one a.m., and the club closed at two. Time enough to sneak in for a peek. But with only one exit, I'd have nowhere to run if they returned early.

Voices trickling through the end of the hallway exit answered my hesitation.

I backed into the stairwell but left the door partially open to watch. So much for getting any information on my Guardian friends.

Humming an unfamiliar tune, Beka strode toward the apartment door. With slender fingers, she slid the key into the knob and cranked it open. When the door shut, I vaulted up the stairs to the roof. Once out into the night, I hurried to the edge. The light from the window reflected off the metal

~ ☾ ~

staircase.

"Shit." I hurdled over the short wall enclosing the roof and landed on the fire escape stairs.

Hopefully I could navigate the sharp turn and get down before she was settled and would see me through the window. Down a flight, I paused.

Beka.

She bent over the kitchen sink, washing a glass. The ceiling light spilled its illumination over her, emphasizing her frame. A sliver of smooth, pale skin on her lower back peeked beneath the hem of her silky blouse at her movements. A quick turn to the table gifted me a glimpse of her corded stomach.

I feared I'd let out a growl, but Beka didn't make a move indicating she heard the beast. I must have refrained. The base of my spine tightened, and a blast of desire rushed up my back.

She'd twisted her flowing hair up into a bun, revealing her long, swanlike neck in full form. I inched toward the stairs, but they whined beneath my two-hundred-pound body.

Fearful she'd see me, I swung my legs over the railing and landed two stories below. The jolt resonated through my bones and up my spine, but barely registered.

Another demon trait.

I rushed around the corner and slouched against the building, listening. The dull, thudding bass of the dance club echoed my heart pounding my ribs. The sharp brick bit into my skin through my thin shirt, and I slammed my hand against the unrelenting surface. But the self-induced pain didn't erase Beka's image or the feel of her body.

Mine.

I was in big trouble.

~ ☾ ~

CHAPTER 6

"What'd you learn?" Gage asked when he caught up to me at the SUV.

"Nothing. They came home as I was on my way in. Tomorrow. I'll need you to do lookout for me. Nowhere for me to run should they come home."

My chest heaved, and I propped my hands on my thighs. Sweat dripped from my brow and splattered against the sidewalk. I needed the run, though. My entire being had been cooped up and immobile for so long, it might take me another century to work out all the kinks.

"Master won't be happy."

"It's only been two days, Gage. Not even. I can't make the Mark just appear. If he had more details for me other than a fifteen-year-old orphan. . . ." I stomped through the rock landscape surrounding the garage. "I plan to visit some orphanages tomorrow during the day."

There had to be something more going on here. Two Guardians, Gage hovering and watching my moves closer than any of my babysitters had, and Master constantly reminding me of the consequences of my failing to get his target.

I slid my fingers around my throat. The choker wasn't visible to anyone, human or demon, but it existed. Cinching tighter and tighter.

Gage's laughter followed me to the car. "I don't know how your last chaperone handled you, David."

I stopped and turned, allowing a fraction of my demonic half to surface. Its jagged features stretched my human form. A feral rumble thundered through the darkness between us. Fear tugged at the corners of Gage's eyes and mouth.

~ ☾ ~

"My last chaperone didn't *handle* me, Gage." My chest burned. "You'd do well to remember that."

I had no patience for him tonight. Beka had rattled my soul, but she was a Guardian. Not only were romantic relations forbidden for me—lest I wanted to become full demon—never could I be with someone so pure. Only Angels were more pure than Guardians.

And she thought *me* to be special.

"I'd like to see you try and *handle* me, David." Gage fastened his narrow-eyed stare on me.

The animal within me awakened. My human side didn't want to fight. I needed to get the girl and leave. Beka's appearance complicated things, teasing me with her elegance.

"Did you mean to challenge me, *babysitter?*" I allowed the evil closer to the surface. The pointy tips of my elongated canine teeth pricked my bottom lip. My eyesight sharpened.

The quiver of his chin told me he hoped I wouldn't call his challenge.

"Why push me, Gage? You know the contractual bonds around my neck and wrist prevent any being from killing me."

He paced, keeping his eyes trained on me. His mouth clamped shut, firing a ring of muscles along his jaw.

Having been in solitude for so long sharpened my senses. The rush of power flowing through my veins was intoxicating. My fingernails grew long, inching me toward transformation.

I bit at the air, tasting Gage's acrid fear. But it wasn't only fear of me. "What aren't you telling me about this mission?"

He resumed pacing but said nothing.

Gage was lucky I was in such control. Had this happened last night, there would have been bloodshed. His blood.

"Be careful the next time you issue a challenge." I marched toward the car. "My last babysitter would tell you the same—if he was still alive."

Gage backed away. "Half-breed."

Wait. If Jessica Hanks was so valuable to merit two Guardians and a heightened interest from Master, then maybe if I got to her first, I could negotiate my contract.

~ ☾ ~

CHAPTER 7

"Okay, hon." The waitress set the coffee cup on the table. "Your food will be up in a few minutes."

I dipped my chin to her and poured in the creamer. My spoon dinged against the sides as the cream lightened the dark pool of steaming caffeine to a caramel color.

My phone vibrated against the Formica table and Gage's face filled the screen. *More checking up.* I pressed answer and propped the phone between my shoulder and ear to keep my coffee going.

"Where are you?"

"Eating."

He huffed, evidently not appreciating my three days of evading him. "What have you discovered?"

"I must not have your charm because I was unable to gleam any information from social services." I sipped the coffee and reveled in its bitter yet creamy taste. "You would think my demon side would come with some mind-altering abilities to enable us to get information."

"This is taking too much time."

I relaxed into the stiff, red leather booth and brushed away the crumbs from the black topped table while Gage moaned on about my lack of progress. Clanks of silverware hitting plates echoed around me. The scent of frying grease and sweet pastries triggered a roar in my stomach I was sure the people sitting behind me would hear.

"David."

"What, Gage? If Master's Seers were a bit more effective, I might have found her by now." I glanced around the café and lowered my voice. "I will scour the schools and malls after my meal. Goodbye."

~ ☾ ~

WASTELAND

I tapped end in the middle of his sentence and tossed the phone to the side. My search for Jessica Hanks had revealed nothing, and I refused to experience another quarter millennia in punishment for missing a Mark. I smoothed my fingers over my chest, remembering the flame.

Beka's image dashed into my brain. When I'd first seen her, I'd flippantly teased she might be worth another stint in solitary, but I was wrong. The only thing worth punishment would be finding a way out of the contract controlling my existence.

To be free was all I wanted.

"This seat taken?"

Beka's voice startled me, and the back of my hand grazed my cup, knocking it over. A stream of coffee spilled over the table and onto the floor.

"You really are a jumpy guy, David."

I shot to my feet mindful of the dark puddle collecting near my shoes. "Beka?"

Her bright smile could chase the thickest clouds away. I'd not yet seen her in daylight, and she was even more stunning with the sun spotlighting her flawless, porcelain skin, and long straight nose. With her hair secured away from her face, her high cheekbones stuck out, demanding equal attention as her sea-green eyes.

"I saw you through the window." She stepped over the pool of coffee. "How are you? Haven't seen you in the club in a few days."

"Busy." I glanced out the window. "Work." I'd lurked around the outside of the club and tried two different times to get into Beka's apartment only to be detoured when either she or Russell returned home.

"I see." She analyzed the floor, while my eyes were drawn to the outline of her ample chest beneath the fitted red blouse.

I steered my attention back to the coffee encroaching my shoes.

"So, what do you do for work that's kept you so busy?"

"Research. Very boring." I eyed the empty booth across from me, knowing I should ask her to join me, but also

~ ☾ ~

knowing I shouldn't. "Want to sit?"

Her cheeks flushed, and she bobbed her head.

"Here, let me." I took her shopping bag. "Don't slip."

"Thank you. I didn't mean to startle you into spilling your drink." She smiled, and the bright sun caught the corner of her eye, highlighting flecks of amber.

She slid onto the booth and settled in the middle. I threw a quick survey of the store. A man with silver hair, sitting two booths down, eyed me over the tip of his newspaper.

I set Beka's bag beside the booth. If Gage located me, I'd simply say I was researching the club, investigating employees. Maybe Jessica Hanks was on the wait staff.

I settled back and tossed a pile of napkins on the spilled coffee. The desert suddenly claimed ownership of my throat. Although my assimilation into the world was nearly complete, Beka's lilac scent still devastated my senses, and my fingertips ached to touch her.

She reminded me of an athlete in her khaki shorts and white tennis shoes.

"Hey there, sweetie. Can I get you anything?" the redheaded waitress asked, carrying a coffeepot and a glass of water. A young, pimple-faced boy trailed her, pushing a mop in front of him and went to work on the mess I had made.

"Water's good for me."

The waitress set a new coffee cup down and poured the dark liquid to the rim. A lanky, nearly bald man, carrying a tray of food took her place beside the table. "Hamburger and fries?" He lifted his chin in my direction.

"Yes." He sat the plate in front of me and my other meal, chicken salad with ranch dressing, before Beka, then turned on his heel and left.

Her eyes went wide. "I'm sorry. I didn't mean to barge in on you and your—" Her cheeks reddened as she glimpsed the departing waiter. "I didn't realize you were sitting with someone. I—" She scooted to the edge of the booth.

I dragged the salad beside my burger and fries. "They are both for me. I am eating alone."

She paused, one hand planted on the tabletop while she stared at my food. "Two meals?"

~ ☾ ~

"Yes. But if you still want to leave, I will understand."

Please stay. But I knew she should leave. More for my sake than hers.

She slouched, letting out a long breath. "Gosh, I thought…"

"What?" I slathered ketchup over my fries. I sure missed eating while in punishment. In the last five days, I'd eaten enough food to feed a small country and relished every minute. The only part of the demon's power I appreciated was the quick healing. My muscles had recovered nicely.

She scooted back to her spot and rested her elbows on the table. "Nothing. Just weird that you're eating two meals."

"What brings you out and about today?" I asked.

"Shopping. You?"

I dunked a fry in the ketchup. "Research."

"Library's on the other side of town." She nursed the glass of water.

"Hotel is near here."

"Marriott?" She swept a stray strand of hair from her forehead. "You look like a Marriott-type."

"Should I be insulted?"

"No. I like Marriot-types."

A French fry lodged in my throat. She liked Marriot-types. She'd told her brother she was drawn to me, too. I was a four-hundred-year-old half demon bound to the life of a slave to Satan's right hand man. She was an immortal Guardian. Opposite ends of the spectrum. One dark, one Light.

Impossible.

I cut my burger in half and took a bite. The salty, meaty taste burst in my mouth. I would never tire of eating again.

I held the other half up. "Would you like some?"

"Sure you have enough?" Her lips curled into a smile.

"You could have my salad if you prefer."

"I like burgers better."

I pushed my plate to the center of the table. "Please."

She accepted the food from my hand, dipped it in ketchup, and took a bite. Her tongue darted out and snatched a stray bit of ketchup from the corner of her mouth.

Along with my breath.

"They have great food here," she said.

~ ☾ ~

"How long have you worked at the club?"

"I just help out whenever. My brother bought it. He's into that sort of thing."

"You seem to enjoy the dancing."

"I saw you watching me that first night." Her eyes narrowed. "But you didn't want to dance with me."

"It was my first night in town. Tired from travels."

"Hmm." Her eyebrows elevated. "Yeah, well, I help him at the bar a little. It's fine for now."

"For now?"

"Here you go, sweetie." The waitress refilled Beka's glass of ice water. "Just holler if you need anything else."

Beka looked to her left. With her hair tied back into a ponytail, I got a clear view of the Guardian's Mark behind her right ear. My breath stalled. A Guardian, someone so pure, sat not two feet from me. My demon stirred, but I denied his urge to pounce.

To destroy.

"So, is it just you and your brother?" I took another bite.

"Mostly. I mean, he has a staff of a few part timers, but mostly he and I take care of the place on our own."

"I did see a few waitresses and security people."

She nodded, taking a bite of the burger.

So, this was what humans did. Enjoyed pleasant conversation, while sharing a meal. I could learn to enjoy this.

From the corner of my eye, Gage's hulking frame caught my attention. He made eye contact with me from across the street and hopped down from the curb. *Damn that meddling demon.*

"Beka. I noticed you wore your hair up today."

"Hot out." She swirled the ponytail around her forefinger.

"I'd love to see it down again. It's so beautiful."

"You want me to take my ponytail out?" She scanned the café and returned her gaze to mine.

She frowned as she continued swirling her golden lock with her finger, teeth raking her bottom lip. Yes. It had to be a nervous habit, one that relentlessly tempted me to take her mouth with mine. She had no idea the effect it had, probably

~ ☾ ~

WASTELAND

didn't even know she was doing it.

"Yes. Please. Would you mind terribly?" *Hurry.*

Gage quickly approached. I tipped my head to her and smiled.

"You are a strange one, David." The corner of her mouth lifted into a crooked smile.

"It's so beautiful draped over your shoulders."

Keeping her gaze directly on me, she reached for the thick piece of dark leather holding her mane in place, and I looked out the window again. Within seconds, Gage would enter the eatery. I couldn't chance him noticing the Guardian's Mark, and her long hair would cover the symbol. One quick motion, she pulled out the binder, and her hair cascaded over her shoulders.

The scent of lilacs bombarded me. "Beautiful."

She combed her fingers through her hair, but stopped mid-motion. Jaw clenched, she straightened in her seat and opened her eyes wide. She scanned the restaurant, nostrils flaring.

"Are you all right?" I fought the urge to touch her hand perched on the top of the table. The tips of her fingers blanched as she flattened them against the surface.

"I'm fine." But she stayed focused on our surroundings as her gaze swept over the room.

"David, there you are," Gage said.

Two long strides past the door, and he towered over our table. I slumped into my seat. Beka pinned Gage with a stare so intent I thought it'd tear him apart.

"Who is your lovely new friend, David?"

"You know this man?" Beka asked.

Her chest heaved, and she must be squeezing her hands beneath the table as her biceps flexed. Still, she didn't face me.

"No. Just met him upon my arrival here for my job."

Gage speared me with a glare. "David—"

"He is assigned to me as my assistant to help me with my research. I do not know him beyond that."

Finally, she met my gaze, but quickly pushed herself out of the booth and stood before the massive demon. He backed

~ ☾ ~

off, ogling her toned body, which in turn made mine tense with anger. Gage will pay for regarding her in such a manner.

I knew I was in trouble for sure if I'd already staked her as mine. And I had done just that, because his lustful gaze triggered my feral sense, which only came out when protecting what I considered mine.

"Where are you going, Beka?"

She moved to my side of the booth and crawled in next to me. "Nowhere. Just wanted to…ah…make room for your friend if he's staying." Beneath the table, her toasty hand rested on mine.

Then the reason for her actions hit me. She sensed Gage as a demon, and her Guardian nature took hold, thinking I—a human—needed protection.

~ ☾ ~

CHAPTER 8

"She is working behind the bar, mixing drinks." Gage strode toward me.

I'd perched myself two blocks from the club at a covered bus stop waiting. "The brother?"

He dipped his head.

"Good. Alert me on my cell phone if they near the entrance to the apartment. I will go in."

Gage snared my elbow. "Your woman has taken quite a liking to you."

I twisted from his grasp. "The quicker you let me get into her apartment and have a look, the quicker I might discover something. I am anxious to leave this small town."

"Are you?"

I stomped away. "I'll be quick."

Gage snarled, but I let it roll off my shoulders. Beka had shadowed me since the restaurant, probably worried for my safety from the *demon* she sensed in Gage. Although I enjoyed her company, it made things difficult to investigate and challenged my resolve.

We'd walked through the town, stopping at two shopping malls and three local coffeehouses. The efforts proved futile, but with Beka so close, distracting me, I didn't have much choice.

Her Guardian nature to love and protect beamed through her entire being. She gave her whole heart to it the way she detected Gage's demon nature and stood up to the beast before coming to my side at the restaurant.

She was an honorable woman.

I made my way to the roof again under night's dark cover. No matter what feelings or bodily urges I had for Beka, I still

~ ☾ ~

had to find my Mark, which, ironically, was her Mark as well.

Squeaking floorboards announced my arrival to her door. Of course it was locked, so I dug the picking tool out from my back pocket. I should break the lock and make it look like Gage entered. Maybe she would kill him for me.

The metal tool slid from my sweaty hand and clanked against the door. I snatched the tool up and jammed it in the lock until it clicked open. Gage had only shown me this technique hours earlier, and I'd inaccurately doubted its effectiveness.

Crossing the threshold gifted me with the sweet scent of lilac.

Beka.

I had to stay focused on the Mark. It was best for us all. Even if Beka protected me from future demons, she couldn't protect me from Master calling my contract due. If that happened, I'd be dragged back to the Manor regardless.

Even my strength was no match for the contract binding me to Master.

I eased the door shut behind me. To the left sat a diminutive kitchenette that opened to a living room. To the right, a dark, short hallway lined with four closed doors.

I moved to the end of the hallway and opened the first door.

Bathroom.

The next door opened to a bedroom. Must be Russell's by the emptiness of the walls and lack of decorations. I'd come back to that one. Finding Beka's room interested me more.

I creaked open the third door and a thick wave of her scent washed over me. I absorbed the sweet air deeper into my lungs. *Beka.*

A cream-colored comforter covered the twin-sized bed in the left corner of the room. A two-door closet with mirrored panels to the right sat open, and I peered in. Several hangers full of dresses, specifically the red one she'd worn when I first met her.

I brushed my fingers down the shiny fabric. Cool to the touch now. Yet I remembered the warmth radiating from her body when she had stood near me that night.

~ ☾ ~

WASTELAND

"No." I bit my cheek hard enough to draw the metallic taste of blood. Without touching anything more, I backed out from the closet.

A wooden, corner desk housed a laptop computer. *Let that hold some answers.* Two steps brought me to the desk, and I lifted the cover. The screen jumped to life. No password needed to open the home screen. *Trusting.* A picture of her and Russell, hugging, surrounded by snow. Her long, blond hair cascaded from beneath a pink cap. Her cheeks and nose a rosy red.

I swiped my finger over the square touch pad and guided the cursor to the magnifying glass in the upper right hand corner of the screen and clicked. A rectangle search box appeared, and I typed, *Jessica Hanks.*

The computer brought two files to the forefront, and my stomach flipped. Beka had found information on Jessica.

I eased onto the padded leather desk chair, the wood creaking beneath my weight, and double clicked the first folder. A document opened with a picture of a freckle-faced girl. Possibly four or five years old. Straight red hair cut below her ears. She held the hand of a taller woman, with matching red hair.

Must be Jessica and her mother. I imprinted the chestnut brown eyes into my memory along with the pale, skin and pudgy cheeks.

I exited the document and opened the next. Another picture. Same girl, same age, standing near a gravestone, holding the hand of a plump, dark-haired woman with a ramrod straight back. But there was a caption to this picture.

I leaned in, squinting to read the fine print

"She will change the face of the earth. Find her. –G."

Who is G?

I clicked out from the documents and stared at Beka's picture again. I feathered my finger along the screen, just below her chin and couldn't help the smile twitching my lips. *If only...*

My limited knowledge of computers left me no other choice than to close the screen. I'd gotten enough. I now knew what Jessica looked like. Despite the years that had

~ ☾ ~

past, I would pick out her eyes in a crowd.

I opened the top left drawer to the desk. A mirror, some lipstick, and a hair brush. I picked up the brush and brought it to my face.

Mmm. My Beka.

I shoved the grooming device into my back pocket. Alarms rang like a bell tower gong in my head about my growing affection for the Guardian, but I didn't care. Soon, I would find my Mark and leave, but with the brush in my possession, I'd always have a part of Beka.

I arranged the chair to its original position and glanced to the left. The covers on her bed were peeled back, as if she'd gotten up and forgotten to make it. One step brought me to her bedside, and I knelt down. The pillow, still dented from the weight of her head, emitted her scent. I closed my eyes and pictured her in my arms, snuggled close to me in restful sleep. Soft, blond hair draped over my bare chest, the sheets tousled from making love.

Mine.

The rumblings of my demon sliced through my fantasy, and I stood on shaky legs. I gave one last scan of the room, then backed out and closed the door. Three strides carried me to the last door. The handle didn't give when I cranked it. I knew this to be the room with the tinted window since it was next to the living room.

I dug out my picking tools and tried, without success, to disengage the lock. If I forced my way in, Beka and Russell would know someone had been there. They would probably blame Gage because of his demon status, but I might be implicated because I knew him.

A risk to be taken to get the Mark.

I jerked the handle. It gave. I pushed the door open and a stale, metallic laced darkness met me. Black walls, ceiling and floor. My phone pulsated in my pocket, and I yanked it out.

Get out.

I stole a gander into the room. Small bed. Teddy bear on the floor. Nothing else.

"Shit."

My heart pounded as I closed the broken door and burst

~ ☾ ~

out of the apartment. I shut the main entrance and engaged the lock, then hurried through the roof access door but stayed close to listen.

"Beka, I need your help tonight," Russell said, following her through the doorway on the far end of the hallway. "Stacia called in sick."

Beka strode forward, tall and confident, dressed in a white dress that ended above her knees.

"I can't. I must locate David. I haven't seen him this evening. I fear he's in danger from his associate Gage. The demon left, and I couldn't get away to try and vanquish him."

"So, Gage was the one I sensed in the club before, not David." Russell tilted his head to the side. "I wouldn't have guessed. I thought I sensed it with him as well."

"No. It was not David. Gage is after Jessica. We must find her quickly." She shoved the key into the door. "But first, as Guardian, I must protect the human, David. Our paths crossed for a reason. I believe that."

Russell curled his fingers around his sister's elbow. "It's more than that for you, Beka, I can tell."

"No," she whispered. "It's not."

"You love him."

Electricity pulsed through my body at the word love. She could not love me.

She rested her forehead against the door. "I've never felt such an intense connection like this before, Russell. I can't explain it, but there is something about him."

"Fight it, Beka. We must find Jessica and get her to safety. You cannot get distracted from the mission."

Beka thrust open the door. "You're right. But—" She palmed her forehead. "You're right, Russell. Thank you for your loyalty, for protecting me. But please, allow me leave to check on David first. The demon works with him somehow. He's in danger."

Russell squeezed Beka's shoulder. "I understand."

"Then I will be back to help you."

They disappeared into the apartment. No shrieks or anything, so they must not have noticed my intrusion.

But they would eventually.

~ ☾ ~

I shut the door and scrubbed my face with my hands. *She couldn't love me. She knew nothing of what I was. No way Light could be with darkness.*

I had to find Jessica before Beka and Russell so I could finish this assignment and leave. But locating a fifteen-year-old girl at a dance club didn't make sense. Something felt off.

Time to push Gage for answers, because if Jessica Hanks really could change the world, she might be powerful enough to get me out of my contract.

Yes. Definitely time to press Gage.

And I intended to press hard.

~ ☾ ~

CHAPTER 9

"Please tell me you found something," Gage said.

"I found something." I strode by him and into the parking lot of a brightly lit gas station.

Two cars were parked near the entrance and one at a pump. A young woman propped against her car held the hose to her gas tank while tapping her phone. Otherwise, the station was relatively quiet.

"Hey, where are you going?"

I kept moving, slowly allowing my demonic side to surface. This time, I would challenge Gage and see it through. He would tell me everything he knew or meet death. Too many things reeked of set up. Two Guardians protecting the girl, Master releasing me from punishment five years early, and issuing a six-hundred-year-old demon to babysit instead of the usual low-level demons.

"David, get back here. I must report your findings."

I grumbled. Searing hot nails pierced my heart. Hair prickled on my arms and up my spine. My fingernails darkened and grew to pointed ends as I neared the darkness beside the gas station.

My eyesight sharpened and fastened on a cat perched on the dark green dumpster beside a door to the stucco building. I let a hiss slide past my fangs, and the feline scampered across the top, its nails scratching the plastic cover.

"David—"

I pivoted, wrapped my fingers around Gage's throat and lifted him in the air. With one swift movement I rammed him into the wall, pinning him a foot from the ground. Bricks crumbled at the impact, dusting the tops of my shoes and clattering to the asphalt.

~ ☾ ~

The smoky scent of Gage's anger plowed over me, and my demon's bellow echoed off the walls flanking us.

His eyes went black. Then his skin darkened, and his fangs slid from beneath his top lip. A hand came down on my elbow, and he swiped at my face. I met his blow with my forearm, but kept my grip.

I snapped my canines, glaring at him directly in the eye. Blood raged through my veins, pumping me full of the demon's confidence. "Tell me everything."

"I know nothing." His nails grated my cheek.

With my free hand I drew my blade and held it to his neck. But at the same time a prick stung my side below my rib.

"Not so good after all." Gage snickered.

"You're not too bright, are you?"

He bared his teeth. Veins bulged at his temples, and his nostrils flared.

"My blade is at your neck. Yours, at my side. Which is lethal?"

His tense face softened as realization dawned on him. Demons were killed by beheading.

I pressed the silver blade to his throat. Blood beaded.

"You can't kill me." Gage's voice cracked.

"I think I can. And I will if you do not start talking." I eased him to his feet, keeping him in check with my growl and my fingers squeezing his neck. "It is I you cannot kill."

"I could try."

"You would fail. Why did Master really send me here?"

"The Mark." Gage squirmed.

I loosened my grip. "And . . . ."

"And what, David? It's always about a Mark. The next demon, nothing else. Same as always." He batted my arm away and advanced.

His blade slashed my stomach. Burning pain crept up my side. My dagger penetrated his neck, and black blood spewed from the cut. I hadn't exerted the pressure needed to sever the head, but enough to make an impression.

I pounded his stomach and scored my nails down his face.

He snapped at my fingers while his other hand covered his gushing wound. He pointed his blade, with a shaking hand. I

~ ☾ ~

paced in front of Gage, allowing more of my demon to emerge and heal my stomach wound.

"Yield, Gage," I said. Energy pricked my skin like needles.

He struck again. His nails tore at my shirt. I spun and cracked my elbow to his temple. He stumbled forward, and I jumped behind him. My arm unyielding around his neck, I trapped his body to mine and dug my lethal fingertips into his throat.

"You've heard stories of my time in solitary, but do you know about my fingernails?"

He grunted.

"Sharper than the dagger you hold." I carved into his skin. "Do you want to test them?"

Another grunt.

"Do you yield to this challenge?"

His body stilled against mine.

I jostled him. "Do. You. Yield?"

"Yes." His dagger clanked against the asphalt, and his arms rose in surrender. "I yield."

I loosened my hold, but let a fingernail glide over his flesh. Sure, the wounds would heal in minutes, but I still needed to remind him of my dominance.

He shivered, and I shoved him away. He palmed the brick wall to steady himself, then faced me. His hand went to his neck. "Damn it."

"Change back," I said in a low tone. "Before someone comes, then you will start talking, or I will finish what I started."

My demon was taking hold more than I preferred. The energy. The power. I could have this all the time if I permanently transformed.

No.

I palmed my knees and focused on my human nature. *In through the nose out the mouth.* My nails and fangs receded, and the blaze simmered. The fight sated my demon's needs for the moment.

Gage's jaw tightened, and his human mask surfaced. The bleeding from his neck stopped, and he glared at me. Shame flickered in his dark eyes. No one hated losing a challenge

~ ☾ ~

more than Gage. Especially to a demon two hundred years his junior.

"Talk." I stood straight.

"There is nothing else to say."

"There's more to this Mark, Gage." The caption beneath her picture confirmed my hunch. "Master drags me out of solitary and throws me into a pit of sensory overload, so he must have other plans. What are they? And how is a fifteen-year-old connected to a dance club? Is there not an age limit to these types of establishments?"

"Yes. Twenty-one."

"Then how?"

"I do not know."

I twitched my lip up, as I paced in front of him. My claws darkened, and Gage's gaze lowered to my hands.

"What did you find in the apartment?" Gage asked.

"I now know what she looks like. You need to answer my question." I inched toward him. "My patience wears thin, *brother*."

"Master's Seer saw darkness and the name of the club in a vision. A faint glow, in the shape of a heart." Gage's jaw muscles tensed as he pulled his hand from his neck. The wound was meshing together.

I didn't want to kill Gage but I had to know. "Why me? You're more than capable to handle a fifteen-year-old female. Why pull me from punishment early?"

"Because you're part human. The only one able to get past any Guardians sent to protect the girl."

"Guardians?" Damn, he must know about Russell and Beka.

"I believe Russell to be one; however, I do not see a mark on him." Gage glared at me with his dark eyes. "And he is brother to your woman, Beka."

"She is not *my woman*."

"Says you."

"Beka and Russell are good friends, just call each other brother and sister as a term of affection." Hopefully he would believe the lie. "What is so special about this girl, Jessica?"

"Master never told, but I suspect it is something very

~ ☾ ~

dangerous or helpful to him. He became quite anxious when his Seer told him of the girl."

"Indeed. He released me from confinement five years early. Why would he not just tell me of the plan? Instead, he fed me to the wolves. I may have slipped with so many humans nearby. I've been away so long and very tempted with the seductive, half-dressed women prancing around."

I ordered the demon inside and my fingernails to normal length. The rush of dark power flowing through my veins felt like a drug. And like my feelings for Beka, that was dangerous.

"Yes. And why do you think he did that?" Gage asked.

"Hoping I'd give in and become full-fledged."

"Indeed."

"If I did, I couldn't get past the Guardians."

"You'd still get your Mark. *That* he knows. You always get your Mark. Despite whoever or whatever stands in your path." He chuckled. "Mostly."

I gritted my teeth. Master was playing games. More than usual. Something had him spooked. That was the only explanation.

"He did that to test your resolve."

I fisted my hands in my hair, tugging until my eyes stung.

"But, surprisingly, you have prevailed. You are very strong, David. Inexplicably strong."

"And that scares him, does it not?" My deadly sharp nails returned to their human color, and I again felt my heart pound instead of the agony of the demon's grip.

"Indeed. You are a half-breed, you should not be this strong. Not able to control how much demon comes through when you need its power." He regarded my hands. "The nails. You called only a part of your demon, whereas the rest of us can only go full demon or human, not partially. That is power, indeed."

"But not enough to break the contract."

"Doomed to servitude by your lovely mother." Gage smirked.

He'd been on the receiving end of my wrath when he spoke of my human mother. But right now, I needed to think.

~ ☾ ~

Because somehow I knew Jessica Hanks was the key to my freedom.

   If I could only find her.

~ ☾ ~

CHAPTER 10

"What'll you have?" Russell said, not deviating his attention from the glass he wiped. He shuffled to the side and picked up another glass but kept himself tilted in my direction, still not looking.

"You are busy tonight," I said. A woman grazed my arm as she settled in next to me, probably wanting to purchase a drink. Many people crowded the bar.

"Yeah. I'm short on help—" He finally straightened and made eye contact. "Oh. What do *you* want?"

"You are short on help. I am available if you need assistance."

He diverted his focus. "What can I get you, ma'am?"

"Gin and tonic, please."

"Hey, buddy. Can I get some help down here or what?" a guy at the end of the bar called out.

Russell scanned the span of the bar, then rested his gaze on me. "You know how to bartend?"

"I am a quick study."

"Beka ran out on me, searching for you. But since you're here, come on and pitch in." He shook his head.

"Why do you shake your head?"

"I don't know what she sees in you, but I need help, so you're it."

Glass shattered behind me, and I turned. Two guys tumbled over a table and a crowd began to form. Russell perked up.

"I will handle this," I said. "You pour your little drinks."

I parted the sea of people surrounding the scuffle. Two young guys wrestled on the floor while a group of ten rooted them on with fists pumping toward the ceiling.

~ ☾ ~

Such immaturity.

But if I diffused the disagreement, I may gain the trust of the skittish Guardian, Russell, which would help in my quest for Jessica, so I pushed forward.

"Hey," I yelled. The thumping music muffled my voice. No one moved. In fact, the circle of people tightened.

I yanked two miscreants aside, making room for me to break through the crowd. One of the guys elbowed my side. "Hey, dude."

I stared into his eyes and growled. He must have sensed my anger and stepped away, bringing the girl standing next to him along.

"Smart choice, son."

I stomped toward the two boys rolling on the ground and reached for the arm of the blond juvenile. I yanked him up. He swung at my face, but I caught his hand in mine. "Enough."

Obscenities rolled off the drunken kid's tongue. I kept him to the side at arm's length.

Next the redhead pounced. "You asshole. You can't—"

I cracked my knuckles against his cheek. He fell to his knees and slumped onto his back, unconscious. The guy I held flailed, his elbow snagged against a dark-haired female standing behind him, and she stumbled sideways.

I tossed the blond near the unconscious one and caught the girl's bicep before her face smacked against the floor.

"Hey, get your hands off her." The scrawny blond charged with wild eyes.

"I'm okay," the girl whispered, looking dazed.

I grabbed the front of the kid's silk shirt. His eyes widened, and I jerked him close. "I think it best you leave."

His lanky, five-foot-eight frame shrank before me. My sheer size alone should have scared him, but I threw in an extra snarl for effect. Adrenaline stampeded through my body. I'd almost hoped he fought a little more.

"Come on, babe. Let's get out of here." Blondie's leer bounced from the unconscious kid to me. "This place is a meat market."

"I'll walk you out." I shoved him in the direction of the

door.

Within five minutes I'd escorted the blond outside with his girlfriend. I turned to the bouncer standing guard. "Don't let him back in, please."

The darkness of the alley beside the club proved a perfect place to cool down from the action. I stopped near the end of the passage way and leaned forward, resting my open palms against the gritty brick wall.

The breeze rushed over me, cooling my damp skin. The action inside triggered my raw senses. They were misfiring something fierce. I'd nearly let too much of the beast out while fighting those kids. Maybe befriending Russell in attempts to snatch Jessica wasn't such a good idea.

The constant crowds, all the touching, and now the fighting. It got me too worked up. Then to discover Master had specifically put me in this situation. Using my human side for his demented needs, hoping I'd fail.

But he'd initiated a Mark, and per my contract, I had to obey.

I turned and let my back rest against the brick wall of the establishment. When I opened my eyes, Beka stood propped against the opposite wall of the narrow alleyway.

"Beka?"

"Didn't mean to scare you."

"I didn't hear you." Strange. I heard most things, but again, my senses were rioting, still trying to calm themselves.

"I was looking for you."

I stood tall.

"Russell texted me you were here."

"He needed some help."

"You took out the garbage, I see." She thumbed toward the street intersecting the alley.

"Young punks causing trouble."

She chuckled. "Young? They pretty much look your age."

"Punks nonetheless." If she only knew how many years I had on those children.

The moonlight bathed her figure in a silver spotlight. She leaned against the wall, one foot propped against the building and her hands hidden behind her.

~ ☾ ~

My breath hitched. Time to leave.

"Are you okay?" she asked.

"Yes."

She pushed away from the building. Every nerve ending peaked with attention. My body hummed for hers. I glanced to the street adjacent to the alley. Empty. The scent of lilac caressed my senses, heating my blood.

"I'm glad I found you." Her voice was low, husky. She rested her palm on my chest. "I'm glad you came here tonight."

"We should get back inside."

"Not just yet." She edged closer. Mere inches separated our bodies from contact. "I can't figure it out."

"What's that?" I sucked in a sharp breath and edged back a fraction.

Her intense stare pinned me to the brick. Her eyes searched my face as if figuring a mathematical equation. She raked her teeth over her bottom lip and slouched, looking disappointed, like she couldn't read my mind.

I coughed at the stinging fire blooming deep within my chest. The demon pricked its venomous talons into my heart, urging me to take her. He sensed the same goodness oozing from her every pore and wanted to abolish it. My mouth watered at the thought of being closer to Beka. How she'd feel against me. Beneath me.

No. I must stay strong. Can't. Lose. Human. Half.

"Why do you keep me at a distance?" she asked.

"I'm sure I don't know what you mean." I fought hyperventilation my breaths came so fast. But they matched hers.

"I don't understand how I could feel this for you. I hardly know you. Not even your last name." Her gentle voice caressed my beaten soul. "And you're not. . . ."

She inched closer. Her soft breasts molded to my chest. I kept my hands at my side. Lust triggered an ache, a need I knew couldn't be fulfilled.

Her gaze focused on my mouth. She ran her tongue the span of her upper lip, and my body screamed to take her.

"We should get back in . . . ." My voice trailed off the last

~ ☾ ~

word. Beka didn't move. One more step, and she now stood so close she had to straddle one of my legs.

"You do not feel the same for me."

"It is not—" My voice faltered. "I will leave soon." I couldn't give in to her. I'd lose my human soul.

"I know. That's why I do not understand this," she whispered. "I should not feel as I do for you."

"Probably not a good idea, no." A groan reverberated deep in my throat as I fought the urge to wrap my arms around her. Four hundred years I'd resisted lust's temptations. I must remain steadfast.

Her fingers grazed up my arms and cuffed my biceps. She turned her gaze to my chest as her hands skimmed across it. I yanked in a sharp breath. Her touch was like a match striking to light. It singed my skin beneath the fabric. I leaned forward as if bewitched, but resisted, resting my head against the wall. More like pounded it.

I can't.

Her hands moved up my chest. When she hit my flesh, her fingers curled around my neck. I unfolded my hands, losing my battle with restraint. I ached to touch her. To revel in the softness pressed against me. I'd never allowed such luxuries. Too intimate. Too difficult to resist. I shut my eyes.

"Look at me, please."

If I did, I'd lose control. I'd dive in and there would be no returning. My entire being would be lured into darkness.

"David."

I finally complied. Her lids hung heavy over her eyes. A deep breath brought her body flush with mine again.

Acting on their own accord, my hands reached for her face. One cheek per hand. Silk, just like I'd imagined. Her eyelids fluttered. My fingers glided down the sides of her throat, her pulse hammered against my skin. Down I went, drinking in her softness until I reached her chest. I hesitated at the edge of the fabric, knowing what would happen should my hands continue. But I must not have cared, because they navigated over cotton barrier and cupped her breasts.

Her eyes rolled back, and her teeth trapped her bottom lip. She swayed her hips against me. "David." She clasped her

~ ☾ ~

hands behind my neck, anchoring herself to me as if battling a turbulent storm.

Enjoying every incinerating moment, I caressed her body, claiming it. I slid my hands behind her, pulling her against me. So close her body molded to mine until I couldn't tell where I ended and she began.

She tilted my face toward hers. Inches separated our mouths, but it felt like an ocean. Closer. I needed more. Her pupils swallowed her entrancing irises. Fingers tightened around my neck, then wove up into my hair.

Stop this, David. Step away. I shoved the unwanted advice my logic spewed and dove in. Those lips belonged to me. Mine to taste.

Only mine.

Contact with her silky mouth stole my breath. Her grip tightened, but she didn't wrench away. A current pulsed to my chest. My rabid demon wanted to rip off her clothes and take her, but I stomped him down. Leaving one of my hands on her warm, lower back, I let the other trail up, following the dips and grooves of her spine.

I imagined it was her bare flesh, not the feel of her cotton shirt. My hand found her neck, and I tilted her head for better access. A moan filtered through her into my mouth, and she parted her lips, inviting me in. My tongue sought hers with a tentative brush, chasing her sweet taste and lilac smell. She deepened the kiss.

I crushed her to me, my hand massaging her lower back so her core rubbed against mine. The delicious friction the movements caused fueled my excitement.

Mine. Take her now. All I wanted to feel what I knew lay beneath her clothing, to touch her all over. She was mine to have. To—

The back door creaked, signaling someone coming out from the back of the club. Beka severed our connection. She stumbled back, taking in ragged breaths. Her stare bore through me, but her swollen, shiny lips demanded my attention. They still glistened from our kiss.

I leaned in for another taste. *More.*

"Beka?" Russell called out.

~ ☾ ~

His voice stopped me centimeters from Beka's mouth. Her warm breath rushed against my face. I bit back a throat vibrating rumble. The beast knew what it wanted, and he would take it if I let him. So, I battled the animal trying to emerge and pushed Beka away.

"Beka? Are you out here?"

"Yeah." She brought her dainty fingers to her mouth. "I found him. He's out here." She kissed my cheek and walked away.

I showed her my back and clamped my eyelids shut, willing my body to calm down. No doubt she'd felt my desire for her. What her kisses did to my body. What she tempted me to give up.

"What's going on?" Russell's voice trickled from around the corner.

"Nothing. Just needed some air after kicking those dirtballs from the club. We're coming in."

"Good, because it's getting swamped in there again."

The riot in my mind subsided. I pressed my hand against the brick to keep my balance. Maybe the burning followed by confinement would be worth missing the Mark this time. I could leave now, claim I couldn't locate Jessica and accept my punishment.

Then, I'd be away from Beka. She and Russell would protect Jessica, and I would be lost to the utter silence.

Or, I could lay with Beka, experience the love of a beautiful woman, triggering the transformation into a full-fledged demon. I wouldn't care about anything. All this torture and agony would vaporize. I—

A dainty hand touched my shoulder. Even that gesture knocked the breath from my lungs. I stepped out from the physical contact and faced her.

"Beka. That can't happen again." I wasn't quite sure how I found my voice, but I was glad I did.

However, I didn't enjoy the flash of hurt that flickered across her face. She drew in a breath and nodded.

"You're right. It can't. I don't know what came over me." Her gaze lowered to my lips, then to the ground. "I'm sorry I did that. I—" She brought her fingers to her mouth. "I—Will

~ ☾ ~

you still come in and help us tonight?"

"Yes." Because no matter how intensely I wanted Beka, I still had a job to do. And I would do it.

At least that was the plan.

~ ☽ ~

CHAPTER 11

I stood by the door, hands clasped behind me, surveying the inebriated patrons stumbling around establishment. Evidently I wasn't fast enough when it came to mixing drinks. So many new ones had emerged while I was away.

Since I'd broken up the fight earlier, I'd been moved to security detail. It was probably better, because behind the bar, there was little room. I found myself constantly brushing against Beka as she rushed to make drinks.

At least I had a clear view of the room. My keen eye examined every woman with red hair and brown eyes.

I caught Russell's glance while scanning the place. He lifted his chin and tilted his head, beckoning to me. I waded through the stream of bodies to the bar.

I propped myself against the thick wood, admiring Beka as she interacted with the patrons. Her smile lit the entire room more than the flashing lights. The dark-haired guy she spoke with stared at her with wide eyes, as did the short, stubby man standing beside him.

His tongue slid out while he scrutinized Beka. My blood ignited. She reached for the money he'd set on the counter, and he laid his hand over Beka's. I moved to intervene, but Russell reached over the bar and snared my forearm. "Can you grab another keg from the back?"

Nobody touches my Beka.

"David. Keg?" Russell said.

I tore my gaze from the man testing my patience with my woman and faced Russell.

"And David?" His eyebrows puckered together. He peeked at Beka. "I see you watching my sister. But please. Just stay away from her."

~ ☾ ~

"She looks old enough to make her own choices." I knew I should stay away, but for him to tell me this—

"You're just sweeping through town, though, you'll be gone soon. She's never had a boyfriend. I don't want you to up and break her heart. You hear me?"

Noble gesture made by the brother. I respected that. But what he said about Beka having never been with a man, I couldn't figure that out. She had to be more than a hundred years old from what I'd overheard her telling Russell. But to have been without a companion, as I have been, surprised me.

I dipped my head and moved to the back door. I spotted Beka at the edge of my vision, and I gave pause. Her gaze met mine, and a smile curved her full lips. I'd kissed those lips. Tasted that mouth. An elbow jabbed my rib, slicing my connection with Beka. I stepped aside and continued on my task.

Once in the supply room I let out the breath I'd held captive in my aching chest. The constant throb of the demon's desires grew tiresome. Darkness dominated the packed storeroom, and it soothed my frayed resolve. Shelves of bottles and various supplies lined three of the walls, floor to ceiling. The silver barrel of alcohol sat like a shiny Altar in the corner to my right. How the humans drank in worship of the amber liquid, it had rightfully earned such a reputation. I'd seen it many times over the centuries.

I grabbed the rims of the cylindrical barrel and twisted it toward the door. A small figure shadowed the doorway.

"Excuse me, Sir?" she said.

I recognized the chocolate colored hair immediately. It was the girl I helped during the scuffle when her boyfriend knocked her over.

"Do you remember me?" She gripped the side of the doorframe.

"I do."

"Since you helped me before. Could you help me again?"

I stood tall, holding her gaze steady. "What is the problem?"

The girl's matted hair rested on her shoulders. Dirt

~ ☾ ~

smudged her bare, tiny arms. "There are some scary men in the parking lot, near my car."

"Where is your companion?"

"He isn't my boyfriend. I was just trying to get someone to buy me and my sister some food." She sniffled. "I'm scared to get to my car, and my sister's asleep in the back seat. I need to check on her." Tears streamed down her cheeks.

"Show me."

She led me out the back of the club and into the dark alley. We went to the left and veered right, toward a back lot.

"I snuck in the back of the club, hoping you'd be there. I didn't see you standing guard at the front anymore."

"You were watching?"

She bobbed her head, curls sweeping over her forehead. "You helped me before. And—well—you're so big."

How ironic. This young, frail human wanted me, a demon, to help her when two Guardians owned the club.

She raised her hand, motioning for me to stop, and pointed to her right. I steered her behind me and maneuvered to the end of the silver-wired fence. Gage and two other demons circled an old, rusted car, heads tilted back, nostrils sniffing the air.

I knew that posture. They were hungry for a soul. I didn't recognize the two demons flanking Gage. Short bushes, acting as a fence, edged the far end of the gravel lot, and the four-door sedan backed up against it. I followed a stench to my right and found two green dumpsters. To my left, a tall brick building loomed.

I pointed to the ground at the girl's feet. "Stay."

A hiss diced the darkness. A third demon lumbered from the shadows the dumpsters offered. He advanced. I took two long strides and leapt into the air, meeting him four feet above the ground. His nails sunk into my forearm, but I allowed my nails out and slashed his throat. His body flopped to the ground, a pile of ash and tar.

"What are you doing, Dav—"

I raised my hand motioning him to shut up. "Get away from here." I sped to Gage. "We're being watched," I whispered and jammed my open palm against his chest,

~ ☾ ~

knocking him back.

Another hiss from the side. I stood, chest puffed and faced the demon.

"Don't," Gage ordered the young minion. "Back away."

"But the light. It draws me to it." The demon approached the car.

"Light?" I asked.

"David?" Beka yelled from behind me.

"Go," I said to Gage.

He waved the remaining demons to follow him, and they faded into the shadows.

"David." Beka's voice cracked. "Where are you?"

I faced the entrance to the dirt parking lot, and she rounded the corner. The darkness didn't mask the fear in her eyes. She reached back, and the girl grabbed her hand. Beka led her toward me.

"Elizabeth said you were in trouble with some bad men?"

"I scared them off."

The girl sidestepped Beka and sprinted to the car. She cranked open the door and climbed in the back seat. I eyed Beka, and she raised her shoulders, indicating she didn't understand either.

The gravel crunched beneath my feet as I pivoted. Gage's outline loomed near the car.

"Elizabeth?"

She crawled out of the car. "She's okay. Still sleeping. But I think something's wrong."

"What, honey?" Beka went to her knees in front of the girl.

"Her chest is glowing."

Trees rustled behind Elizabeth and Gage's figure materialized. I dove over Elizabeth and tackled him at the waist. We rolled but I gained the top and buried my fist in his face. I hopped to my feet and leapt to the car. Inside a tiny girl, long red hair, chest glowing, lay on the cracked leather seat.

Jessica Hanks.

I reached in and gathered her into my arms.

"David?" Beka said.

"Get back. There are more here." I hugged the sleeping girl

~ ☾ ~

close and backed away from the open car door. "Beka. If you have your sword, get it out now."

"Sword?" She froze. "How—?"

"Do it." My voice echoed off the trees.

Metal scraping metal rang through the air. She held a dagger up and settled her pant leg over a holster around her calf. Darkness surrounding the car came alive as seven demons surged forward.

"Elizabeth. Run to the club. Get my brother, Russell. Do it now."

She whimpered, but I heard the gravel shifting so she must have obeyed.

"Jessica. Wake up." I jostled the girl. Her glow intensified, but she didn't move. I needed her awake so she could hold onto me while I fought.

Although I wasn't sure I could fight Beka. Because if I did I would kill her.

And I didn't think I could kill one whom I loved with my entire human, and even maybe my evil, soul.

"David. Hand the Mark to me," Gage said.

I flashed my fangs. "Stay back."

"David?" Beka asked.

I continued backing away, keeping Gage and his henchmen in sight. Beka moved with me, three feet to my left. I cradled young Jessica in my right arm.

"Think about what you're doing, David. You can't breach your contract."

"I'm not. I got my Mark. I will turn her in." I glanced at Beka. Her eyes went wide, realization beginning to settle in. "After I learn more about her. Or in exchange for my contract."

Gage stopped. His black eyes flashed. "You wouldn't dare go against Master."

"If Jessica Hanks can help me gain my freedom, yes."

~ ☾ ~

CHAPTER 12

"David, no. You don't realize what you're doing," Beka said. "Please, hand her to me. I will keep her safe."

Shuffling from Gage's direction demanded my attention. I inched toward the entrance of the parking lot, keeping Beka and Gage in front of me. Only five feet until I met the brick wall of the neighboring building. I could set her down and get in front of her. They would not get through me to my Mark.

Gage and his group closed in. "David. We will take the girl now."

I met the wall and settled my treasure against it, while staring at the demons and Beka approaching. Gravel crunched beneath their weight, kicking up the sun-baked dust. The breeze carried a smoky scent of anger mixed with the acidic hint of fear.

First Beka pointed the dagger at me, and then at the demons encroaching her, then back to me. The confusion and anguish flashing across her angelic face made my blood smolder with rage.

I wanted her. To discover a way out of my contract to Master and be with her. Even though she'd be immortal and me human, I didn't care. I wanted her and nothing else. If the price was Jessica, I might pay it.

At least I'd be free from Master. If I explained everything to Beka, she might understand.

No she wouldn't. I was a demon. If a battle ensued she would soon see how evil I was. I would repulse her.

"I can help, David." She held her head high. "Let me help you."

My heart hammered. She could never love me. I allowed some of my demon to surface. He readily obliged. A vicious

~ ☾ ~

WASTELAND

snarl thundered deep within my chest, warning the demons not to challenge.

Beka froze, arms tensed. "David." Her chin quivered.

A minion lunged at her.

"Beka, on your three." My voice was no longer mine. I fully morphed into the despised creature within me. Her scream tore at the remnants of my soul as she witnessed my transformation. It had to be done. Three demons approached me, fully transformed, weapons drawn.

A silver sword appeared and blocked the first demon's advance, slicing his neck.

Russell.

I lashed out at the second and third. The force rammed me against the wall. But their strength was no match for mine.

At my feet, Russell reached for Jessica, and I planted my foot against his forehead, knocking him back. A demon's nails scored my neck. I returned the favor, only deep enough to sever his head.

The other stabbed at my thighs, mauled its way to Jessica. I barely recognized the roar streaming from my mouth. Fully morphed, my humanity weakened by the second. I clapped my hands over his ears. My nails dug into his skull, just above the creature's ears, and I twisted his head. With a flick, my dagger-like nails slashed the neck.

Gage approached Beka from behind.

"Russell, get Beka," I yelled while handling another demon making his way to Jessica. I cranked my knee into his gut. I snatched the dagger from his hand and impaled his chest.

Metal hitting metal rent the air. Russell's sword met Gage's dagger. Beka poked at his chest, then squatted for a sweep to the legs.

Gage jumped and came down heavy on Beka's leg. The snap reverberated off the building, fueling my already brimming rage. She crumbled to the ground, still swinging her blade. Another demon tackled Russell from the back, leaving Beka to handle Gage.

I glanced between Jessica and Beka. Agony shredded my chest. I lugged Jessica up and threw her over my shoulder, then sprinted toward Gage.

~ ☾ ~

I steeled my grip on the dagger I'd stolen from one of his henchmen and leapt into the air. As I passed over him, I flicked the blade and ran it across his neck. Blackness sprayed over Beka, covering her in soot, but Gage slouched to his knees.

He threatened that which I considered mine.

For that, he died.

Gage's body disintegrated into the gravel. The remaining demons froze, paralyzed without their leader. Russell finished the two battling him and the third ran.

Surely he would get word to Master. And in the moment I'd killed Gage to save Beka, I'd sealed my fate. I'd sacrificed one of my kind to save a Guardian, our archenemy.

There was no saving me now.

~ ☾ ~

CHAPTER 13

"Where are you taking her?" Elizabeth asked as I passed the back door to the club.

"To safety. Get inside, Beka and Russell will come soon and care for you."

I clutched Jessica to my chest and sprinted around the corner. Not safe to go back to my hotel room. But I'd stashed plenty of money in the SUV in case of an emergency, so I would stop there first, grab it, then seek out a place to hide with this child.

She hadn't moved yet. She couldn't be sleeping. Not through the fighting earlier and now the movement of me trudging down the sidewalk. I slowed to a brisk walk, keeping to the shadows of the pre-dawn darkness. I pressed my fingers to her neck and a strong, steady pulse drummed. I jostled her body so she draped over my arms, exposing her chest more.

A dark, cotton t-shirt covered her, but the subtle glow seeped through. Heart shaped.

"So, Gage was truthful in telling me what the Master's Seer had seen." A car approached on the street, so I crouched next to a tree, three feet off the sidewalk.

I rested Jessica's bottom on my thigh, holding her steady and lifted her arm. No cuts or bruises. Same with the other arm. I twisted her forward to examine her back. No blood or holes in her shirt. Legs were clear, too. I nestled her back, weaving my other arm beneath her knees and stood.

Straight, red hair framed her pudgy, girlish face. Not much had changed since the picture I'd memorized.

The car passed, and I got on track for my SUV. Within ten minutes, I had the bag of cash strapped to my back and the

~ ☾ ~

girl still in my arms. I was strong, but not strong enough to carry her indefinitely.

I spied a hotel, near an old railroad station. I needed time to figure out my next move. A quick inspection of the area showed me no one had followed, and within fifteen minutes, I latched the door shut on a tiny, dirty hotel room.

The queen-sized bed dwarfed little Jessica Hanks. Her frail body sunk into the thick comforter. I settled a blanket over her.

I doused the lights and paced the length of the bed, staring at the girl.

Master wanted her, badly. The Guardians thought she would change the earth by her very existence.

So, that meant she had to be a powerful source of good for them to protect.

My phone ringing launched me to the bag I'd tossed on the table beside the bed. I dug in search of the blaring device. Only Master and Gage had this number, which meant it must be Master calling.

Finally my fingers landed on the sleek instrument, and I pulled it out.

Gage's face scrolled across the screen.

~ ☾ ~

CHAPTER 14

"Housekeeping." A female voice seeped through the closed door.

I hopped to my feet, checked the peephole, and peeked out the window. A tall, dark haired woman stood next to a cart. It neared eight a.m., I had stayed up sitting in the unforgiving wooden chair watching Jessica lay unconscious all night, she never moved.

I plopped back into the chair.

A knock jolted the door. "Housekeeping."

The familiar beep of the plastic key disengaging the lock had me to my feet again. Evidently they didn't observe do not disturb signs.

"No thank you," I yelled.

The door burst open, splintering the frame and Russell, sword drawn, barged in. His cold blade pierced my midsection.

My demon's fury raged. I clapped my hands around his wrist and guided the blade further into my stomach, bringing him closer to me. My demon-side emerged, and Russell's eyes went wide. He jerked, but my grip on him was relentless.

I peeled his fingers from his weapon and stepped back, pulling the silver blade from my body. I lurched forward and yanked him by the neck toward me, spun and kicked the door closed.

He lurched forward, smacking my forehead with his. His knee pelted my stomach, thankfully missing anything vital. I released him, turned a circle and had the sword to his neck before he registered I'd moved.

"I could kill you so easily, Russell."

He choked out an unintelligible word. A curse maybe.

~ ☾ ~

Surprising.

"How did you find me?"

"We have connections." He huffed. "And Gage's phone."

"That explains the call I received. You tracked me with it?"

Russell's Adam's apple bobbed, and he stiffened in my grasp. I held the weapon fast to his neck but maneuvered us so I stood between him and Jessica.

"Where is Beka? Is she safe?"

"Like you care, *Demon*."

I smacked the flat of the sword against his temple.

"Yes. She's safe."

I glanced to Jessica, keeping the blade to Russell's neck. I phased out from the demon's hold on my heart.

"What in heaven's name are you?"

I faced Russell and saw utter wonder in his eyes. "I am not from Heaven."

"You're demon."

I stood tall.

"How did you evade my senses, and Beka's?"

"I shall be asking the questions, Guardian. I hold your sword, do I not?" I nodded to the seat next to the table. "Sit."

I sat on the bed, next to Jessica, weapon trained on Russell.

"Where is Beka? You said she is safe."

"That's all you need to know, Demon."

"Noble to protect your sister." I pointed at Jessica. "What is this girl?"

"You don't know?"

"I thought it obvious by my question."

"Why'd you take her, then?"

"She is my Mark. I must or suffer the consequences. What is she?" I raised my sword again to show my impatience.

"We know little about her other than she will change the face of the supernatural earth." Russell's gaze bypassed me to the girl. "Somehow."

"You do not know?"

Russell edged forward in his seat. "Only that she harbors a power greater than any on the earth. She will fight for Light."

"Light?"

~ ☾ ~

"For everything good and pure."

Everything I wasn't. "No wonder Master wants her."

"Master?"

"Why did you come here alone?"

"Beka and I were tasked with finding and guarding Jessica." Russell planted his elbows on his knees. "Save a few familiars helping, it is just Beka and myself."

I laughed. "You are not doing such a good job."

A wave of smoky anger burst from Russell. His fisted hands blanched at the knuckles. "How did you evade our detection?"

"Where were you to have taken little Jessica when you found her?"

"It has not been revealed to us yet."

"Explain this to me." I rested my hand on Jessica's wrist. A slow, steady beat pulsed against my fingertips.

"You do not know Guardians do you?"

"Only those I've killed. Not much call for conversation during battle."

Russell grimaced. "We follow the will of *our* Master."

"As do I."

"Obviously not. Or you would have returned to him with your prize."

"I will. I am just taking a detour first." The sword began to feel like a weight, and I rested the hilt on my thigh, but sent Russell a feral reminder to him I had the advantage.

"Why have you not killed her? Or me for that matter," he asked.

"It is of no concern to you. Tell me everything about Jessica."

"I will not."

I tapped the flat end of my weapon against his knee. "You would die for her?"

"Yes," he said without a moment's hesitation.

"A stranger, yet you would sacrifice your life for her? That's absurd. You're what, two centuries old?"

"Try four."

I dipped my head. "Four hundred years. That is a feat in itself to survive such a long time."

~ ☾ ~

"You?"

"The same. And Beka?"

"I'd rather not say."

"Then I'll assume four hundred since you address her as sister. It must be in your family."

"Assume what you like."

My body ached for Beka. To see her eyes and touch her face. To kiss her and feel her body. Only a brief taste of her and I'd become an addict. But Russell wouldn't betray his sister's whereabouts. Not that I could go to her now. The betrayal her eyes revealed when I morphed into my demon will forever be engrained in my memory.

"Jessica." I tucked her hand beneath the blanket. "Tell me about her."

"No."

"Then we are at a stalemate. What would you expect me to do in this situation?"

"I cannot say. So far, as a demon, you have surprised me."

"Surprised?"

"You protected Beka when her leg was broken, and she was vulnerable to the one you called Gage. You killed him. One of your own." He pushed himself further back into his seat and rested his elbows on the wooden arms. "Even now you protect Jessica by putting yourself between me and her."

My stomach rumbled. Should I tell him I am not a full demon?

"But it is not I who will harm Jessica. Your kind wants to see her dead. To banish a creation that will send a ripple through the fight of good and evil." He smiled. "In our favor, of course."

"If you were to have her, what would you do next? How would you learn your next move?"

"*Our* Master will share with us when we should leave and where we should go," Russell said.

"But you own an establishment."

"No. We only run it as part of our cover."

"Seems I was not the only one dishonest during our relationship."

"Relationship?" Russell's jaw clenched. "Please."

~ ☾ ~

"So, where does this leave us, Guardian?"

How could he sit there with such peace on his face? His hands lay folded in his lap. Not one wrinkle of worry or fear creased his forehead. I kept a sword within a lethal distance. I held Jessica, who was predicted to change the face of the supernatural earth, captive. She was a beacon of Light from what I interpreted from Russell. Yet he didn't appear frightened.

He was willing to die for this girl.

This might be a Master I'd enjoy working for.

~ ☾ ~

CHAPTER 15

"I will not take you to Beka." Russell launched out of his chair.

"I have shown my trust by not killing you. Does that not stand for something?"

"Can you hear yourself, Demon?"

"I shall not betray my oath and kill you." I stood, sword at my side. "Unless you try to kill me or take my Mark."

"Your *Mark?*" Russell buried his fingers in his thick, dark hair. "She is not a *Mark*. She is a human, going through something that will forever change her, change our reality."

"You do not know that for sure."

"I take it on faith. As you do on your assignments from your Master."

"It is not faith I have in my Master. It is obligation."

"That's the difference. I *choose* to follow mine." He faced me again. "Why would you opt to follow evil, kill innocent people, just to please your Master?"

"It is not your concern, Russell." I pointed at Jessica. "She hasn't moved since I retrieved her. Do you know what is wrong?"

He snuck toward the bed, and I patted his shoulder with the flat of his sword. "No farther. Just answer."

"She has not moved? Eaten? Used the restroom?"

"She is catatonic."

"Supernaturally, maybe. Preparing her body for a change."

Russell stared at the child while rubbing his stubble-dusted chin. I sensed the desire to snatch her and try to escape oozing from his body. To try anything to save her from me. As much as I hated to admit it, I trusted this Russell, dare I say even liked him.

~ ☾ ~

"What change?"

Russell's lips turned downward. The nobility he'd shown toward Beka and now to Jessica and the honor rolling from his mouth when he spoke of his Master was enviable. My chances of successfully removing the contract for my soul might best be served by siding with the Guardians.

My demon side slashed at my heart so fiercely I clutched my chest wondering if his claws had poked through. The constant inner war between demon and human was growing tiresome.

"Sit." I ordered Russell. "I shall make a deal."

He eyed me as he descended into his chair. "I am not in the business of making deals with the devil. We kill demons like you, David."

"I am not—well, hear me out and then decide."

He sat back in his chair and clasped his hands behind his neck, holding my gaze.

"I will accompany you to where Beka and Elizabeth stay. You will share with me your plan. And I will share mine with you."

"You would do that?"

"Use your brain, Guardian. In four hundred years, have you come across a demon such as myself?"

He shook his head.

"Then you must realize, I am different."

"Is that why you toyed with Beka? You're more of a devious demon. You do not just go for humans' souls, you devour their hearts and will to live for sport?"

"Will to live? Explain this to me." My heart suddenly chiseled my ribs. This time, it wasn't in response to the demon but fear for Beka. Her safety. Anger at the thought of anything happening to her stabbed at my chest, which my demonic side loved. It fed on the agony and clamped its piercing fingers around my heart. "Is there something wrong with Beka?"

"What do you want with her?"

"Nothing. Your words confused me. You said something about her will to live. Did you not mean Beka?"

"I can't figure you out." He planted his palms on the arms

~ ☾ ~

of the chair.

I tensed, unsure if he planned to attack again. I thought him smarter, considering I held his sword, and easily overpowered him when he first charged in the room, but he seemed bewildered suddenly. Confused.

I stood, holding the sword out. I peeked at Jessica, and she lay silent, still. "Explain yourself. My patience grows weary."

"You act as if you worry for Beka, yet, you're a demon, how could this be?" He let out an audible sigh. "What I meant was, you broke her heart when you turned out to be—" He gestured in my direction. "When you turned out to be what you are. Whatever that is."

"Is she well?"

"Her broken leg healed, of course. We Guardians are not so fragile. But hearts do not heal as easily, even for us."

I had to see her. If only one last time before I left with my Mark. "Take me to her."

"You would come with Jessica?"

"Yes. Only to learn more about her. I shall not allow you to take her. She is my Mark and I will complete my contract."

"Demon."

"Decide." I twirled his blade in my hand.

"It is not far from here."

"Then we shall walk."

"But it's mid-day." Russell rubbed his eyes. "Do you not have an aversion to daylight?"

"I rather enjoy the sunlight. I can see things so clearly. But you are right, we will wait until the cover of dusk."

My thoughts fell immediately to Beka. The day in the restaurant. My first vision of her in daylight. It will be forever etched in my mind, which would be torture if confined to solitary for the rest of eternity for killing Gage and loving a Guardian.

~ ☾ ~

CHAPTER 16

"Would you like me to carry her?" Russell asked as the shadows of evening crept around us.

"Thank you, yes." I handed the limp girl to the Guardian.

He received her with wide eyes and raised brows. "You trust me to carry her without running."

"You couldn't outrun me, even if you were not carrying an eighty-pound girl. I am not worried." I eyed him. "And I know you do not want to die, which you would if you chose to run, as I mentioned earlier in the hotel. Jessica is mine, and I will kill you if you try to kill me or take her."

"Demon."

I almost said, 'not yet' but held off. That revelation will be made at the appropriate time, should I make the last resort choice.

"Have you been with Beka for all of your four hundred years?"

Silence. Russell stared down at the girl in his arms. He rested his cheek against her forehead.

"You refuse to betray any information about Beka to me."

Russell's lips pressed into a thin line.

"I respect that."

He looked at me. "I told you too much as it is already."

"I shall not betray your confidence to her. I must see her. Ensure she is well. Your slip has left me worried. The will is a very powerful thing. Without it, one would surely crumble." The familiar hardware store near the club came into view. "We are near your club."

"Yes."

"I am sure it will be under surveillance."

"We are not going in the front door." He cast a glare over

~ ☾ ~

his shoulder. "Give me some credit."

I stopped on the sidewalk in front of a vacant building across the street. The *For Sale* sign cluttered the front door and boards covered the main picture window. Possibly an old gas station or drive thru in a former life.

I turned to Russell. "Give me the girl."

"No. I'm fine."

"I was not inquiring about your status. I was instructing you, which means you do not get to choose. You do it."

He faced me. "If I might be so bold to say, I sense great conflict in you, David. I know you will make the right choice, despite what you are." He handed me the treasure.

The breath rushed from my lungs as Jessica's limp body sagged against mine. "I am not afforded the luxury of choice."

"I believe you made one by taking the girl and not giving her to your Master yet."

Choice. He knew nothing of *my* choices. One was to bring the girl in, complete my assignment and move on to the next, continuing my enslavement. Second choice would be to give her to the Guardians and declare my Mark missed, earning me another two hundred and fifty years in sensory deprivation. Third, keep Jessica, and discuss a trade with Master for my contract.

Not much for choices. All had dire consequences.

Shuffling to our left paralyzed me. Russell must have sensed it, or my sudden slowing, and mimed my reaction. He reached behind him, but grabbed only air and cursed. I still had possession of his sword. It was bound snug to my back while I held Jessica to my chest.

Not exactly a great position for battle.

It was only a matter of time until Master sent a legion after the girl and me. It appeared my choice was being made for me.

"David." Someone called out to me from around the corner of the vacant building.

"How close are we to your fort?" I whispered to Russell.

"Two blocks down, through the side door of the Coffee Grind."

"Then where?"

~ ☾ ~

Silence.

He still didn't trust me. I could hold no fault in that. I'd earned it.

"You killed Gage." The demon that had been with Gage came into focus. Two demons on either side.

Okay, five was manageable. Maybe the rest hadn't gotten to town yet.

"Now you walk with Guardians?"

"What is your name?" I asked while scanning the darkness to the sides and behind us. Russell did the same.

"They call me Ignis."

"That's too bad. Do you dare challenge me, Ignis?"

He bared his fangs.

"You saw what happened to Gage. Six hundred years of servitude to Master, and he fell within seconds. You cannot harm me." I glanced at Russell. "Keep moving."

I hugged Jessica tight. For the first time since I'd grabbed her, she moved. Her glowing chest pulsed brighter, and it shimmered against me. She must sense my demon starting to surface. Starting to sizzle and claw at my chest.

"You hold the Mark in your arms, you must return to Master." Ignis drifted closer, a dagger in each hand. Three more demons rounded the corner.

Eight wasn't so easily manageable.

"I shall. I am not in breach," I said.

"We will escort you."

"No thank you. Be gone. I will return in a few days time. After I learn more about her."

"You are a runner. Not a researcher, there is no need. Come now."

I twitched my lip over my descended fangs. "You do *not* command me."

"I speak on Master's authority."

Pain seared my heart. I couldn't hold back a grunt. "I will return."

"David, don't," Russell said.

"I must." I nailed Ignis with a glare. "Come help me with the girl, but the Guardian lives."

"We cannot allow that."

~ ☾ ~

"He is of no consequence. He cannot hurt me, and I have the child. He can go." I glanced at Russell. "I suggest leaving now."

"I will not."

"Stubborn fool." I backed toward him. "Don't forget your sword."

He shot me a look of utter surprise. Hopefully that meant he understood what I was about to do, though I was unsure I did. I couldn't turn this girl over, yet if I didn't, I would be punished. *Again*. But if she had the power to free me, make me human, somehow . . .

"Ignis. Give me your word the Guardian lives."

He offered a brief nod.

"I will come with you."

The demons crept forward, like timid dogs. I let my evil surface enough to give me the long nails, fangs, and heightened senses. Two more demons stayed back in the thicket across the street. Their outlines barely visible, even with my sight.

I lifted Jessica to Ignis. Delight brightened his tar-black eyes, and a smile creased the red skin at the corners of his mouth. He reached for the girl.

With lightning speed, Russell withdrew his sword from its sheath, circled me, and sliced the hands from Ignis. Another spin decapitated him with the ease of a true warrior. Russell stood in front of me, facing four demons while I held the girl. A Guardian protected me. A demon.

Four demons stepped out from the darkness. They wore the badges of my Master on the left breast of their shirts. Elite warriors. Ones sent to impose punishment. They could incapacitate me enough to get the collar activated, rendering me weak enough for transport.

Their all too familiar seven-foot-frames sent the hair prickling on my forearms. Metal to metal clanked as Russell engaged three demons.

One got through.

I shifted my treasure to my hip and finished morphing into my evil half. I held my big hand out and ducked at the first swing of the sword. My fingers slashed his neck. His head

~ ☾ ~

tipped, and thudded to the ground.

Two of the Elite approached. "You have missed your Mark. We have come to impose punishment."

"I have not. She is in my arms. By contract, you cannot."

The warriors stopped. "You agree to return with her?"

"Yes. I am not in breach of contract."

"You must return with us," they said in unison, like programmed robots.

"I shall return in two days. On my own, as I always do."

They surged like lightning bolts of energy. Flashes of silver ignited as they drew their swords. I raised my forearm to meet their strikes, holding Jessica with my other arm.

Their swords rushed me, but they were intercepted by two others and sparks rained. Russell on my left, Beka on my right.

Beka spun, snipping the legs out from the warriors while Russell worked simultaneously to run his sword over their necks, toppling their heads. The two remaining bolted into the air and came down on us.

One collided with Russell, knocking him to the side. The other sliced his weapon down the side of Beka's arm. She sprung back onto her hands, and her foot rammed the demon's face, knocking him off balance.

I charged, reaching for his neck. He swung his sword. I ducked and slashed his mid-section. The demon darted toward Beka, drawing a second sword. He crossed it over the other, aiming for her throat.

I vaulted over Jessica's small body, into the path of the crossed swords, familiar with their lethality. I planted my palm in Beka's chest, knocking her over. The blades connected with my neck. Sparks sprayed.

I dug my fingers into the demon's chest and lifted him from the ground. His swords grated against my neck again, rendering more sparks into the air. With my other hand, I swiped at his neck, and he faded into the ground.

I snatched Jessica into my arms. A prick stung my throat.

I looked down a long, silver blade and met Beka's vibrant eyes. Blood followed the curve of her high cheekbones and dribbled off her jaw.

~ ☾ ~

Her moist eyes flickered and chin quivered. "Give her to me, Demon."

I'd been called demon many times, yet it stung more than ever coming from Beka. "I cannot."

Beka's blade waivered. "Please. David," she whispered. Her shoulders sagged.

"I cannot."

A tear escaped from the corner of her eye as the tip of Beka's sword dented my flesh. "Then I have no choice but to kill you."

~ ☾ ~

CHAPTER 17

Beka swung, and I blocked the blade with my wrist. Sparks flared. Her eyes widened, but she forged onward.

Jessica's weight held me captive, not that I intended to fight Beka. She surged forward, full strength, with another swing. The demon burst from inside me with a roar.

"How could you do this?" She swung, and I ducked.

She turned, aiming for my legs, I jumped, but with her speed, she got in another revolution. The tip of her blade nipped my hip. Metal to metal behind us told me Russell still fought off demons. I hadn't tracked how many were there. My focus was on Beka.

I had to concentrate very hard to keep my demon from killing her.

"Stop. I do not wish to harm you." I backed away.

The demonic instinct for self-preservation warred with the conflicting instinct to save that which I viewed as mine. Holding Jessica was the only thing preventing me from mounting a full force attack. I couldn't get the momentum carrying eighty extra pounds.

"Give her to me." Beka and I circled each other. Her sword pointed at me, but I remained weaponless. I had a dagger bound to my ankle, but I couldn't make myself grab it. I would kill her if I let my demon have a chance.

But I loved her and couldn't allow him to harm her.

An impossible union. She was Light. I was darkness. I'd only met her days earlier. Maybe the two hundred and forty-five years of solitary had dented my sanity, not that I was exactly sane to begin with.

"Back away, Beka. I do not trust my control." My nose twitched at the metallic tainted lilac scent. "Please."

~ ☾ ~

"Never." The anger and hate for me rippled the air around her. I'd stabbed her to the core with what I was. A demon. A thing she killed to preserve all that was good. The betrayal she must feel.

I despised what I was. All I could hope for was to get the contract removed and try to exist in this world as a human, somehow. Some way.

It would be much better with her by my side.

She struck again, and I dodged the sword aimed for my neck. "You will hurt Jessica. Please stop."

"Give her to me, Demon."

"I cannot."

"Why?"

"She is my Mark. I'm contracted to turn her in."

"You speak riddles and deception, David. How could—" Her breath caught. "I—"

Russell grunted from the side. A sword pierced his stomach. I lunged and buried my claws in his attacker's shoulder. Beka leapt to the demon and beheaded him, then trained her weapon on me again.

"You fight both sides. I do not understand this." She inched forward.

I backed away, gravel shifting beneath my boots. The beast overwhelmed my heart the longer I stayed in my demon form. Jessica felt like a thousand pounds in my arms. I set her down under Beka's scrutiny. "Please, Beka. I don't want to hurt you."

"Too late."

With one hand gripping Jessica's shoulder, I knelt before Beka and showed my human form. "Tell me of her importance. What is she?"

"A treasure. Purity at its finest. Something you know nothing about."

"Purity?"

"Her goodness is so potent, it leaks from within her. See how her chest glows?"

The light pulsed.

Beka stood tall and widened her stance. "I will not let you have her, David."

~ ☾ ~

WASTELAND

"You have no choice in the matter."

"I believe I am holding the sword."

I bent at the waist, exposing my neck. "Try it."

She whimpered. "Don't make me do this, David. Just give me the girl."

"I cannot."

"You keep saying that. Tell me why. Tell me what you are. You evaded my senses. Drew me in."

She'd drawn me in as well. I'd come so close to giving myself to her, which would condemn me to darkness. "I did not mean for that."

"But you did." She straightened her back. "You're a—" She sagged to the ground, dropping her sword, shoulders shaking. "Demon."

Sadness oozed off her and nearly flattened me like a steamroller. I looked at Jessica's limp body.

"Beka!" Russell's panicked voice tore me from my stare. A sword penetrated Beka's torso from behind and stayed planted, while another blade rested across her throat.

I lunged to my feet and phased to full demonic form so forcefully my human bones protested. A roar ripped through the air, one so deep and raspy I wouldn't have known it as mine had I not felt it leave my throat. "Release her."

"Walk away from the girl," the demon said. One of Master's Elite. Must have been hiding in the darkness awaiting his opportunity. He held a collar in his hand. If it touched my wrist or neck, I would be rendered immobile and returned to Master for sentencing.

Another quarter millennia of darkness.

I diverted my gaze from Jessica to Beka. Tears spilled from her wide eyes, and her hand gripped the demon's blade. Blood flowed from her palms, oozed down her wrists and dribbled off her forearm to the gravel. She was holding the sword, preventing it from severing her neck.

Russell appeared by my side, sword drawn. Beka alternated her attention between us. My chest heaved as I debated. I needed the girl. Somehow I knew she could free me from my contract if she was purity like Beka declared.

Nails pierced my throbbing heart. The demon took hold. I

~ ☾ ~

scanned the darkness. Not a thing moved. The air hung heavy and still. No demons left. Just this one. I could best him, but he would detach Beka's head before I reached him. If I walked away from Jessica, I prolonged the inevitable.

Russell stood tall by my side, as if my partner in fighting the very thing I was. Or at least partially was. His shoulder nudged mine. Light and dark with a similar objective.

To save the one we loved. And I did love Beka. But did I love her enough to hand Jessica over to the demon to spare Beka's life? Or let Russell take the girl and watch the demon behead my woman.

Beka whimpered. Tears streamed down her face as her gaze stayed focused on me. "Don't let them get her. David. I beg you."

Blood spurted from her neck, igniting a hurricane of fury raging through my body.

"Stop." My voice thundered. "You will trade."

The demon laughed. "The girl for this Guardian."

"No. The Guardian for me."

"You are of no consequence to me, *half-breed*. I want the girl."

"For what?"

"Master shall be her mentor. Now step away or your Guardian's head will roll."

My demon's talons punctured my heart. Beka's hands and neck ran crimson, and her body struggled against the blade.

I lifted my hands in surrender. "Your word she lives if I step away."

"No, David," Beka said with a rasp. "Girl. More. Important."

"Not to me."

There, I'd decided. I choose Beka's life. Once free, she and Russell would get to Jessica somehow. I had to believe that. But Russell alone would not survive this demon. Beka and Russell would get the girl. While I got solitary.

"I will step aside. You release the Guardian when I do."

"Why do you care for this one? She is of the Light. You are demon."

I reared my fangs, and inched to the side.

~ ☾ ~

"The other Guardian as well," the demon said to Russell.

"I will not." Russell knelt beside Jessica.

Beka whimpered.

"No! Russell," I said.

He picked Jessica up and backed away, eyes focused on Beka. "The girl lives."

"Run, Russell," Beka said. She squeezed her eyes shut, and the demon slid the blade. Her head fell back, and she sagged to the ground.

I leapt into the air and collided with the demon. His blade punctured my hand, then chest, but I saw only red. With one swipe of my nails, his head tipped. I landed on my shoulder, the gravel shredding my shirt. I rolled and scrambled to my Beka.

I wove one hand behind her head, cupping her blood-soaked skull, and my other clasped her neck, holding it together. "No!"

My hands turned human, and the blood streamed through my fingers. "Beka." My human voice cracked. Her head didn't roll off completely, so the cut had not gone through the entire neck. *Please let her survive.* Her strength was great, hopefully enough to have prevented complete separation.

So much blood, though. Pools formed beneath her head.

I'd battled many Guardians before. They were strong. Fighters. No angelic dust yet. She could still survive.

"Beka." I held her neck tight. "Heal. God. Please heal."

A sting, like liquor drizzled on an open wound, enveloped my hand. Electricity jolted up my arm and over my shoulder, leaving a wake of flames licking the surface of my skin. I bit back the instinct to jerk away.

My bellow rent the air.

All that connected her neck to her body were my hands. I must bear the agony and hold her together. I just hoped her Guardian nature fused her neck together instead of dissolving into the ground.

The burn zipped over my shoulder and into my chest. My heart seized. An ache froze my lungs, and the air rushed out. Nothing worked to draw in another breath.

I could not die, but it felt as if I had. My body sagged to the

~ ☾ ~

side. I held Beka's neck steadfast. She'd yet to move.

"No." I morphed into my demonic form. My heart stampeded back into action.

Beka choked out streams of red. Her body convulsed within my grasp. With one hand encompassing her neck, I wove my other arm around her waist and gathered her body to mine, her back to my stomach as I sat. "Breathe, Beka. Breathe."

Her heart pounded like a drum, strong and fast. Funny, mine beat the same rhythm. Her lungs expanded with mine. It didn't make sense, but I didn't care. I hugged her, reveling in the wonderful beating within her chest as I released the demon's hold.

Sitting on the cold, hard asphalt of the deserted parking lot, I buried my face in her matted, crimson-stained hair. I still detected a scent of lilacs above the metallic blood and dirt crusting her mane.

Mine.

The cold reality of what I'd done settled in. I'd lost my Mark to the Guardians, killed many of my kind. Soon, Master would call my contract in, compelling me to return to him.

But at least Beka lived.

I loosened my grip around her neck, convinced it had healed enough to not tip off her shoulders. A faint, thin ruby line ran the width of her throat. I skimmed my forefinger over the mark and savored her warmth.

Yes, she would be fine. I should leave now. Go face my judgment before Master ignites the contract and the burn drags me back to him.

I would feel enough torture for the next fifty years, no need to add to it by staying. I scanned the area. All clear. Russell had probably taken Jessica to their stronghold. I'd lost my chance with Jessica, but saved Beka.

I traced my fingers over her cheek and along her lower lip. I leaned forward and pressed my mouth against hers, then slid my arm out from around her. Her body eased off mine and onto the asphalt. I pushed myself up and stood over her.

Her head tilted, and her eyes remained closed as if in a deep slumber. I scooped her up into my arms and crossed the

~ ☾ ~

empty lot toward the coffee store Russell had mentioned.

I would see her safely there. Hopefully she would awaken and find her way to the safe house. She and Russell would protect the girl. Once Master learned the Guardian's had my Mark, he would call me to him. Nothing could stop that now.

Beka's cheek rested on my chest. Long eyelashes dusted her smooth, pale cheeks. The intimate contact stirred my demon. Not so much in violence like usual, more subtle. Subdued. Beka had seen my beast. Disgust ruled her eyes more than once. A memory I would not relish in solitary.

I tilted my head and rested my cheek on her forehead. Strands of hair tickled my nose, infusing her scent deep within me. *That* scent would get me through my punishment. The memory of our kiss. Her body molded to mine in the alley.

The tan stucco coffee house came into view, and I stopped at the curb across the street. The store's windows were dark, save the dim security lights casting a meek shadow on the empty chairs visible through the window.

A sapphire awning hung over the door, and a red bench sat empty, to the right of the entrance. The perfect spot to set her down for Russell to find. I inspected the treasure in my arms and tightened my hold. Her head tilted back, exposing her neck. Through the darkness I made out the line marring her skin. Forever marked by one of my kind.

"I love you, Rebeka Abbot." I peppered kisses along her forehead. "I know you can't hear me. But I had to say it out loud at least once."

I crossed the deserted street, my heart cracking with each step.

I settled her on the bench and rested her hands on her stomach. I knelt before her and caressed her cheek. Her head tilted toward me.

"You'll always be mine."

I pressed my lips against hers, for one last memory of her warmth, taste and smell. Maybe after two-hundred and fifty years, when I was released, I could find her again.

She would still reject me. She *should* reject me. I was demon.

~ ☾ ~

But a demon who had found love. I would concentrate on that for the next quarter millennia.

I stood and turned my back on the only person I would ever love.

"Don't go." Russell's voice flooded the overhead speakers. "Jessica can save your soul."

~ ☾ ~

CHAPTER 18

I froze on the sidewalk, beneath the sodium lights of the overhang, and faced the building. It might have been wishful thinking that made me hear Russell's voice. Maybe I'd finally cracked, mentally, and imagined his proclamation.

"Hello?" I said, facing the dark picture window. Further scans of the area showed me empty sidewalks. A short distance away, at the corner, the mechanical voice of the crosswalk counted down until the light turned to walk.

Beka lay motionless on the bench.

"Pick her up and move to the door," Russell's voice came out of the darkness from the speaker. "Do it now."

I gathered Beka in my arms. She nestled her face to my neck and breathed a deep sigh. It was the first movement she'd made on her own since the injury. She must be healing.

"Jessica ... safe," she whispered.

Even while straddling consciousness and unconsciousness, she worried for the girl's safety above her own. She'd sacrificed herself for the girl. But even more aggravating, Russell had been all too willing to sacrifice Beka for Jessica.

"She is safe. Be still, my love," I said with my mouth against her forehead.

I faced the front of the door, and the lock disengaged. I stepped back, analyzing the structure. The door was shaded, blocking me from seeing inside the establishment. Much like the tinting on the window to the room in Beka's apartment.

Balancing her weight, I reached for the steel handle and pulled it open. A wave of cool air funneled out, along with shuffling and heavy breathing. I stopped in the middle of the doorway. Icy fingers cuffed my wrist and dragged me in, nearly dislodging my grip on Beka.

~ ☾ ~

Cold metal pressed against my neck, while a figure skimmed by me and shut the door. The lock clicked.

I froze, fighting the raging instinct to morph into my demon half. Logically, I knew the person holding the sword against me to be Russell, but with all that had happened in the last day I fought to maintain control over the beast.

"She lives," Russell whispered. "I feared the worst."

I scanned the barely lit room. Eight round tables littered the floor and two plush couches in the corner made up the meager coffee house. The back of the room had a door, propped open and a sliver of light tinted red from the exit sign, glowed.

The blade disappeared from my throat, but in the next breath it chilled the base of my neck.

"Walk," Russell said.

"There is no need for the weapon."

"I'll determine that, thank you."

"It would do you no good."

"I did see the sparks ignite when the blades slid against your throat when you stepped in front of Rebeka. I do not understand this."

"Then why do you insist on jabbing me with the blade?" I moved toward the open door. The sign next to the door said *electrical*. "You are taking me to the electrical closet?"

"You can see that?"

"I see most everything in the darkness."

"Demon."

"Yet you bring me into your safe haven and allow me to carry your sister and fought by my side."

"Anything to save Jessica."

"That includes sacrificing your sister." I stopped by the door.

"If it was the price to save Jessica, yes."

"You are lucky I do not share your convictions."

"You saved her?"

"I believe that obvious since I hold her in my arms at the moment." I growled. "You, however, sacrificed her without a second thought. I am not pleased by your actions, Russell."

The cold, metal hilt of the sword cracked against my

~ ☾ ~

temple. Pain radiated down the side of my face to the base of my neck. My fangs slid out, and I snapped at Russell's blade, my full demon surfaced.

"How dare you say I did it without a second thought. She is my—" His shoulders widened. "I did what was needed."

Moisture pooled at the rims of his eyes. He stared me down, his jaw tense. He must not realize his behaviors were a direct challenge. I bit back a roar. He knew not what he did with such actions. I embraced Beka, my anchor to sanity. She was mine. Her safety was all that mattered.

"Back away," I managed a whisper, fighting for control.

I focused on Beka's face. Her delicate skin and full lips. I called on my human half, but the fiery demon refused to back down from a direct challenge.

Russell must have sensed the rage billowing off me and broke eye contact with me. "I did not mean to challenge you, David. I apologize."

My claws and fangs retracted.

"Jeez, David," Russell said.

"Do not stare me down again if you wish to live." My human voice was barely audible. Sweat trickled between my shoulder blades. I stood frozen, waiting for him to direct me.

He reached around me and swung the door open. "Keep moving."

I walked through the threshold, into the small closet. The hum of electricity emanated from the metal boxes hanging on the white walls, and the air carried a trace of sulfur.

Metal rang against metal as Russell sheathed his sword. Light flickered on above us, and the door shut. At the same time a gate, inches before us, slid to the side and latched onto unseen hinges. The floor shifted beneath me.

An elevator. I held Beka close.

"Relax. It's just an elevator."

"I have heard of them."

Russell coughed. "Heard of them?"

"Until I arrived at the hotel in this town, I had never been in one." I regarded the dark door boxing me in next to a Guardian and chuckled. Never envisioned myself locked in a wee room with an agent of Light, holding another agent of

~ ☾ ~

Light, with whom I'd fallen in love.

Master may call my contract due at any time, igniting an agony in my chest that wouldn't subside until I went to him. But when Russell admitted Jessica might be able to save me, I couldn't walk away. I had to risk punishment.

The sickening motion of our descent ended with a jolt, and sent me bouncing back. I'd heard about elevators when they first came into invention; however, the hotel's was smoother. I'd prefer not to ride either again.

The doors creaked open and a long, dark, narrow hallway greeted me. "Where are we?" I steadied myself on the now-solid ground.

"Tunnel under the street to the club."

"You constructed this?"

Russell ducked beneath the door out from the elevator. "It existed, we modified for our needs."

"We?"

"We have connections, remember?"

"Humans assist you?"

Russell reached for Beka. "I'll take her."

I hugged her close and twisted away from him.

"You are a strange demon to figure out." He moved down the hallway.

He wasn't the only one confused by my behavior, my emotions. The demon hadn't chipped away all of my humanity, and my feelings for Beka, my need to protect her, trumped logic.

Had I taken a deep breath and stood tall, my shoulders might touch both sides of the concrete walls and my head the ceiling. I cradled Beka close and slouched enough to move without scraping her or myself against the concrete shrouding me.

Thick, damp air, carrying the scent of dirt and mold filled my lungs. I pressed my cheek to Beka's forehead and let her familiar scent replace the dankness of this place.

Russell stopped in front of a metal door and peeked through the square window. He eased the door open, his hand on the hilt of his sword strapped around his waist. Cries from the rusty hinges echoed down the hall.

~ ☾ ~

WASTELAND

Grateful to be done with the claustrophobic tunnel, I welcomed the sight of stairs in the well-lit stairwell. We climbed three flights and met another door.

My arms twitched with fatigue, and I adjusted Beka higher to lean more into me. Her head rested on my shoulder, near my neck, bathing me in her fragrance. Dried blood ringed the neck of her copper shirt, tainting her lilac smell with a metallic scent. Strands of stiff, crimson-stained hair fell over her forehead as her head swayed with my movement.

Russell cranked open another steel door, holding it wide for me to pass. I stepped into the hallway I recognized as the one outside their apartment. I strode onward.

The door swung open and a massive guy, long raven hair draped over his broad shoulders, stepped through the doorframe holding a sword.

My heart discharged like a hand grenade. The demon burst forth and let out a hiss that would have scared a rattlesnake. My teeth elongated and talons emerged ready for battle should I have to drop Beka to fight.

The man's golden eyes flickered. He struck. I ducked, freed my arm from beneath Beka's knees and held her upper body to mine as I swiped at the blade. Sparks ignited as my wrist met the metal.

"No," Russell yelled. "Abraham, stand down."

I turned my body to shield Beka. Her legs swayed limp like a rag doll. So vulnerable.

Mine.

My instinct to protect her rivaled a wolf's protecting his mate. And she wasn't even my mate—officially.

The giant retreated to the doorframe, holding the sword up. "Demon."

Russell reached for the one he called Abraham. "I know." He glanced at me. "It's complicated."

"What is the complication, sir? Red skin, fangs, and black nails. Kill him."

"Do you not see who he holds?"

Abraham analyzed me with wide, golden eyes. He must finally recognize the long, blond hair draped against my chest. I had her face cradled close, shielding her from

~ ☾ ~

possible injury. "Our—"

"Back off or you shall die."

"A demon protects our —"

Russell raised his hand. "Silence. Sheath your weapon and back away."

The giant gave me another look but obeyed. Russell approached me, palms up. "Calm down, David."

"You and your people would do better to not surprise me."

He dipped his head in acknowledgment. "We are all on edge. It is only Abraham, Jessica, and Elizabeth in the room. Please, you will scare the girls if they see you like this."

I bent my knees and wove my arm beneath Beka's legs, cradling her limp body to my chest once again. I rested my cheek on her temple and focused on my human half. The one longing to join with Beka. To be with her always. Russell's tension-creased face softened. He brushed his knuckles down Beka's cheek.

"Your Abraham started to call her something. Our what?"

"We will talk later. Once Beka awakens." Russell stepped toward the open door but stopped and looked back. "But know this. You saved more than one treasure tonight."

~ ☾ ~

CHAPTER 19

Abraham stood outside the door leading to the dark room, his hands propped behind his back. He donned a supply of knives tucked into a dark vest, a long sword strapped to his side, and black boots with steel tips.

A thick band of leather encompassed his neck and wrists. Long black hair draped his wide, muscled shoulders. He turned in my direction and grumbled, then faced forward again.

"He guards the girl?"

"Yes." Russell exited the kitchen holding two plates of food. Beka lay on her side, back against the couch and head resting on a bright orange pillow. I sat on the edge of the soft, leather couch, my backside near Beka's stomach and planted my elbows on my knees, hands clasped before me.

"How long will Beka be like this? She's moved only twice," I asked.

"She's healing. Let me look at her." He set the plates on the table before me, then knelt near her head and brushed the hair from her face.

I didn't move. Instead, I picked up the plate and swirled steaming noodles around the fork.

"What's this?" Russell asked.

He pointed to the ruby line across her throat. "That is where the blade severed her neck."

He faced me. "Severed?"

The image of her neck detaching cinched my stomach like a noose. "I held her together until she healed enough to move."

Russell held my gaze. His mouth opened, then shut again. He returned his focus to Beka. "She should not have a mark.

~ ☾ ~

Once we heal, all traces are gone." He bowed closer, touching the mark. It spanned the entire front of her neck and was a quarter inch wide. "Was it deep?"

"Very." I choked down the noodles lodged in my throat. "I am surprised she survived."

Air rushed from Russell's mouth in an audible sigh, and he settled onto his heels. He bowed to Beka and pushed back from the couch. He snatched the other plate and regarded the room that housed Jessica.

"Where is the other girl?" I asked.

"Elizabeth is on Rebeka's bed, while Jessica sleeps in the protected room." Russell jutted his chin up. "You stayed with Beka. Protected her. Why?"

I wanted to say, *she's mine*, but I knew she wasn't. Didn't stop my wanting her to be, though. "Knew she could survive. She is strong." I sat up.

Russell's left brow crinkled, creasing his forehead.

I scooped another forkful of noodles. "What is Beka's age?"

"Much older than my four hundred years." He shoveled in the food.

"You are cryptic with your responses. It's irritating," I said. "Tell me what you are."

"You know what we are. I think I should be the one asking you that question, don't you?"

"You said Jessica could save my soul. Tell me what you meant."

"You are bossy, aren't you?" Russell set the plate on the table. His long, dark-brown braid flopped over his shoulder, but he flipped it back and settled into his chair. "Jessica is purity personified."

"Beka said that. Her chest glows. What can that do for me?" I swirled the last of the noodles around my fork.

Russell gripped the armchair. "It's all about you, isn't it? All of this. What do you want? What are you?"

"You first. Jessica is in high demand. Each side wants her. Is she one of us or you?" I regarded the small room I'd broken into earlier. Besides the furniture, on which we sat, only a table flanked by two floor lamps, decorated the simple room.

I could easily overpower Russell and his guard and snatch

~ ☾ ~

Jessica for myself. Facing Master with such a prize would surely grant me reprieve for killing my demon siblings. Possibly release me from my contract.

Russell's gaze drifted beside me. Following his line of sight landed my eyes on Beka. Peacefully quiet, sleeping. Hopefully regenerating to full health.

She had said Jessica was more important than her. Was willing to sacrifice herself. Russell as well.

"I'm waiting, Guardian."

"It was predicted a child, on her sixteenth birthday, will transform into Merus. Within her, she will house pure Light."

"And. . . ."

"We only knew her name and had a picture from when she was young. We were sent here to track her." Russell sank against the back of the leather chair across from me. "It took many months. I feared we'd failed."

"You were here many months with no leads? Why would you stay?"

Russell smiled. "Faith."

"Fools."

"We trusted we were here for a reason. Destined to protect the Merus." He scrubbed his stubbled face. One last glance at Beka, and he closed his eyes. "Then you showed up."

I cleaned the rest of my plate and set it on the table. Unconsciousness still exerted its dominance over Beka, yet she coiled her body around the back of mine so I touched her stomach. Her closeness wrapped me in warmth. I curled a strand of bloodied hair behind her ear and swiped a smudge of dirt from her cheek with my thumb. "How'd you know to come here?"

"We have our ways as I'm sure you do."

"Cryptic." I faced him.

"Cautious."

"Understood." I glanced out the window Russell's chair backed up to.

Strokes of purple licked the bottoms of small, puffy clouds hanging in the sky. The sun would rise soon, and the day brought the unknown for me. I fit in nowhere. Neither a full demon nor a full human. Bound to my demonic Master by a

~ ☾ ~

contract, yet bound to Beka, a Guardian, by love.

"What are you?" Russell planted his elbows on his knees and speared me with a stare.

"You know what I am."

"One called you a half-breed."

"I am unique."

"You evaded our detection. That means you must be—"

"Part human, part demon," Beka said from behind me.

The sound of her voice bathed me in heat, but the cold, steel blade pricking my neck stole that warmth.

~ ☾ ~

CHAPTER 20

I froze, my fingernails growing, digging into my skin. My teeth extended and brushed my bottom lip. I willed myself to remain human, to fight the instinct, but a snarl made it through my clenched jaw.

"Your instinct is to kill." Beka shuffled behind me, and the cold blade disappeared, making it easy for me to return to my human form.

"Yet, you retract the beast almost as soon as it emerges," she said.

I chanced a look. She propped herself up on her hand, watching me with intent eyes. Her hair, tinted pink from the blood, draped over her shoulder.

"How do you know I am both human and demon?" I asked.

"I know much, now." She hugged her knees to her chest, then unfolded her body until she sat directly beside me, feet planted firmly on the ground. "I have heard of attempts to mate humans with demons. Doesn't work, though, because the demon is too evil for a human female to carry to term."

The couch dipped beneath our weight, and her thigh touched mine. What surprised me, though, was she didn't move away. I had just partially morphed into the demon while sitting next to her, and she remained close.

"Rebeka. You are well?" Russell asked. "What can I get you?"

"Whatever you are having is fine. I am famished." She flipped her stringy locks behind her shoulder and sat straight. Her long, graceful fingers rubbed her neck as she analyzed me. "Such a tortured soul. Struggling to maintain sanity between the human and demonic worlds."

~ ☾ ~

She grazed her knuckles down the side of my face, leaving trails of electricity in its wake. The energy launched my heart into a steady staccato.

"How?" I asked.

"Here you are, Rebeka." Russell handed her a plate of food and a glass. He sat in his chair and reached for his plate again.

"Jessica?" Beka swirled noodles around her fork.

"Safe in the room. Abraham stands guard."

Beka sagged against the couch, breathing a sigh. "Saved by a demon."

"Half-breed?" Russell perched his elbows on the armchair.

I nodded.

"Tell us," Beka scooped noodles into her mouth.

"Four hundred and fifty years ago, my mother signed a deal with Lucifer. Traded her first born for riches." I stared at my hands. A slight tremor settled in as the anger fueled my blood. "Contracting me to do his running when assigned."

"Running?" Russell asked.

I stared at the light carpet, focusing on remaining composed. "Demons. I go get them and bring them to him."

"Contract with Lucifer." Russell whistled. "That's binding."

"Probably how your mother was able to carry you to term." Beka rubbed her thigh with her free hand. "Powerful, especially signed in blood and with a first born."

"Why would your master contract Jessica as your mark? She is not a demon," Russell said.

"I figured she wasn't." I stared out the window, mind firing in a thousand directions.

"Why her then?" Russell asked.

"Master probably wishes to kill her. He must know she is a powerful Light in the darkness he likes to spread." I sat straight. "I never know more than I need to catch them. It's not allowed."

"Killing Jessica would extinguish the Light, yes, but even more powerful would be to have her for his purposes," Beka said.

"Light to darkness. Whoever possesses her?"

"Yes." Beka's stare bore into me. "And if you don't bring

~ ☾ ~

the demons he asks you to?"

"He calls his contract due, and I'm punished." I rubbed my throat.

"Punished?" she asked.

"Two hundred and fifty years of solitary confinement." Beka gasped.

"But the first fifty years are burning torture. After that, I am left in a pit of sensory deprivation." I palmed my drink. The cool, sweaty glass sent an icy chill up my fingers. I absorbed every essence of sensory input surrounding me, knowing my time was limited. Beka's lilac scent. Buttery noodles. Soft cushions beneath me. A blooming sunrise. The gentle caress of Beka's harmonic voice.

"Nothing? But how do you survive?"

"I cannot die. No matter how long I'm deprived of food—anything for that matter—I will survive. Weakened slightly but not much more than a human with a head cold."

"You've had this torture before." Russell leaned forward.

"My first night at your club was the first day out from the punishment."

"So, you've not brought your Mark back before?" Beka asked.

"Only once. And not by choice. The one for whom I was punished died in an accident prior to my bringing her to Master."

"The failure was beyond your control, yet you were punished?" Beka asked.

I rested my hand on Beka's knee. "Master seems to enjoy punishing me. I am a half-breed. He cannot kill me, no weapon can. He can only throw me into confinement, but there are rules. No longer than two hundred and fifty years as set in my contract and only for failing to bring in a Mark. Not sure, though, what it is for killing my kind. Especially one as old as Gage. Regardless, Master and I are mutually bound by it."

"Why?"

"I do not understand my mother's logic for making such a deal. All I know is that she made it. Signed with her blood." I laughed. "Funny thing. She died giving birth to me. Her death

~ ☾ ~

activated the contract, turning me into what I am today. Master snatched me immediately and raised me as his own in the ways of Lucifer."

"Yet he wishes to punish you," Beka said. "His son."

"He is *not* my father." I swallowed the bile. True, he was the only thing I knew as a father, but he was not.

"I'm sorry, David. I did not mean to anger you." Beka's hand soothed my shoulder. "I simply wonder why he would do this to the one he raised."

"I'm told I scare him. He cannot touch me. Protected by the contract, yet bound to its terms. Not even agents of Light, such as yourselves, can harm me. Doomed to a life of servitude with no way out of it unless I become full demon."

"How?" Russell asked.

"Doesn't matter. I refuse to do it. I do not want to lose what little soul I have left." I stood and moved to the window.

Violet streaks broke through the dark sky. Splashes of pink and orange tinted the hovering clouds. One star remained. The full moon maintained its possession of the night as if fighting the sun's attempts to rule the sky.

I scrubbed my face, the long night beginning to weigh me down. Even with a full stomach, fatigue tugged at my eyelids. "There are none like me, I'm told. But surely Lucifer or other demons have found other females willing to sell their first born's soul."

"Lesser demons may have, but their power is weak and probably wouldn't put out the powerful protections you have. Lucifer is the source of all evil," Beka said. "He surely took an interest in you when he signed your contract."

That didn't comfort me in the least. "What's my mother done to me?"

"Why don't you run and hide from this Master?" Russell tossed his arms up. "Instead, you do his bidding. Killing innocents."

"Can't. He can activate my contract at any time. My mark will burn. The bonds around my neck and wrists will flame, barely tolerable until I get to him. Only then will the fire die, and I shall stand before him to await punishment or receive my next assignment." I glanced at my reflection in the

~ ☾ ~

window, zeroing in on my thick neck. Not even I could see my *leash*, but I'd felt its misery before. "Quite frankly, I'm surprised he has not activated the contract yet. He must surely know I have given Jessica to Guardians."

"You may be protected in this place," Beka said.

I whirled. "Protected?"

She got to her feet, a smile creasing the skin at the corner of her eyes. "We have had this room blessed. Holy water flows in the pipes, and daily, Abraham blesses the rooms and the building. Your humanity, however little you have left, must allow you to be in this place since it is protected from demons entering."

"The blessing does not prevent the beast from its appearance." I glanced in Abraham's direction. "You almost lost your guard because he surprised me."

Beka looked at Russell, and he nodded. "David carried you in from the lot where we were attacked. Abraham startled him while he held you and the demon emerged."

Beka swung her gaze back to me.

"I allowed him into our sanctuary from the hidden entrance. I hope I made the right choice, Rebeka. From the cameras I saw he carried you. He protected you with his life and gave up Jessica as well," Russell said.

"Yes. I am aware." Her voice went raspy, and her hand circled her throat. "You gave up your possession of Jessica and killed your brethren to save me. Why did you do that and risk your punishment?"

"I couldn't let you die as easily as some." I hurled a glare at Russell and showed Beka my back. It was more like I couldn't watch *her* die *period*. The thought of the world without Beka, *my* world without Beka, was worse than any punishment Master could institute. Her smile. Her bright eyes. Her pure soul. Even in the reflection of the window her beauty gleamed.

The heavens got it wrong making her a Guardian. She was angelic. Deserving of the most brilliant wings created.

"I took Jessica here and was on my way back down to get you when I saw the demon—"

"Russell. Do not call him demon." Beka's fingers curled

~ ☾ ~

around my elbow. "His name is David."

"Pardon me, David."

I glanced to the side and was met with Beka's stunning emerald eyes. Acceptance, tainted with a sprinkle of fear, flickered. A subtle sting pricked in my chest as my heart began to pulse faster. She saw me as David, not the demon?

"You carried me." Beka's breath warmed my bicep, her lips centimeters from my skin. Peace beamed from her face and slight smile.

I want that peace.

I tore my gaze from her mesmerizing eyes. "Russell said this was where we were going when we were ambushed. I brought you here for him to take care of and was leaving to turn myself in when he told me Jessica could help—" The words clogged my throat.

"Yes." Beka smiled.

"She can save my soul?" Did I dare hope?

Beka grazed her knuckles down the side of my face. "She is *meant* to save your soul."

~ ☾ ~

CHAPTER 21

"If it's all right, I shall check on Jessica, then retire for some rest," Russell said as he scooped up our empty dishes. "I am quite tired."

"Sure. Thank you, Russell," Beka said.

She stood by my side, watching the sun chase the darkness of the night away with me. The tips of the trees swayed with the wind. Clouds dotted the skyline, but they were no match for the sun's dry, blazing rays.

I liked this state called Arizona. The heat was suitable, penetrating, yet comforting. Or was it Beka's hand grasping my elbow. She'd inched it into the crook and settled in as if it belonged. Her light skin contrasted my dark, leathery skin.

I did not understand Beka's interest in me. For hundreds of years she fought those of my kind, protecting the human race. Yet now, she stood shoulder-to-shoulder with the evil she vowed to battle.

"What troubles you, David?" Her soft voice sounded like a familiar melody my mother used to hum. Impossible. I'd never known my mother, only imagined what she would have been like. The songs she'd hummed. The color of her eyes and hair.

"I cannot stay in this room forever, if that's, indeed, what is protecting me from Master's call."

"You do not have to. Jessica's sixteenth birthday approaches," she said.

"What will happen on that day?"

"We aren't exactly sure other than the Light will transform her into a new being."

"And it'll be too late for Master to poison her?"

"Yes. If she transforms in the presence of evil, she will

~ ☾ ~

become evil. Her Light will become darkness."

Fear coiled its frigid fingers around my chest. The demon bubbled to life at hearing the news of how to foil Jessica's transformation. *I was* evil. I disengaged from Beka's hold. "I must leave, immediately."

"Why do you say such a thing?" She snagged my hand in hers.

Maybe staying in this room for eternity would be okay, if Beka stayed with me. But she would not. Could not. She was meant to be out protecting innocents from the likes of myself.

"David?"

I gripped the front of my shirt, willing my heart to slow. "I must leave. I might harm Jessica's conversion. Evil flows through me."

"So does Light."

I stopped beside the couch. "Light? How can Light and darkness both flow through my veins? Impossible."

"You are part human, are you not?"

I stiffened. "A small part, yes."

"Years of doing Master's bidding has whittled away at your humanity."

"The demon often tries to take hold."

"But now, something else pulses through your veins, that which counteracts the darkness. Do you not feel it?"

I faced her. The sun spilled in through the window, illuminating her smooth skin. The dried blood of her shirt had hardened, and it tainted her light hair, yet she was radiant. Like an angel.

"Quiet your mind, David. What do you hear?" She closed her eyes, and her chest puffed out, lungs filling with air. The fabric went taught across her chest, and I jerked my focus to the sunrise. The streams of violet, red and orange streaking the sky didn't compare to Beka's radiance.

I could never get lost in Beka. Never taste her the way I longed to. Not without surrendering my human soul. But, oh, she was tempting.

"Try it, David. Tell me what you hear."

Darkness enveloped me as my eyes shut. The image of her face burned into the back of my lids. Her graceful neck, her

~ ☾ ~

supple body. Heat licked at my cheeks, and my fingers itched to touch her.

I froze, holding a breath captive to listen. An echo in my ears, like a faint drum. It was my heartbeat, but not only mine. One tick after it, another pulsed, with the same rhythm.

Two hearts. And warmth. My cold veins simmered, like the sun baked my skin. I opened my eyes to check if rays of sun splashed against me through the window. They filled the room, but not directly on me, not near my chest like I would have thought.

"Do you hear it?" Beka asked.

"I hear something. Feel it."

"While holding my neck. Did you have a wound on your hands?"

"Yes." I turned to her.

She stood, her eyes still closed and head tilted back. "Did your hands burn? And it traveled through you like electricity?"

"How do you know this? You were not conscious."

"My heart stopped. I felt its last beat."

"Yes."

"My blood spilled into your wound and yours into mine." Her eyes opened, revealing dilated pupils. "I feel you within me, David. Your struggle. Your fear."

"How?"

"My life force flows through you now. And it is strong. I've lived many years." She faced me. "How did you start my heart again?"

"My heart stopped when yours did. I called on my demonic side to heal my wounds so I had the strength to hold you steady. The dagger didn't completely sever your neck." I choked down the emotion welling in my throat remembering the blood. Feeling it pour out from her neck and into my hands. "But it nearly did."

"Yes. I held the blade out as much as I could. But the demon was strong."

"One of the strongest. Elite Warriors. Master sends them to activate my collar and take me back."

Her hand rested on my chest, over my heart. Heat vined

~ ☾ ~

out from her fingers. "Your heart beats steady and strong."

"Yes," I whispered.

"Touch my heart."

Prickles of heat stung my chest.

"You won't hurt me, David. I know it."

"It is too difficult."

"To touch me. It overwhelms your senses?"

I nodded.

"It'll be okay." She reached for my hand and placed it on her chest. "Feel it pounding?"

My spine tingled, an electrical jolt streaking through my back. Blood pulsed against my ears. Breaths turned into gasps.

"Listen. And not just with your ears. Feel it, David."

The dull thudding serenaded my ears. Her heat pulsed through the thin fabric of her shirt. Despite the blood caking her clothes, lilac was the only thing I smelled.

Then I understood. "Our hearts beat as one."

~ ☾ ~

CHAPTER 22

I kept the water on the cool side of warm as I showered. To be in a Guardian's home, washing in their shower, eating their food, and desiring to be with them hurt.

Literally.

My demon sensed their goodness. Its sharp talons relentlessly lacerated my heart. Especially when I was near Beka. She often stood close to me or touched me, like I was a new toy or my skin held a special texture.

With water flowing over me, I ran my hands down my chest. It felt normal to me. A subtle burning sensation bubbled with each pulse of my heart, but that must be her essence within me. If Beka affected me this way, Jessica's touch, if what they said was true, might turn me to ash.

The thought of a chance of freedom from my contract triggered a spike in my heart rate. To not have to do Master's bidding any longer. To end the killing. I should not get my hopes up.

I cranked off the water, still in awe of the luxury of indoor plumbing. The steaming water pounding on me relaxed my tense muscles, but didn't shut off my brain. I needed to stay cautious, guarded. I refused to rest all my faith in one girl and her supposed ability to possibly free me from my demonic prison.

I towel-dried and slid into the clothes Russell provided. The cotton stretched tight across my chest, but it would have to do. Beka's blood soaked my other shirt.

I opened the door and stepped through the threshold and rammed into Elizabeth. The half-pint girl squeaked as my massive foot landed on her bare toes. My shoulder barreled into the wall of the narrow hallway. A growl escaped.

~ ☾ ~

"You're kinda clumsy," Elizabeth said with a snicker.

"You are small and sneaky, little one." I palmed the smooth, beige wall, steadying myself. I would crush the tiny teen if I toppled onto her.

"Don't call me little one. I'm seventeen." She crossed her frail arms over her chest. "And you took longer than a *girl* in the bathroom."

I stared at her, not familiar with what she meant.

"You know. Long time in the bathroom." She rolled her eyes. "*Girls* are supposed to spend hours in there, not guys."

"I'm still getting used to having such a luxury in the house. It's quite enjoyable."

"You're so weird." She gawked. "And tall."

"Like I said. You are tiny, little one." I moved toward the living room. Abraham still stood outside Jessica's room. He watched me with narrowed eyes and a tensed jaw. I'd not seen him without such a scowl.

"Wait." Elizabeth snared my hand.

I jerked it from her grasp. She was too small. Too brittle for me to be near, let alone touching.

"What? Jeez. I just—" She waved her hand toward me. "Come here. Bend down."

I glanced at Abraham and back to the small girl. She stood five feet tall, maybe less. My six-foot-three frame towered her. I bent at the waist, giving her a few inches.

Her big brown eyes pierced through me. "I just—um—" She slid her forefinger beneath her eye, smearing a tear laced with black make-up. "I wanted to say thank you," she whispered. She studied the floor, rocking from heel to toe.

Then, she reached for me.

Her tiny arms wove around my neck. Her little body trembled against mine. I melted to my knees before her, hands out to my side, unsure what to do.

"You saved my sister," Elizabeth said. "You look very scary when you're mad, but you saved my Jessica, so I'm glad."

Her little body quaked. Beka stood at the end of the hallway and nodded. I took that as permission to hug little Elizabeth, and I put my arms around her slight waist. Only seventeen, yet she'd seen so much. Put on such a brave face,

~ ☾ ~

yet she was so young still.

"I thought those bad men were going to get her."

"You were smart to come find me." I combed my fingers through her glossy hair, smoothing it against her back. "Brave."

"I knew you'd help. I just knew it." She brushed her lips against my cheek and buried her face in my neck. Tears dampened my shirt. "What will happen to Jessica? No one will tell me."

"I am not sure." I stood. Elizabeth didn't release her hold so she went with me. Wetness trickled onto my skin, and she let out a whimper. "Don't worry, little one. Beka and Russell will protect her with their lives. You, too."

"I'm scared," she whispered.

I guided her legs to my side with one hand while my other kept her snug against my chest. I pivoted at the waist, seeking Beka's instruction. She pointed into the room behind me, and I carried the girl to Beka's bed.

Elizabeth clung to me as I imagined a child would clutch her father. I kneeled, setting her onto the mattress, but she didn't release her grip so I knelt beside her.

"It's okay, sweet one. You're safe." Her hold loosened, and I reached for a blanket at the foot of the bed and tucked her in. Her big eyes analyzed my movements, tears streaking her face.

"Sleep," I said. My heart stuttered.

"You'll stay here, too. You're strong enough to take care of us all. I saw you."

"I am strong, yes. But not entirely safe to be around."

Her nostrils flared again. "They called you demon. Said those other ones were demons, too."

I dipped my head at her, acknowledging she was correct.

"Demon means you're bad, but I don't think you're bad." I sat on my heels by the side of the bed as she gripped my fingers in hers. Her tiny hand got lost in the enormity of mine.

"But I am. Dangerous to be around."

"Then why did you help me and Jessica if you're bad?"

"Still working on that one."

~ ☾ ~

"I think you want to be good. Just maybe can't be all the time." She yawned, her dark lashes fluttering.

"I have a monster inside my chest. It comes out sometimes when I don't want it to."

"Take it out of you then."

"That's what we're going to figure out how to do." Beka stood in the doorway, propped against the frame, and her hands buried deep in her pockets. Wet hair cascaded over her shoulders like a waterfall. Gone were the bloodstains. She wore a fresh, white t-shirt and clean army-green shorts.

I faced Elizabeth again. Her eyes were shut. Sleep smoothed the worry wrinkles from her forehead. I disengaged her hand from mine and stood. Her chest fell and rose with a steady rhythm as she drifted into unconsciousness. Her brown hair contrasted the bleached pillowcase, and her slight body disappeared beneath the thick, cobalt blanket.

It felt like acid burned my eyes. Such a precious, innocent little person, and she trusted me—a monster—to protect her and Jessica.

Yet it was me who could destroy them. If the demon took charge, it might affect Jessica's transformation. I must leave. I must accept my fate and go back to Master. I refused to face eternity knowing I killed these people in a fit of anger.

"She's so tired. Been through a lot." Beka twined her fingers with mine.

I studied my Beka. One instance of loss of control with her would end this all within minutes. Maybe that was why Master had not called my contract due for losing Jessica to the Guardians. If I had sex with Beka and became full demon, I would kill anyone to get to Jessica.

"You were right to tell her she was safe." Beka's thumb swirled against my hand. "She's strong. All will be well."

I melded my fingers with Beka's. She was wrong. Master would win. He always won. I should not delude myself.

"I feel your torment." She stepped into me, clasping her free hand over our joined fingers. "Is it quite a struggle to be here? To be near such purity?"

"Sometimes." I pried my hand from hers. "It reminds me of what I will never possess, Beka. It is more torturous than

~ ☾ ~

two and a half centuries of punishment." I backed away from her.

"David. No." She moved toward me. "Don't go."

"I must." I cast a glance over to Elizabeth and back to Beka. "It's for the best."

CHAPTER 23

I shoved open the door to the roof. The stifling heat seared my skin, but it could have been my pounding demon. Anger triggered its lust for power. Its thirst to douse any goodness within my radius.

And I was angry.

Angry at Master. Mother. The Contract . . . Myself.

I was a fool to believe I had a chance to become human. The evil in me was too great. If it came out as Jessica transformed, everything would be ruined. I couldn't risk it. Couldn't risk Beka's safety, either.

I wanted her so vehemently, I didn't trust myself.

I peered over the short ledge. People scurried along the sidewalk in front of the club. It neared opening time so the workers came to start their shifts. The evening sky staked its claim on the daylight, striking splashes of slate and muted purples against the clouds.

Out from the protection of the apartment, I expected to hear Master's call, beckoning me to him as he had hundreds of times before. But I didn't, nor did I feel the misery his voice evoked. The day with the Guardians, surrounded by their goodness propelled me into a heightened level of irritability, but the softhearted girl, Elizabeth, had made it unbearable. She trusted me as a child would a father. All of it was something I couldn't have.

I should leave, and hope Master's call doesn't come for a while. If I evaded the demons they wouldn't know my whereabouts, maybe Master would think I died.

"Fool." I tugged at the neck of my shirt. Nothing could allow me to escape the supernatural leash cinching my neck and wrists.

~ ☾ ~

Or maybe I should just take Beka. Make love to her and become a full demon. I would be free. No worries ever again. No guilt over the scores of innocent people I'd killed. Or led to a demonic life.

I followed the little wall until the alley came into view. Deserted, save fluttering papers and crumpled cans. I hopped up onto the wall.

"David, don't," Beka called out.

I tensed. Her voice acted like a command my body couldn't disobey. Like she owned my will as Master did. I didn't look back. Instead, I tipped forward in defiance. My shirt strained across my chest, drawing me back.

I pressed forward, fighting the tug. "Release me, Beka."

"No."

"You walk a dangerous line with me."

"You will not hurt me."

"You know not what you speak of. I must go. It is not safe to have me around you. Around Jessica."

"I can't understand it, either, David, but we're connected. You are where you are meant to be. Now. In this moment."

My shoulders sagged. God I loved her. "How can you say that? I am demon. Surrounded by Guardians and—" I reached around, and ripped my shirt from her grasp. "Children."

The loose gravel of the roof crackled, and in the next breath Beka stood beside me on the ledge. "You were so good with Elizabeth earlier. She trusts you with her life. And Jessica's. You are more human than you think, David."

"She knows not what she does. She is but a child."

"She witnessed your demonic form."

"The shock of it all hasn't hit her. Once it does, she will see me as I really am." I chanced a peek. "As will you."

Beka may think she can overlook my demon, but she was wrong. Too pure and innocent to see reality. To accept it.

"I'm not used to people not following my orders. You were going to jump, even after I told you not to. You're very frustrating sometimes."

"I follow no one's orders, other than Master's."

"You must stay. Jessica turns sixteen soon. Let us help

~ ☾ ~

you."

"Why do you want to help me, Beka? I'm demon. I'm—"

"You're also human." She snatched my hand in hers. "Human, David. Remember, in the alley? Two nights ago when you touched me?"

A jolt of electricity sizzled down my spine.

"When we kissed?" she asked.

My demon knocked my ribs, rumbling for release. For pleasure. For Beka.

"Focus on that. That is what I want." She stepped down, still holding my hand.

"No." I tugged, but she remained steadfast.

A grumble rattled from my throat.

"You do not scare me, David. Even with your scowls."

"You should be scared of me, Beka. I cannot be killed, yet I can kill very easily. Sometimes it is beyond my control." And with Beka, I doubted my control.

"Your neck sparked when the blade hit it. Explain that to me." She waggled our connected hands.

I finally took her into my sights. Standing on this ledge, I towered over her. Yet she didn't seem small. Only beamed with hope and light.

"Bonds around my throat and wrists protect the vulnerable spots. Nothing can penetrate them. Not even my talons."

"You've tried?"

I bit my cheek. Of course I'd tried. I'd never wanted a life such as this.

"Your claws." Her thumb circled my forefinger knuckle. Peace rippled over my skin.

"My demon nails are lethal. One well-timed wave of my hand, I can send a head rolling, vanquishing any being."

"And you have done this often."

"Only two hundred and forty-five years of my four centuries have been spent in solitary, so yes, I have a long list of those I've killed or brought to Master." I toed the ledge on which I stood. "Including Guardians."

"Yes. I am aware."

"Excuse me?"

~ ☾ ~

"I am aware of Guardians lost to demons. I even lost family to them in battle." She tucked a strand of hair behind her ear. "I've been around a while, too, David. Seen many things. Know even more."

"You've lost family? You have other brothers than Russell?"

"He is not my brother." She tugged again, but this time I allowed her strength to guide me down from the ledge. "We only call each other brother and sister to fit in better with the humans."

"Who is he, then? And Abraham?"

"Guardians, like me. Only younger."

She glided closer.

"Younger, so that's why they follow your orders."

"In part." Her hand rested on my chest. "Abraham just arrived to help us protect Jessica."

"Please, don't."

"You don't want to touch me?" she asked.

"That is not the issue. It's not right."

"Why?"

"Besides the obvious reasons—I am demon, you are Guardian?"

"Yes. Besides the obvious."

"Why would you want a demon to touch you?"

"Stop calling yourself demon. I hate it."

"It's reality."

"No. You are a friend to the Guardians." She yanked me to her. "I shouldn't want to be with you like I do, but I do. I want to touch you. I can't explain it. But I trust it."

My heart cramped, squeezing the air from them with a sharp whistle. My mouth watered for her. One taste before I left. I could stop it before it went too far. Before I lost control.

Yes. Take her. The demon swirled beneath the surface of my chest. Blood pulsed.

Her heartbeat stuttered with mine.

"I feel your struggle, David." Her hand skimmed my neck as if working to feel the invisible bond.

My fingertips traced the scar marring the width of her neck. The red line had remained, despite being fully healed. I

~ ☾ ~

retracted from her.

"I can't," I whispered.

"I shouldn't," she said. "But it is you I belong with. No one else." She pushed herself up, and her mouth latched onto my neck. Her tongue flicked. Her lips swept the width of my neck, as my fingers had done to hers. I grasped her shoulders, knowing I should push her away. Instead, I followed the contour to her elbows and pushed her arms so they wove around my neck, opening her to me.

Mine.

I traced her body until my hands found her breasts. Her chest heaved, her breaths coming in pants. Her head tilted back as I massaged her tempting body. I ached to feel her without the obstruction of clothing. To see all of her.

Mine.

I brought my mouth to her neck and nipped at her skin. Needles prickled my chest. The demon urged me on, wanting me to dive into her to complete my transformation. He'd live freely then. I pushed his taunts from my mind and kissed my way to her jaw line. Her fingers tangled in my hair, and I suckled her earlobe.

Lilac mingled with the heady scent of her arousal. Mine, too.

"David," she whispered.

I trailed up the side of her face. Her smooth skin stung. It must be her purity torching the darkness within me, but I absorbed the feel. A pleasurable torture. My hands navigated from the softness of her chest and skimmed her neck until I held her cheeks. I swallowed the warmth bubbling in my chest.

"Kiss me," she commanded.

Her shining lips called to me with an authority I couldn't resist. Didn't want to resist. She opened, allowing me entrance. Her moan drew me in. Arms coiled around my neck, elbows digging into my shoulders, pulling her taller, closer to me, and she deepened her kiss.

My body rippled with need, building an energy that threatened to burst through my chest. The demon thundered deep within me, urging me forward. *More.*

~ ☾ ~

I disconnected from her and gasped for breath. "Beka, wait."

She nipped at my bottom lip. "It's okay. I want this. Want you." She filled my mouth with her tongue again. My hands gravitated from her face, down her neck, and cupped her firm breasts.

It wasn't enough. I needed to feel her.

I found the hem of her shirt and shot my hands up the front. "Yes," she breathed.

I pushed up her shirt just below her breasts. Logic stopped me, trying to lure my brain from lust's haze.

"Don't stop." She raised her hands over her head. "I want you to see me in a way no man ever has."

I slid the thin piece of cloth off and tossed it to the ground. She stood before me only wearing a brassiere. Her pale, smooth skin flushed beneath the raspberry rays of the setting sun. Flesh spilled over the fabric holding her breasts captive, hiding her beauty from me. A tiny, dark mole disappeared beneath the cloth straps, near her collarbone.

"It's okay." She guided my hand to her chest.

Our hearts thundered in unison as I stroked her. My other hand slid around her waist. I feasted on the sight of her, the feel of her satin skin, and the smell of her lilac perfume.

"Wait. Let me see you." She placed a hand over mine.

Her lips shone with the essence of our last kiss. I licked mine and tasted her. I should stop, but couldn't. I needed more. Never had I seen such elegance. She must be the daughter of gods.

Her hands slid beneath the hem of my shirt and foundled my stomach. Branding irons would have produced less anguish. The intensity nearly brought me to my knees. What power was this that she rendered me captive with her hands and her beauty?

"Lift your arms."

I obeyed as if possessed, and she peeled off my shirt. Her mouth skimmed my chest. Teeth scraped my collarbone, nibbled up my neck and over my jaw. In the next breath, her mouth claimed mine.

I clutched her to me. Our skin met, and together we

~ ☾ ~

moaned. Tongues tangled, as our hands learned each other's bodies. Hungry. Claiming.

Mine.

I traced her spine to the small of her back then gripped her backside. She opened herself and hooked her thighs around my waist. Such warmth. Peace. I wanted to lose myself in her body.

I wrenched my face from hers and gulped a breath. The edge of the cliff beckoned, and I was about to jump off. "Beka. I must stop—" My voice cracked. "I can't—"

Teeth scored my neck, and she nipped. That drove me beyond the threshold, and I pulsed against her, taking her mouth with mine.

She tilted back, chest heaving with every breath, and I buried my face in her cleavage. Never had I tasted anything so sweet. She felt like silk against me. Her feminine core against my waist, the delicious friction her movement created. Her hand tangled in my hair, pulling me to her.

The smell of lilacs overwhelmed me as my hand moved into her hair.

"David, you will be my K—"

The door burst open. "Stop."

Beka's body tensed against mine. I pivoted, shielding her from Russell.

The beast emerged with such a force it made me stumble.

Russell drew his sword. "Step away, my lady."

"Russell, go," Beka said. She released her grip on me and slid behind me. I kept my eyes on the approaching Guardian.

"Step away from the demon. Has he hurt you?" He charged, but my feral roar stopped him.

"Do not come any closer." I bared my elongated teeth and stabbed my talons into my palms, restraining the urge to pounce. "She is mine."

Russell cocked his head, and his gaze went above my shoulder. "Rebeka?"

"Back away, Russell. You are not allowed to see me in this manner."

Russell's focus drifted to the ground, where our shirts lay in a heap. His gaze snapped to mine. "What have you done?"

~ ☾ ~

He advanced, swinging his sword.

The weapon clanked against my wrist. Russell twisted and poked. The icy metal pierced my chest, below the heart. Beka grunted.

Russell retracted his sword, and Beka slumped against my back. I reached behind me and turned slightly, keeping the attacker in sight. A circle of red below her collarbone beaded on her soft, pallid skin.

Fury raged like river rapids in my veins. I let the beast take hold and leapt at Russell like a lion. My teeth tore through his feeble skin. Metallic blood spurted into my mouth, bones snapped, tendons severed.

No one hurt what was mine.

I sank my nails into his chest, and we rolled.

Beka screamed. "David. Stop!"

I shoved Russell off me. The door dented beneath the impact of his body.

"You hurt that which is mine." I paced the gravel before him.

He clasped his crimson stained throat. "She is not yours. She can never be yours. She is—"

A bellow, from the depths of my stomach rent the air. He was right, but still, I loved Beka. She was mine in every way but as a bedmate.

"She is—"

"Russell. Don't," Beka yelled.

Russell glared at me with flaming eyes. "She is betrothed."

~ ☽ ~

CHAPTER 24

Still in my demon form, I snatched my shirt and dove off the rooftop. I flipped mid-air and landed on my feet. My human form burst forth. I couldn't let my demon stay out. He'd kill someone.

Violently.

I slid my thin shirt over my head and sprinted down the alley.

"David." Beka's voice echoed off the towering brick walls.

More voices murmured behind me, but I couldn't decipher them, and I didn't stay to figure them out. I burst out of the alley and dashed to the left. The brick buildings blurred into dull hues of red and brown.

I had no idea where I would go, but I needed something to destroy. My demon roiled, wanting release. Wanting to cause pain.

Beka betrothed?

The time we had kissed in the alley, she'd said it couldn't happen again. Then, on the roof just now, she said she shouldn't care for me as she does. I figured it was because of my demon. No Guardian, keepers of the Light, should care for a demon. Even one who was half-human.

I turned the corner of a gas station and bolted northward. I'd spotted some open desert near there while out exploring. I needed solitude and darkness to think.

A cluster of men, holding bottles, stood near an open trunk. Loud music poured out from the open car windows.

"Whoa, buddy, what's your rush?" one said as I evaded their group.

My roar echoed off the wall as I ran. My heart stung. The blood pumping through my veins ached, throbbing with an

~ ☾ ~

WASTELAND

electrical current.

The feeling reminded me of when I held Beka's neck together. She said we were fused because of sharing our blood.

A black void ahead. *Open desert.* A blaring horn ripped me from my mental tirade. Bright lights rushed me, and I leapt. I toed the roof of an SUV and lurched forward, hurdling it. The cement met my head with a thud as I fell into a summersault. Gasps and sighs enveloped me, but I shook them off, hopped to my feet and took off again.

I must leave this town. Evade the demons sent to retrieve me until Master activated my contract. Then, I would go, serve my sentence. Darkness and the absence of senses would be better than the feeling ripping through my body at the moment.

My Beka is betrothed. She and I could never wed, but still, the ache of the thought of her joining with another man. "No." It felt like razors slid down my throat I yelled so loud.

Damn my mother for selling my soul before I was even born. I hopped the curb and burst through thigh-high shrubbery. Thorns snagged my jeans. Slashed my skin. But I went on, welcoming the pain. It didn't compare to the agony constricting my chest.

I slid my tongue over my lips. Beka's essence. My blood pulsed.

I traversed a ditch to the sandy ground, sending a plume of dust into the air. Chest heaving, I palmed my waist and gasped for air. Stale, floral-scented particles tickled my nose and throat. Save the moon and stars in the sky, darkness ruled. Exactly what I needed.

The moon beamed silvery rays over a fifteen-foot tall cactus before me.

I let my demon out and stomped to the massive plant. Its needles existed to protect the cactus, and they protruded at least two inches, promising utter misery should someone toy with them.

I fanned my hand and impaled my palm with the pointed tips. The pain scorched my red skin. My black nails clicked against the needles, but I pushed through. Needed more. A

~ ☾ ~

distraction.

A throbbing ache sprawled from the base of my neck.

Sweat trickled down my forehead, and stung my eyes with saltiness. Beka had ripped my heart out, promising possible redemption with Jessica. Teasing my resolve with her soft body and tender kisses. Never had I been so tempted to lay with a woman.

Her very essence, a beacon of light in my dark world, lured me to her. The first night I saw her at the club dancing. Confidence oozed off her as she swayed with the music. And when she pulled me through the Jezebels.

The tips of the needles poked through the back of my hand, having skewered my palm.

Yes. The pain. More.

I withdrew my hand from the needles. My dark blood coated the spikes but they didn't sizzle. Didn't melt from the potent evil flowing. Beka now had my blood pulsing through her veins. Did it burn like hers burned me?

Probably not. The goodness and Light flowing through her was more potent, no doubt. Overpowered my evil, fighting it like a cancer, expelling it from her purity. Light and darkness couldn't exist in the same body, it went against the dichotomy of good and evil.

The needle holes faded, and my hand return to normal. The sting died, but not the sizzle of my heart.

I snatched a rock from the sandy desert floor and threw it at the cactus. It bounced off, thudded to the ground. I faced the black sky, stretched my mouth open as wide as it could go and yelled. The noise resembled the cry of a wounded lion or bear.

I loved Beka. With every human fiber in me, I loved her. Her angelic face flashed in my brain. Her flesh spilling from the brassiere. The taste of her skin. Her tongue against mine.

Even in my demon form, my body responded, picturing her beneath me as we became one. I took off running again. I let the anger and rage rush through me, clinging to the demonic side. The power was addicting.

Maybe as a full demon I wouldn't remember her. Remember the love. The peace. I could erase her memory by

~ ☾ ~

lying with every woman I wanted to.

I dug my nails into my palm. I would never forget Beka's purity. She'd branded my human and demonic soul for eternity.

A white-hot pain ignited in my back, near my left shoulder blade. I stumbled forward and skidded to a stop. I reached behind me and met the cool metal of a small dagger embedded deep in the bone. I yanked it out and lost myself to the demonic side even more as I turned around.

Russell cleared a small bush.

A curtain of red descended over my vision. I leapt and met him mid-air. I latched my fingers around his throat. We spun one revolution and landed on our stomachs. The thistles of a small cactus ripped through my shirt, slicing my skin.

I jerked him to the side and we rolled.

"David," Russell said. "Wait."

I cracked a fist into his jaw. He planted his foot against my chest and launched me into the air. One twist had me landing on my feet, and I attacked again, tackling him around the waist.

We collided with another cactus, and Russell's scream permeated the thick darkness of the desert. I wrenched him from the needles piercing his back and raked my talons across his chest. I snapped at his hand, nipping the medial edge.

Sparks lit up as his blade met my neck.

"See. You cannot kill me." I guided the dagger back and tried it again. "No one can."

"David,"

"I wish you could take my head and end this agony." Tears stung my eyes.

"Get off me, David. Listen."

I pushed off and towered him while he jumped to his feet.

He patted his chest and shook the sand from his hair. "You didn't need to do that."

I paced before him, my animalistic side maintaining control.

He tensed and drew his sword from the sheath on his back.

~ ☾ ~

"Don't bother, it is of no use," I said. "Did you not see the sparks from your dagger? You cannot kill me."

"Nevertheless, I'll hold it anyway."

Stupid Guardian. "What do you want?"

"Beka ordered me to track you down and explain."

"Ordered?"

Russell kicked a rock. "Yes."

"You are her servant." I paced. "I should not be surprised. You did seem to wait on her more than I thought was normal."

"You don't know everything going on here, Demon—er—David." He faced me, but squinted.

"Guess Guardian eyes are not as good as demon's. How'd you find me?"

"I jumped off the building directly after you did. Beka was mortified and ordered me after you immediately. She fears for your safety."

"I can't die, remember?" I showed him my back. "Although I wish I could many days. If you can figure out a way to end me, I would be most grateful."

Footfalls approached. "But your Master may call you to him. She greatly fears losing you to him."

"You best stay back, Guardian." I flashed my fangs. "I've not been in my demonic form for this long in quite some time. I'm very close to losing control."

"Let me talk to David Sadler," Russell said. "He is friend to the Queen of the Guardians."

~ ☾ ~

CHAPTER 25

"Did you say queen?" I faced Russell.

"I will speak only with David."

Releasing the hold on the demon proved more difficult this time. I faced the dark sky and closed my eyes. My flaming chest cooled as I told the demon to retreat to the dark corner of my heart.

I would wait, for now, to let the beast out permanently until I heard what Russell had to say.

"Much better." He sheathed his sword. "You do look quite frightening as that beast."

"Get used to it."

He cocked his head. "Meaning?"

"Nothing. Tell me what you came to say and be gone."

"Sorry. It does not work that way."

"Excuse me?" I straightened my back.

A cool breeze seeped through my shredded jeans. Darkness pressed over me as I stood in the depths of the desert, surrounded by black void, facing a Guardian.

"First, I must apologize for my actions earlier." He bowed his head. "I misread what happened. I thought you had violated my Queen in a way that would ruin her for her future mate."

"You mentioned betrothed." The word tasted like bile as it left my mouth.

He nodded. "Rebeka is the oldest of the Guardians and our Queen. She is to keep herself pure for the predicted King who will join her. I saw you—" He coughed into his hand and analyzed the ground. "Well, I thought you were taking advantage of my Queen."

"And you stabbed me; therefore, stabbing her." I sprung,

~ ☾ ~

planting my palms against his chest and gripped the fabric. "Now tell me what do you mean predicted king?"

I wasn't sure I wanted to know. Minutes earlier she'd held me in her arms. Kissed my mouth. Touched my body. To think of her with another—

"She is prophesied to join with an Angel, hand chosen by the Light. Their union will sanctify Good's supremacy on this earth. They will rule as king and queen of The Guardians."

"And Jessica? How does she fit in all this?"

"We have yet to receive that revelation. We only know that on her sixteenth birthday, which nears, she will be a vessel of Light, one of the strongest known to earth." He came closer. "We think it is through Jessica the Angel will be revealed, so Rebeka will know her mate, the future king, and join with him."

I clasped a hand to my neck and squeezed. On the roof, she said she wanted me and no one else, but she was not in the position to decide, like I have not been. I wanted her, but could not have her. We have both been kept from love.

"Rebeka is confused by you, David. Your darkness brings her to a place she cannot afford to go. You understand that, don't you? You're a temptation to betray her calling. She wants to give herself to you, but knows she can't, and she is ready to turn her back on her destiny to be with you, a—"

"Demon," I said.

"I'm sorry, David. I am here under her orders, but not telling you what she wanted me to, which is to come back and be by her side. But she's confused. I must look out for all the Guardians. For Jessica."

I stared him down. "You're defying her orders."

"Partially. I came here to apologize as she instructed. But instead of asking you to return with me, I am begging you to stay away from her. For everyone's sake."

His words were like salt pouring over an open wound in my stomach.

"You could never be what she needs. You are demon."

"Half human, though."

"Regardless." He gripped the hilt of his sword.

"I will go." I showed him my back.

~ ☾ ~

"You will? So easily you will go? I don't understand."

I faced him. "Would you like me to stay and make things more difficult?"

"No. I—" He shrugged. "I was just surprised. I expected—"

"A fight? Fangs and claws and swords?"

He nodded.

I tilted back, facing the sky. "I want nothing more than to stay, to be by Beka's side and to join with her the way only a true mate could. But I am not free to be with her in much the same way she's not free to be with me."

"Tell me."

"As she has to keep herself pure for her future King, I have to keep myself pure to prevent full transformation into demon."

"You would lose your humanity if you lie with a woman?"

"Yes." My shoulders sagged. "I am too tempted by Beka to stay. The minute I bed her, I would convert to full demon and lose what's left of my human soul for eternity. And more than likely, I would kill her in the moment as well."

"I had no idea."

"How could you? No one knows. I am doomed to servitude, never able to experience love, and compelled to do the bidding of the devil's right hand man."

A deep sigh from Russell sent my blood boiling.

"You said Jessica may be able to help, yet you ask me to leave."

"Not leave as in disappear. Only stay away from Beka until we can protect Jessica's conversion. If she can save your soul like we think she can, I will bring her to you. But that still would not give you freedom to be with Rebeka." He ran his fingers through his hair. "You'd be human."

"I will stay away, but Master can call me back at any moment. I cannot resist his call for very long." I clutched my shirt where it hid Master's brand.

"I had Abraham bless another location at the south end of town. A secondary location in case we needed it. Would you wait there? I believe the blessing protects you from your Master's detection."

I squatted and snatched a rock into my hand. "Tell me

~ ☾ ~

where this place is, and I will consider it. I may just go and face my punishment for giving you Jessica. I am surprised he has not called me to him yet."

"The four demons that attacked, one had a collar."

"Yes."

"What is that?"

I threw the rock at the cactus. "It renders me weak so they can escort me to Master."

"But not weak enough to kill you?"

"No. Only to subdue and transport if I do not cooperate." I rubbed my neck. "It's been used only once, and it is not pleasant."

"As if two hundred and fifty years of solitude is. Yet you chose it when you gave up Jessica. Why?"

"I'm starting to ask myself the same thing." I faced Russell. "I've considered going in and getting her, but that would hurt Beka."

"You love her."

I nodded. "I love her with whatever amount of soul and humanity I have left in me, but it is that very love that will kill her. So I will go to your lock and key until you can tell me if Jessica is able to save me."

He smiled.

"But, I tell you this, Russell. You left Beka to die once when you left with Jessica." I hissed, remembering the blood gushing from her neck and over my hands holding her together. "Do it again, and I will hunt you down, unleash the beast within me and tear you limb from limb."

~ ☾ ~

CHAPTER 26

I settled into the hard cot near the corner of the small space and closed my eyes. Beka's scent tainted the room. She must have been with Abraham when he had blessed the dwelling. The smell tortured me with the memories of kissing and touching her. But as long as she did not show up, I would survive.

I slid into darkness, losing my mind to the void, but a pounding at the door slashed its peace. I rolled from the bed and to my feet, scanning the room. Only a cot with two chairs against the wall to my left and a short hallway to a bathroom stall.

A whimper leaked through the door followed by a thud. Hairs prickled at my neck. I'd made certain I wasn't followed after Russell and I separated several blocks away.

Another bang and a moan prompted me to stride to the door. A silver tip of a sword split the wood. Streaks of crimson dribbled through the crack. I yanked the door open and Abraham's massive body flinched.

A sword anchored him to the door, but what worried me most was Jessica's body fastened to his. The weapon had pierced her as well.

"Demon," Abraham said. "Pull this out and get the girl inside, we are under attack."

I jumped in front of the door, absorbing a dagger between the shoulder blades to shield them. Abraham coughed, blood trickled from the corner of his mouth, but he never let loose of the girl. I gripped the hilt of the weapon and extracted it from Abraham and Jessica. Turned out the blade skimmed her shoulder.

The Guardian stood. "Take the girl inside."

~ ☾ ~

"Where is Beka?"

"Our Queen fights. Holding them back for me to get the girl here. I—"

"Hold on to Jessica." I pushed him into the room and slammed the door shut. "I will get Beka."

My dark surroundings came alive. Red demons, black nails and silver swords ready for blood crawled out from the surrounding shadows. They marched forward.

Not many places to go. Safe house behind me. Brick walls on either side. A gravel parking lot spanned before me, but seven demons ate up the distance, weapons raised.

"There is the half breed. He is in with the Guardians," one said, pointing his dagger.

Distant clanks of metal hitting metal snared my attention. Must be Beka fighting. So close I scented the sparks of sword battle.

I just had to get through the brutes rushing me. One held a collar.

"You killed Gage," the demon holding the collar said. "Master will be pleased I caught our betrayer."

I morphed into my monster. "You have not captured me yet."

A blade pierced my shoulder, and the demons pounced. They seemed more interested in detaining me than getting Jessica. Or maybe they realized they couldn't get to her through the blessed room.

Dagger in hand, I spun and flicked my wrist. The metal slid through the forearm of the demon clutching the collar. The limb fell to the rocky ground, and I kicked the blasted device away. Sure. He'd grow another hand, but at least it would not be holding my collar.

A dagger pinged off my protected neck. I hoisted him a foot off the ground and sliced, rendering him a pile of ash. A heel cracked my knee, and I tipped. I clutched the necks of two demons on my way down. Another swipe of my lethal weapons met red skin, splicing it open. Two heads drummed against the ground and plumed into dust.

I twisted the hand of another demon and sunk my fangs into his forearm. He howled, exposing his neck, and I

~ ☾ ~

WASTELAND

slashed.

More dust.

My knee cracked into place, and I hobbled to my feet, head throbbing and heart hammering. The sulfur laced dust and ash tainted the fresh, evening air.

Three demons inched back as I charged from the house. Bright light flashed from the one window beside the door, and it bounced off the neighboring brick building.

I lunged at the three and slid my pointed nails along their throats. Momentum forced me into a summersault, and I jumped to my feet. The ring of clashing swords rent the air. I sprinted ahead but snuck a glance over my shoulder at the Guardian's house. White light illuminated the cracks in the wooden door the swords and daggers had mutilated.

The rays flooded out, cutting through the early morning darkness surrounding the small structure. Jessica's time must have come. My human instinct to help Beka drove me forward. I would get Beka and bring her to Jessica and end this.

I bolted toward the span of trees at the end of the lot. I burst through the foliage and into the sprawling front yard of a mansion. A driveway split the middle of the gravel landscaping. Beka battled three demons. Two more approached from behind.

I leapt toward the two and blasted my fists through their chests. Hot flesh and thick blood coated my hands lodged in their chest cavities. One twist removed their dead hearts. I tossed their organs to the ground and finished them with my nails across their necks.

Beka faced me. "David."

A silver blade skewered her gut from behind. Glancing at me had cost her a sword through the stomach.

A shade of red tainted my vision.

Two long strides, and I was by her side, slashing the face of one demon. The other swiped at my neck, his nails snagging skin on my cheek. His other hand rushed me, but not to hit. He aimed the collar to snap it around my neck. I ducked.

Something pierced my shoulder, my thigh. Beka gasped and metal clanked against metal.

~ ☾ ~

I sagged to one knee, still slashing my hand at one of the demons. Beka must be getting the third with her blade. So many demons. We needed Russell.

Beka groaned, demanding my focus. Her chest beamed. Bright white light beamed from her mouth and blanched her eyes.

"Beka!" The demon staggered away from her, stunned. But the two on me charged on with their attacks.

I reached for the one with the collar and cuffed his wrist. He posed the most threat. I planted the heel of my foot in the chest of the other one. He landed four feet away. I cranked the collar-holding demon's arm back behind him and shoved his face into the ground. I snatched the collar and tossed it, knowing I couldn't destroy the thing. I grabbed his blade and detached his head. The other demon ran to Beka, eyeing the light show.

She faced me, eyes white as fresh snow. No more sea-green irises. Paralyzed by the bright sight, the demons crumbled to their knees, making for easy prey as I relieved them of their heads with well-timed flicks of my deadly nails.

Another dash of light burst through the tree line separating the property from the parking lot. It was Jessica, followed closely by Abraham. She ran at supernatural speed toward us, her chest and eyes glowing exactly like Beka's.

That was the first time I'd seen Jessica move on her own volition. Her long, red hair flowed behind her as if facing a strong wind. She fixed her gaze on Beka. Although still in my demonic form, Beka reached for me. "David."

My human form emerged before I'd commanded. I brushed my fingertips against hers. Her glowing skin combusted at my touch.

"What's happening?" she whispered.

"I don't know." I scanned her body for injuries. "Are you okay?"

"I thought you'd left." Tears streamed down her radiant face.

"I was. Russell found me. How are you here?" I twined my fingers with hers, palm to palm. The heat emanating from her penetrated my skin to the point of agony. But I endured the

~ ☾ ~

contact not wanting to release her ever again. My heart hammered my ribs, squeezing the air from my lungs. Lilac swirled around me, imprinting her scent within me.

"Club. Attacked." She looked toward Jessica. "Had to get her to safety."

Her gaze fell on me again. "My David. You will be with me always."

Her light pulsed, searing my eyes. The heat equaled that of punishment. I stepped away no longer able to withstand the ache her touch provoked. My darkness recoiled from her Light. Another reminder of what kept us apart.

She turned to Jessica again and leaned toward her.

"Go." I gasped, working to catch my breath. "You must go to her."

She nodded. "Come with me."

"You first." I motioned to her to go. She faced Jessica and ran.

Each step she took from me, the pain lessened. And my heart ached. A cool breeze soothed my fevered skin.

Jessica fell into Beka's embrace, and they crumbled to their knees. Their light, rivaling the sun, encapsulated them. I brought my hands up to shield my eyes. My heel caught a rock and hard ground cracked against my butt. My throat closed, like my invisible collar morphed into a noose.

Beka.

Abraham knelt before the glowing females as if paying homage.

Pain seared down my spine. *What is happening?*

Jessica peeled out from Beka's embrace and looked to Abraham, then me. The glow between her and Beka dimmed, save a circle of light radiating from beneath their shirts, over their hearts.

Jessica's long, red hair flowed as if still running or met a gust of wind. But the trees behind her remained still. She pulled her shoulders wide and stood tall, her glowing eyes never blinking, only staring at me. She pointed and Beka nodded. They clasped hands as they approached.

I pushed myself to my knees, heart throbbing, demon howling. *Hold on, David.*

~ ☾ ~

The color returned to Beka's eyes, yet the light on her chest flashed like a strobe. I felt it because it matched how my heart beat.

Blood pulsed my eardrums. I looked to the ground and pounded my thighs. Anything to distract from the ache. It had to be Beka's blood within me. Or maybe Jessica was healing me.

Please let it be true.

Only ten feet from me, Jessica pointed at me and picked up her pace. "I must touch him."

Compelled by her commanding voice, I stood and reached for her. Only five feet separated us. The joy and peace radiating from the two women rolled over me, giving me a taste of what I would have if only I touched her hand.

I have longed for this for centuries. I could face life as a human, as long as it was demon free. I would take it.

Two feet.

Thundering pain coursed through my body. A raging river roared in my head. My heart burst into a sprint, and my pulse throttled my ears. My legs and arms morphed into concrete appendages, heavy and tired.

But I hadn't touched her yet.

"I call your contract due." Master's deep voice echoed in my ears.

My knees buckled, and the ground rushed forward. Fire licked at all parts of my skin. I morphed into my demonic side without command and grated my chest trying to put out the flame. It had never been so intense before.

So immediate.

Then, the familiar clank of metal, chased by an instant squeezing in my neck, quaked through my body. My shoulder met the rocks of the gravel yard, piercing my skin.

"No," Beka screamed.

Jessica leapt, hand outstretched. I groped the ground for her, but she crumbled beneath the weight of one of Master's Elite guards. Inches separated our fingers.

"Beka." My voice cracked beneath the pressure of the choker.

The ring of blades clashing surrounded me, but my limbs

~ ☾ ~

grew too heavy to move. Paralyzed by the collar circling my neck, I lay pinned to the ground, inches from my salvation. My fangs descended, and I stabbed them into my lip. Salty tears melded with the metallic blood.

Russell landed in front of me and swung his weapon, beheading the demon wrestling Jessica.

"Get me to the demon," she said.

He faced me, his eyes wide and reached for Jessica.

A set of iron fingers clamped my ankle and yanked me back. I scratched my nails into the hard ground trying to stop myself. "Beka."

But the collar weakened me. A sharp strike to the head triggered flashing white lights. Darkness quickly followed but not before I heard Beka screech my name.

Something I had better get used to, because in solitary, between the scalding torture, that scream would haunt me for the next two-hundred and fifty years.

~ ☾ ~

CHAPTER 27

"I see you have chosen not to resist my guards, son."

I allowed the two Elite Guards to manhandle me, pushing me toward Master. My hands were bound behind me, and I wore the collar, so I really didn't have much choice. Not that it mattered. I'd missed my chance with Jessica and Beka. Distracted by their beaming light and the desire to be human, I neglected to see the threats approaching behind.

Thankfully Russell had shown up. He surely would have protected them. And Abraham was there. I had to trust Beka and Jessica were safe. My mind would shatter if I thought any differently.

"Still the silent one." Master rose from the chair hidden behind the massive, mahogany desk.

The office was different than the one I knew back at the manor in New York. Daylight flooded the room from a wall of picture windows to his left. A sea of rooftops lay before me.

Bookshelves lined the walls from the floor to the ceiling. Behind me sat a full bar, complete with an ice bucket and four short glasses.

Master liked his comforts.

"New office?" I asked.

He motioned the soldiers holding me toward a set of chairs facing the desk. They hauled me to them and plopped me down. Master's witches must have increased the collar's magic, because I'd never felt so weighted. Like lead flowed through my veins.

"You have been with me more than four hundred years, son, yet you eye me with such contempt."

"I'm not your son."

He bared his canines. The creamy skin at the corner of his

~ ☾ ~

albino-red eyes creased as a smile stretched across his thin, onyx lips.

An image of Beka flashed in my brain, and I shook my head. It would be a long quarter millennia with that slipping into my mind so often. I wasn't sure how many days had passed since I'd last seen her.

"You've proven yourself quite strong to resist the Queen's advances, son."

Beka.

"The Queen of the Guardians is quite a prize, and it seems she had her eyes on you." He sneered. "Although I question her judgment if she fell for a demon like you."

"You know of her?"

"Of course. Why do you think I pulled you out early and threw you to the wolves? I knew you wouldn't be able to resist the scantily dressed women of the desert. They reveal much in their attempts to stay cool in the heat." Master rounded the side of the desk. He leaned on the front edge, facing me. His thin arms creased his crisp, alabaster silk shirt as he crossed them over his chest. "But once again, you did not fall. Did not come to full acceptance of your fate to be a demon."

"You planned all of this?"

"Not the part where you fell into favor with the Guardian Queen. You were to have found a woman, mate with her and forgo your humanity, *then* kill the Queen and her precious little Jessica." Master bared his long teeth. "Instead, you protected her, turned over the Mark to our enemies, and killed your fellow demon. *For her.* Did she brainwash you?"

I huffed and hung my head low. The metal clamping my wrists behind my back dug into my skin. Better get used to it. Much more discomfort to come.

Long fingers gripped my face, his nails digging into my cheeks. Master forced me to look into his demonic red, glowing eyes. His rancid breath stung my nose. "I cannot kill you. But your sentence will be carried out with the fullest extent of pain allowed."

"Why do I frighten you so?"

He pushed me away by my chin and my back slammed against the chair. "You do no such thing."

~ ☾ ~

"Gage said otherwise."

That earned me a stinging slap across the face. I ground my teeth, fighting the demon that wanted to emerge. It would do no good, the constricting collar kept my power at bay. Not that I could have killed Master. Only Lucifer was stronger than Master.

"Why can't you kill me?"

"I would, and believe me, I want to, but your contract protects you, you know this. But I will be very creative with your confinement this time." He leaned in close again, his sulfuric breath gagging. "The next time you emerge, you will run to the nearest female and ravage her, sealing your fate as my demon son. Then you will be fair game to kill should you defy me once, even in the smallest way."

Saliva gathered beneath my tongue, and I spit at his face.

He spewed his rancid breath over me and backed away, wiping the side of his face with a white kerchief he'd plucked from his breast pocket. "Why Father allowed a clause in your contract is beyond me." He waved at the guards. "Take him away."

The thugs hoisted me to my feet by my armpits.

"Wait," I said. "What if I were to offer to convert fully to your ways?"

"Stop," he ordered.

The demons turned me, but I focused on the floor.

"Let me speak to my true son. I do not negotiate with humans."

I scrutinized the demons flanking me. Their red skin, long, pearly teeth, and black eyes a reflection of me in my demon form. Could I stand to be like that forever, only taking human form as a mask when needed to mingle in public?

The beast writhed as I considered my options. *Do it.* Either two hundred and fifty years in solitude again, or I could morph into the demon one last time and remain that way.

Master tipped back and pressed a button on the phone. Within seconds a door behind the desk opened and a woman sashayed through. An emerald green dress, covering little of her private parts, clung to her slender body. Long, cascading hair draped over her, hugging the curves of her ample

~ ☾ ~

breasts.

"David," Master said.

I let the burn engulf my heart, and I morphed into my demon.

"You take this woman now, surrendering your human soul, and we will start anew, son."

Master reached for the woman's hand, and she smiled. He led her to me. She stood inches from my body, looking up into my eyes. Her long, red nails abraded my chest, hitting flesh in the holes I'd scratched in the cloth earlier.

I turned my head to the side, drawing in a deep breath as my heart slammed against my chest. "Anew?" Every muscle in my body stiffened in anticipation of the pleasure the woman before me would undoubtedly give.

"A will as strong as yours, son, you would rule by my side. Second in command of a legion of demons."

The woman's hands navigated to the front of my jeans, pausing along the zipper. I jerked away best I could, which wasn't much. "I did not agree yet, woman."

She regarded me with heavy-lidded eyes. "You will." Her breath was hot against my neck and her voice husky. "Your body has already."

"Or, maybe brunettes are not what you crave." The woman stepped away and a dark plume of soot encased her. "Maybe you like this better?"

The smoke faded. Beka's stunning emerald eyes perforated the evaporating dark fog. My heart caved. She crept forward, her eyes wide, lips shiny. The tiny, green dress hugged her firm breasts. Her chest heaved, teasing my body.

The immobilizing grips on my elbows, coupled with the debilitating collar, rendered me powerless to move.

"David. Don't fight it. We can be together. Everything will be perfect." Her tongue lapped against my neck, her teeth pricked my earlobe.

"I can't—"

Her tongue filled my mouth, and she rubbed her core against mine, igniting the excitement within me. "It's not really you. It's—"

"I can be whoever you want me to be, any time you need

~ ☾ ~

it." Her breasts pressed against my chest, and she moaned. "You want to touch me, don't you?"

She resembled Beka, but she tasted like soot. Smelled like smoldering ash instead of the lilacs that represented the woman I loved. But Beka was gone. This woman, identical to Beka, I could take right this moment. My body would get the release it's craved for centuries.

I stepped into her.

She smiled, and her eyelashes shadowed her flickering eyes. "I want you to touch me, David. Would you like that?" Her tongue filled my mouth, but I only tasted brimstone and sulfur.

It was not my Beka. No matter what the woman looked like, it wasn't what I truly wanted.

"No," I said.

Cool air prickled my body as Master wrenched the woman from me. She immediately clung to Master, her body pulsing against him from the side like a dog in heat.

"Get him out of here." Master turned to the woman. His mouth covered hers, and she morphed back into the dark-haired girl as Master slid the skimpy dress off her shoulders.

The demons lugged me away. I morphed back to my human form, chest heaving. No. I would not dishonor Beka by succumbing to temptation. I would endure punishment, then someday, I would find her, and hopefully Jessica, and get my salvation.

~ ☾ ~

CHAPTER 28

    This new torture, created specifically for me, was more than I could have ever imagined Master possible of. Not sure why, considering he was the right hand to the devil himself. Leaking images of Beka's body, face, and glowing skin into my consciousness while I lay in the dark, writhing from the burn. An unspeakable torture from which I didn't think I would survive.
    Master must have found an evil witch who penetrated my thoughts and extracted these images. Or it was a spell to reveal what I held most precious so they could torment me with it.
    Each flash amplified the already raging inferno melting my skin. The first fifty years of the two-hundred and fifty year sentence are spent in fire, overloading every sense of pain and every nerve fiber possible. The remaining were spent in utter sensory deprivation.
    Once the fire ceased, it was a relief at first, until the madness of absolute void set in. I was still in the first phase, only Master added the images of Beka to intensify my agony. So I not only experienced the flesh melting from my bones but also my blazing desire for Beka.
    I should have taken the girl in Master's office and have been done with this. No. I could not. I *would* not. I survived the last sentence, and I will survive this one. How long had passed since I last saw the *real* Beka?
    Another flash of her seized my mind. Flame licked my skin. I pressed my cheek against the cold, hard floor beneath me but it did little to extinguish the fire. I squinted, but the darkness had stolen my vision. Didn't matter, I knew there was nothing to see. No flames. No Beka.

~ ☾ ~

Just a black void filled with agony.

Muffled voices near me cut through my distress. Couldn't be voices. I lay in a room protected from all stimuli other than what Master allowed. Cursed doors and hexed walls imprisoned me according to my contract.

More voices. A scream.

My mind must be breaking. Dementia had come earlier than the last time. Then again, the punishment was fifty times more vicious than the previous one. Mostly because I'd found love and lost it.

Beka.

Crackling wood and shouts invaded my ears. Prickles of electricity sizzled my arms. I lifted my hands to shield my face, but they were too heavy. The burn, paired with the thick, metal clamped around my wrists and throat, the weight was too much. The chains clanked as my hand thumped to the concrete floor.

The darkness lightened. I blinked back blue dots forming from the overload on my senses. Metal clanged, vibrating deep within my eardrums. I opened my eyes, but the blazing light seared them back into darkness. *What new torture is this?*

Fingers gripped my biceps and lifted me up. The chains held me in place. More sounds of metal hitting metal. Pinches of fire pricked my arms. The stench of charred skin wrenched my stomach.

"Hold on, my David," a sweet voice I recognized as Beka's called out.

Yes, Master had found an even more vicious torture. He'd duplicated the exact pitch of her voice, her tempting lilac scent. I sagged against the body cradling mine. It jerked, and more metal strikes rang. More pricks bit at my skin. The grip tightened on my armpit.

I wanted to tell them to leave me be, but time had rusted my vocal chords. I could only grunt. Scorching fingers traced my arm down to my wrist and tugged. Chains snapped. I opened my eyes but met only darkness.

Arms wove beneath mine, hooking my armpits, and lofted me up. My weak legs folded, but the strength beneath me

~ ☾ ~

stood fast.

"Try, David. Try and walk." A male voice this time. Familiar. Couldn't place it.

"What's happening?" I said, but it came out as mumbles.

A cool, refreshing liquid splashed my feverish face. It seeped into my eyes, moistening them. Dim light filtered through the curtain of darkness.

"It's me. Russell. Come. You have to move."

Did that man say Russell? Hope sparked within my chest against my better judgment.

I groped the darkness and ordered my legs to move. I wasn't sure how long they'd been inactive. Judging from my uncoordinated jerks, it must have been a while. "Beka—"

"She's busy right now. Hurry. Walk, David." Russell's body smashed into mine, pitching me forward. Something cold pierced my back, near my kidney. Flames erupted.

"Need your demon, David," Russell said, gasping. "Help."

I visualized Beka's face. Focused on her voice the last time I'd heard her in the yard when I was taken. She'd survived if what Russell said was true. If, in fact, it was really him here to rescue me.

Another nightmare. One of Master's tortures.

Needles stabbed my heart as I called on the demon. He had been asleep for who knew how long, but he readily emerged. A growl scratched my dry throat. My weak limbs pulsed, as my demonic side began healing whatever injury I'd received.

I reached forward but grabbed only air. Russell's body rolled off mine. I shuffled onward, knowing I would have to hit a wall soon. The light in my eyes brightened. Still unable to see through the cloudy blur. Finally, my long nails struck something. Flickers of lights, probably sparks, flashed before me.

I scraped down the wall. Metal to keep everything out. Cursed metal. I groped at the chilled surface and worked myself up to my knees. More metal clanks behind me. Fear shot me to my feet. Using the wall to balance, I stood. A wave of body odor invaded my nose. Sulfur mixed with smoldering hair. Hair prickled on my neck. I swung my hand. A wash of

~ ☾ ~

tainted air crashed into me.

"Demon," I said. That time my voice didn't crack. I swallowed hard, trying to clear the thickness coating my throat.

"On your three," Russell yelled.

I swiped. My nails met another throat.

"Move to your right."

Sparks flashed before me. A blade pierced my ribs, and I toppled. More sparks sprayed over me as I edged on. A hand latched onto my bicep. I swung.

"Wait," Russell said. "It's me."

He hoisted me to my feet. My legs helped more that time. My back sagged against the unforgiving wall. Jagged edges of brick chafed my skin. "Beka?"

"Out there, holding them off with Abraham."

"How long?"

"Just got here." He pushed me forward. My hand found air instead of wall, so it must be the door.

"No. How long have I been gone?"

"Talk later. Escape now." He rushed past me, and I heard the ring of swords clashing again.

I filled my lungs with the fresh air and focused on my body, willing it to work. Willing it to heal. I would carry whatever this was to the end, revel in the belief I was being rescued. Because I knew it couldn't be true. But it was better than sitting like a lump on the cement, letting the flame consume me.

I blinked through the neon blue dots littering my vision and made out the doorframe before me, so I crossed through. Light, not stinging like before, settled over me. Shadowy figures danced in front of me.

"Walk forward," Russell commanded me.

I shuffled, hands out. The moving figures fell into focus as I neared a tall human. I recognized Russell's, dark hair. A cold blade pierced my shoulder, and I collided with a wall. The color red tinted my blurry sights. Demon. I swiped. He gurgled and melted out of view. A swaying, blond cape snagged my attention. Hand grazing the wall to keep me steady, I followed the vision. It had to be Beka's hair. So

~ ☾ ~

much longer than I remember.

Two tall figures charged her.

I followed the wall and reached out to Beka with my other hand. A flash of silver slammed against my wrist, sending sparks spraying. I turned and captured the neck of whoever struck me.

I jerked him close, and his face became crisp and clear. Long teeth, red skin, and sickening breath. I cranked his head to the side, snapping his neck, and he sank to the ground. Let another person decapitate him. I only wanted to get to my Beka.

This might be the torture, though. Her within arm's reach, yet never able to touch.

She plunged her sword into the gut of one demon and twirled, sliding her blade through the neck of the other.

"David," she said with a screech. She grabbed my shoulder and pushed. "Down."

I ducked. She swung. Dust sprinkled my bare back.

"Come on." She snatched my hand and yanked me forward.

Russell joined us and slid his hand under my armpit on the opposite side of Beka. They steadied me, hurrying me along while Abraham followed.

"How?" I asked.

"Do you know this place?" Beka asked.

Light-colored walls, squeaky tile floor, and closed doors lining the narrow hallway. "No. I am not at the New York compound."

"Turn right, stairwell at the end," Abraham said.

"Took some time, but we found you, my friend," Russell said.

"Friend?"

"Shut up," Russell said. "Focus on walking. Can't your demon self heal any faster?"

I dug my talons into my palm, as flames flared within my chest. The all too familiar twinge of my punishment spread through my mind. I was hallucinating. No one broke through Master's defenses, let alone take someone from solitary.

But it was a dream with Beka by my side, so I would go

~ ☾ ~

with it. Just to feel my Beka close again, even if in a torturous dream.

"Russell. Don't pester him. He's volatile right now." Beka peered my way. "David. You remember us do you not?"

"Could never forget my Beka."

"Focus on that. Fight the darkness." She stared ahead. "We still have a bit to go through to get you out."

A sheen of perspiration clung to her glowing skin. Sweat beaded above her upper lip. I craved a taste of her salty flesh. My mouth watered at the thought. To touch her bare arms.

A demon lumbered through a side door. Russell let go of me and lunged, sword drawn. Beka stayed focused, guiding me forward.

"Just get to the roof," she said.

"I cannot leave. My contract is—"

"You mean this?" She extracted a bottle, with a black seal on top, from a small bag strapped around the front of her. "We'll deal with this shortly. Come on."

On clumsy legs, I followed. Russell had vanquished the demon and ran to the stairwell door.

"Up," Russell said.

He took the stairs two at a time. Fatigue robbed my strength. I mostly pulled myself up with the railings to the first turn.

"Five more flights," Beka yelled. "Move it."

She planted her hand on my butt and gave me a shove.

All the senses bombarded my mind. Too much. Too fast. I rumbled at the confusion. My animal voice echoed off the cement walls.

She retracted her hand. "Sorry. Please, just hurry."

My legs throbbed, threatening to seize as I rounded the last stairwell. The door opened, metal crashing into my face. My dulled reflexes didn't catch up to the motion until I lay flat on my back. Beka hurdled me and tackled the demon at the waist. They fell through the doorway.

"Rebeka." Abraham vaulted over me.

I rolled to my side, sprung to my feet and stumbled after them. Abraham pinned the creature to the wall with his sword. Beka lay motionless, back against the sterile white

~ ☾ ~

WASTELAND

wall, head tilted. I stormed to the demon and buried my nails in his throat.

"Beka." I shook her by the shoulder. My chest constricted under the pressure of an invisible vise. Air. I needed air.

Her eyes fluttered open. Blood trailed the side of her face, over her high cheekbones. "I'm okay."

Abraham reached down, and she grabbed his hand, then mine. "Let's go."

We burst through the door, Abraham leading, Beka following, and I stumbled behind. The door at the top of the stairwell burst open.

The bright sunlight set off a rainbow of blue, red, and yellow in my vision. I groped for the railing to stay upright. The cold metal slipped through my fingers. My shoulder crashed into the wall. My chest stung, consumed with fire.

My brand.

Darkness curved the corners of my vision. A roar ripped through my throat. My heart erupted, shooting fire-hot blood into my chest. It brought me to my knees, inches from freedom. The choker tightened. My hands gripped the doorframe, chest heaving, and I leaned forward expecting lava to pour from my mouth.

"David," Beka yelled. She raced toward me. I found her eyes.

Her face began to fade into darkness. "No. Don't leave." My throat stung. I was right. This had all been a nightmare. A torture Master designed to break me.

"Fight, David. Fight it." She cupped my cheeks and, surprisingly, the blaze receded. "Look at me."

"You're disappearing. Don't go, Beka. Even if you're a dream, don't go. Please stay."

"No. No I'm not a dream." Her silky lips brushed my cheek. "You feel that?"

I nodded into her hands, searching for more.

"I'm here. We're together. Don't let the darkness take you. We're almost there. Just a little more running."

"It hurts."

"I know. Fight, David. You did it before. You can do it. It'll be over soon."

~ ☾ ~

"Never over." My throat constricted. I reached for the collar but it was gone. Only the burn remained.

"Get up, David." She looked behind her. "Russell. Help me."

A strong hand threaded my arm and heaved me up. "Get up, Demon. It's time to run," Russell said.

They maneuvered me onto the roof and into the bright sunshine. Flames scorched. The contract was still activated. The flame intensified each step further from Master's homestead. My legs moved, I wasn't quite sure how, but they did. They carried me to the edge of the roof.

We had to have been fifteen stories up, and the closest building over twenty feet away. Abraham stood on the other roof. He waved us to him.

Had he jumped?

Beka's hands on me disappeared. "Hold him," she said.

I glanced over my shoulder. She backed up five feet as if she were about to take a running start to jump over the ledge.

"Wait," I said.

"It's okay, David. Trust us." Russell slapped my back. "Get ready."

"For what?" The wind gushed out of my lungs as someone collided with my back. Two thin arms wove beneath my armpits and held me against softness. My nose twitched at the fragrance of lilac.

Beka's cheek nuzzled mine. "My David," she whispered.

But what confused me more were the white wings above us. I looked down. My feet dangled above an alley, and I neared the roof where Abraham stood.

His legs bent, as if he readied himself to receive me. Beka dove at him, and her wings flapped like capes in wind. We slowed to approach. She released her grip on me, and I fell the last five feet.

My bare feet skidded in the gravelly rooftop floor, but Abraham's strong hands clamping my arm kept me upright.

I shaded my eyes. Beka hovered a few feet above us, hands on her hips. She winked as her body jerked with each flap of her divine, snow-white wings.

"Beka," I whispered.

~ ☾ ~

"Hi, David." She fluttered to the ground two feet from me. "A lot has changed since we last saw one another."

~ ☾ ~

CHAPTER 29

The gravel dug into my knees as they met the ground, my full body weight behind them. Beka had wings. They'd plucked me from Master's possession and had my contract.

Must be a trick.

"Let's go. He's too heavy for me to carry far, we must get back to Jessica," Beka waved to Abraham. "Go ready the car."

He bowed and scurried away.

Pellets of sand and rock bounced off my back, and I spun. Russell skidded to a stop a foot beside me.

"Wow, that's a big jump, My Lady. Not all of us have your wings, you know."

"Come. Let's get him downstairs."

"First. Let's see the *true* David. Can't have you walking through a business office all fanged-out and red-skinned." Russell rested his hand on my shoulder.

I stood, ordering my human half to come forward. The demon refused to let go, thriving on the pain the contract elicited. Claws ripped at my heart, wanting to get out. To extinguish the goodness surrounding me.

I used Russell's shoulder to anchor myself against the riot inside my chest.

"You can do it," Beka whispered.

Her hand stroked the side of my face, leaving a wake of cool comfort.

"Let me see my David." She smiled, creasing the skin at the corner of her eyes.

Finally my human half broke through. Russell held me steady. "You okay now?"

I nodded. "Where are we?"

"Sunny California. Top of an office building." Russell led

~ ☾ ~

me to the door on the roof with Beka close by, wings still out.

The fifteen-foot wingspan cast a long shadow around her. She bent at her knees, reached beside the door and pulled out a bag. "Here." She tossed it to Russell.

He snatched the parcel mid-air and let go of me. He unzipped the bag and presented a dark cotton shirt. "Here, put this on. Damn, we forgot shoes."

Russell's speech was different. Modern. Reminded me of the shows I'd watched on the airplane at the start of this ordeal. "How long have I been gone?"

"We'll stick to the stairwell. It's only seven stories. Unlikely we will run into anyone, but still." Beka said, leaving my question hanging, unanswered. She drew in a long breath through her nose, and her wings folded until I no longer saw the white feathers behind her. "We're almost there. Are you doing okay?"

I nodded. The fire strangled my throat and licked the insides of my chest. I wanted to corral Beka into my arms, but I didn't dare. I fought the demon's rage so much I didn't trust my control.

"Hurry," she said. "Looks like he's going to burst a vein."

Russell ducked and looked behind him. "Demons on the rooftop over there. Time to go."

They shoved me through the doorway, and we stumbled down the first three flights of stairs with only our heavy breathing and clanking shoes bouncing off the cement walls. My lungs seared with each breath I took, as if I breathed fire instead of air.

Despite not being in the darkness of solitary, the pain portion of punishment raged. Maybe I had a chance of surviving it if Beka stayed near. Her touch soothed me before. But she said it would be over soon. How?

They guided me to a stop before the last door.

"David," Russell said. "This leads to the main floor. We have to get through the lobby. Can you make it?"

"Yes."

"Stay between us." Beka presented her open palm. "Hold only my hand, though, so it doesn't look like we're both supporting you." Her fingers combed my hair, and she slid

~ ☾ ~

behind me. More tugging followed.

"My Queen, the hair stylist." Russell rolled his eyes.

"We must get this mess under control. He can't go in there looking like a beast. We only have a couple hundred feet to the exit."

"Can't hide that beastly smell, though," Russell said.

"Smell?" I asked.

"Your senses are not working very well yet, are they?" Russell teased.

"They have been bombarded suddenly, they are a mess within me." I analyzed him through hazy eyes. "Vision is starting to sharpen, and you are still just as ugly as I remember."

He grunted.

"But you do look different. How long has it been since I last saw you?"

Beka appeared before me again, closer this time. "We'll tell you everything later. Okay, stand up straight."

"Hard to."

"I know. You can do it, David."

Her long, blond hair cascaded over her shoulders. She wore a black, long-sleeved fitted shirt, with black stretchy pants and dark shoes. Her hair was longer, and her emerald eyes clouded. Dark circles cradled her eyes like she hadn't slept in many moons.

"Where are your wings?"

"In hiding. Don't need them now. Take my hand." She reached for me. "Let's go, Russell."

He cranked the door open and more brightness accosted my nerves. Beka tugged my hand, and I moved forward, standing as straight as possible, fighting the urge to shade my eyes.

Windows made up the entire three-story high walls. Through the glass, zooming cars filled the streets. Inside the building, people scurried back and forth, their shoes clacking and squeaking against the marble floor. The noise echoed in my head like a gong.

A short, dark-haired girl took a second look at me, and her mouth dropped open. Despite being at least seven inches

~ ☾ ~

shorter, she managed to glare down her nose, at me. I wore a dark cotton t-shirt, clean, still creased as if just bought from a store. Dark splotches spotted my worn jeans, though. The ends were frayed, and I was barefoot.

I'd take a second look at myself as well.

Russell walked a step in front, as if to shield people from the sight of me. Beka stayed directly to my side, her hand clasped with mine. I'd missed the warmth of her touch. Yet now, her touch was cool. Calming.

"Hold on. What's going on here?" a deep voice rumbled. I couldn't see past Russell.

"Just taking the trash out," Russell said.

"Pardon me?"

"If you idiots would do your job a bit better, you wouldn't let the homeless get up to the VP's office." Russell waved toward me. "Now, excuse me, he's rather rank, and I would like to escort him out."

A short pause. Beka's grip intensified. A radio crackled. "Let me check with—"

"Check with who? We're fifteen feet from the doors, let us pass and we'll be on our way."

"The person trespassed, we have to call the authorities."

"Already did that." Russell tilted his head forward. "Like I said, I'm taking care of this, back off."

I finally got a view of the guy who had been talking. Tall, broad shoulders. The overhead florescent lights bounced off his shaved head. His shoes squeaked as he stepped aside. Another security guard, dressed in identical dark army fatigues, stood behind a marble desk fifteen feet away. He tapped his finger to his ear. The guard near us did the same.

We must be at a banking establishment to warrant such security.

Beka led me forward.

Tall, metal pillars on each side of a narrow passage separated by a horizontal bar stood ten feet before us. A woman slid a thin, white card beneath a scanner. The light on the top of the pillars beeped and flashed green. She pressed her waist against the bar, and it shifted, letting her by. The contraption beeped and flashed red once she was through.

~ ☾ ~

I'd seen something similar in an underground place called a subway in New York.

The beeps rang in my ears like a bell tower. The incinerator in my chest ignited again, and I couldn't stop the flinch before the tension engulfed my spine.

"I'm going to have to see some ID please." The guard put his arm out, blocking Russell.

"Sorry. No time." With lightning speed, Russell's open palm smashed into the guard's chin. His head snapped back, and he stumbled. But while he did, he reached for his sidearm.

A dull rumble resonated, the beast desperate to emerge and rip his throat out, but Beka's firm hand grabbed my elbow and urged me onward.

"Jump."

I faced forward and saw what she meant. The scanning mechanism was our hurdle. I bent my legs and lunged. With Beka's added strength and her massive wingspan I managed to clear the contraption.

Screams erupted, but I couldn't focus on any of them. I must keep the beast within me quiet. My nails hardened and darkened.

"Hold on, David," Beka said as we descended to the floor. "There's Abraham, see him?"

The tall Guardian stood by the curb, near a shiny, black vehicle. I'd never seen one so long. The back door was propped open. He stood with hands clasped in front of him and wore face-filling, reflective glasses. His long hair was slicked back into a ponytail, and he donned a tuxedo.

A group of five females hovered near him, watching, but the stoic Guardian faced straight ahead. Russell burst through the first set of glass doors. "Hurry up, they're closing in."

Seven guards swarmed the desk. Three more had gotten through the scanning mechanism, and they sprinted toward us, boots chirping against the slick, marble floor.

My heart pounded as my dark-nailed hand pressed against the glass, keeping the door open. Beka pushed me through first and followed close.

~ ☾ ~

Russell propped the second set of doors open with his foot, waving me forward. I ran out, bursting into the brightness of day. I clamped my hands over my eyes, dizzy with neon-blue spots tracing the corner of my vision. The windows of the building must have been tinted, because the daylight singed my retinas.

A hand squeezing each elbow, Beka and Russell ushered me toward the car. Abraham darted around to the driver's side. Russell pushed me in. My head rammed into the handle of the opposite door. That elicited another lament as the burn flamed again. Too much was happening at once.

The car jolted. Through the open door, I saw a guard catch Beka by the shoulder. She cranked her free arm, connecting her elbow with the man's temple. I crawled to the door to help, but Russell nailed the man in the jaw. He went down.

Beka dove into the car. Her shoulder collided with my stomach, and we fell into the seat. Air whistled from my lungs.

The car jostled again.

Russell jumped in. "Go. Go. Go."

The car jerked forward, and my body slammed against the soft seat. Beka rolled off but stayed close. Our shoulders touched as she settled back, her chest heaving.

I gasped for breath trying to cool the fire and fill my lungs. Russell sat off to the right on a long, padded seat. Dark, tinted windows, running several feet long, lined the side of the vehicle. A TV screen in the corner against the back end of the car. A narrow sink with glasses clanked, tucked beneath the TV. Straight ahead, separated by plastic, I saw the back of Abraham's head.

Tall buildings and people zoomed by me, but all I wanted to see was Beka.

She sat, staring at me with wide eyes, her head leaning on the headrest of the seat we shared. I relaxed into the leather. The discomfort faded from my consciousness as I absorbed the sight of her face.

I swiped my knuckle along her cheek, wiping away a crimson splotch marring her skin. She leaned into my touch. Her scent flooded me, and I swallowed the ache. Her thumb

~ ☾ ~

swirled the skin below my eye, leaving a wake of coolness.
Her touch doused the flames.
"I've finally found you," she whispered.
An inch separated our faces.
"How long have I been gone?" I buried my fingers in her hair.
"Doesn't matter. We're together now." Her lips captured my mouth.
A wave of coolness infused my body as if I'd been submerged in an ice bath. She chased away the blaze of the demon trying to burst out of me. Of my punishment. She was really here. Holding me. Kissing me. I gripped her silky hair and angled her for deeper access.

My Beka.

Her lips swept across my cheek, and she buried her face in my neck. She settled onto my lap. "Finally." Her breath teased the hair on my neck.

I combed my dirty fingers through her silky strands, reveling the touch. It had grown so long. Gentle kisses peppered my neck.

"Careful, My Lady. He is still demon." Russell coughed. "We have to get to Jessica first."

A grumble from Beka's mouth vibrated along my neck. She tilted her head. "Soon, my angel," she whispered. "Rest now, I will keep you cool, and we will get you some food."

She settled next to me, keeping one arm around my shoulders. She guided me close to her and wrapped her other arm around me, cradling me. Darkness tugged at my vision. Fatigue weighed my body down.

"How long?" I wanted to stay awake and look at my Beka's perfect face. I had so many questions, but my tired brain couldn't pick one to ask.

Beka's sweet breath washed over me. "It's been a long, thirty-five years without you, my angel. But I've finally found you."

~ ☾ ~

CHAPTER 30

Squealing tires and a quick jerk forward ripped through a peaceful, cool, darkness. Gone was the bright sunlight. My demon eyesight allowed me to see trees whizzing by. Streaks of light cut through the darkness beside us as a vehicle approached, inches from ours. It veered, ramming into the side of the car. I crashed into Beka.

"Open the moon roof, let me out," Beka yelled.

I grabbed her wrist. "No. We stay together."

She winked. "I'll just be gone a minute. Need to deal with this car trying to push us off the cliff."

"The cliff?" Behind her lay a black void. Not even treetops.

Russell pressed the buttons on the door handle, and the moon roof whizzed open. Another wave of whining metal rang out as the SUV collided with ours again, jostling me to the side.

"Beka. No."

She reached for the open window, but I immediately saw what she meant to do when feathers began to protrude from a long slit in her shirt.

They inched out while her hands gripped the sides of the open roof. She closed her eyes. The wings hastened in their mission. Soft feathers stroked my face, but she curled them close to her body. Amazing how things so big hid within her small body.

She hugged them to her back like a cape, gave me a quick smile, then pulled herself up and out of the car. The sound of a parachute snapping open as it caught wind had me jumping to the window to see. Her wings were open and we zoomed ahead of her.

"Beka," I yelled as the car approached us for another hit.

~ ☾ ~

She appeared, flapping her powerful wings, and she matched the speed of the vehicle next to us. She punched her hand through the top and peeled the metal back.

A sword shot through the roof, nicking her arm. She projected upward, still matching their speed, and went to the driver's side and smashed her hand through the window. Another set of headlights sped up behind us.

"Abraham, you better hit the gas, we have more company," Russell said.

"What's happening, Russell?"

"Guess your Master didn't appreciate us coming in to get you and your contract." Russell moved to the end of the long car, near Abraham and mumbled something to him I couldn't make out.

Demons pursued us in cars. This was so new to me, always having fought either on foot or on horseback. Vehicles, especially one this big, moving at high speeds, complicated things. I stood, half of my body out the top of the moving car through the moon roof. Beka fluttered beside us, dodging swords while trying to grab the driver. The car from behind rammed ours, and I lurched forward, the side of the roof cracked into my ribs. The wind whooshed out from my lungs, and bones popped.

I howled, and my demon took control.

"David. Don't. We can't let them get you again," Russell said.

Beka squealed and catapulted into the air. "Russell, give me my weapon," she yelled.

He popped up the other moon roof holding her weapon. "My Lady," he yelled.

With two powerful flaps, she zoomed toward him and snatched it from his hand. Her long hair trailed behind her as she moved, defying gravity with the grace of a swan, but the lethality of a powerful Guardian.

I ducked into the cab of our car and shuffled toward Russell. I snatched a blade from his belt, then hurried back to my window and hoisted myself onto the roof. Beka stabbed her sword into the top of the car beside us, opening it like a can opener. The car behind us rammed our bumper.

~ ☾ ~

Our car swerved and skidded on the rocky shoulder. Rocks from our skidding wheels pelted the metal pursuing us. We'd nearly gone over the edge. Sure, we'd all survive the crash, but still, I couldn't tell how far the drop was, and it would take serious time to recover from injuries of that magnitude.

I let out a snarl as I faced the car behind us. I crawled onto the trunk, dagger in hand. Flaming, red eyes glared through the tinted window. Elite Guard, of course. Difficult to kill, but possible. I refused to return to darkness.

"David. Don't," Russell yelled.

I jumped onto the hood of the car behind us and dug my nails through the metal to secure my position. I drove my dagger through the windshield and directly into the chest of the driver.

I retracted my hand, snagging the cracked windshield and tossed it over the side. I grabbed the steering wheel and cranked it to the left, toward the trees.

Squealing tires skidding on pavement rang out. The stench of burnt rubber assaulted my nostrils. With my other hand, I slid my demon nails over the driver's throat. He disintegrated into nothing. A set of talons scored my forearm as the passenger fought for control of the steering wheel.

The car I'd been in must have braked because I saw its long frame go by us and come up behind. The vehicle Beka worked on veered to the side. She soared into the sky with a solid flap of her wings, and the car plunged over the edge into the void.

Beka streaked toward me. "David."

I sliced off the hand of the demon reaching for the steering wheel. He swung his blade. It clanked against my wrist. I collared his neck with my fingers and tossed him out. His body flopped onto the road. The car seesawed and swerved. Gravity yanked me to the side. Our vehicle rammed the back end. Abraham cranked the steering wheel. The tires locked, throwing it into a skid.

"Jump," Beka yelled.

I did as she commanded. My hand met hers, and she heaved me up. We hovered, as our long car flipped to its side and slid. Sparks speckled the darkness. Metal creaked.

~ ☾ ~

Gasoline tainted the fresh air.

The demon's car skidded, but momentum pushed it over the edge.

Beka dropped me to the road, and I planted my feet on the centerline. She darted toward our rolling car, and I took off running. Our vehicle finally stopped. Smoke and flames ruptured from the pile of mangled metal.

I peeked over the ledge. Russell hung onto a rock ten feet down. I stretched for him, but he was out of reach. "Where is Abraham?" I asked.

"Here," he said from behind me. He lay flat on the gravel shoulder fifteen feet away.

A gust of wind sprayed me with a fine layer of dust. Beka hovered, flapping her powerful wings, above Russell.

"Need a hand, Russell?"

"That would be nice, My Lady."

With a couple graceful swoops of her wings, she descended to him and wrapped her arms around his chest from behind and lifted him up.

"You men are so heavy." Beka hovered near me and dropped Russell.

He landed with a thud and stumbled toward me. I steadied him by the shoulders. Russell shook his head. "You just had to help, didn't you, David?"

I pushed him away.

"Relax. I know. You were just trying to help." He faced the steaming pile of metal. "This is going to delay things, I'm afraid."

"Delay what? Can someone tell me what is going on?" The scorching flame within me flared again despite the strong breeze Beka's wings provided. "Where are we?"

Beka set down beside me. Her feathered limbs retracted behind her so I only saw a few feathers swaying in the breeze. "David. We must get you and your contract to Jessica. Remember I told you I thought she could help you?"

I willed my demonic self to its dark corner and faced her as David. A cool breeze filtered through my shredded clothes. Seems the demon got in some well-timed swipes. "Yes. You have found a way that she can help me?"

~ ☾ ~

"Not so much as a way has found us." Beka stepped toward me. "But yes. Jessica can break the bonds of this contract. She need only touch you and the contract to allow you to become what you were meant to become."

Finally, after four hundred years, I would be rid of my demonic half. Not bound by any contract. I let out a long breath and sagged forward.

"But, we need to get you to her. And with no car, that will slow things considerably," Russell said.

"My Lady," Abraham said. "We must take shelter." He nodded to the trees lining the road. "I am sure more demons will come, we must put distance between us and these broken cars."

She faced me. "Are you okay, David?"

"Not really."

"Does the burn consume you?" Her left wing unfolded and draped my shoulders. "I will keep you cool."

The soft feathers brushed against my skin, and they felt like ice cubes to my flames. "How do you do that?"

She threaded her arm around my waist and led me forward. "Like I said, David, much has changed since we have last been together."

~ ☾ ~

CHAPTER 31

The cool water washed over my skin as I descended into the stream. The current hacked away the filth clinging to my body. Thirty-five years with no bathing, no food. Nothing but the sense of fire and torment.

The agony remained, deep within my chest, a constant reminder of the punishment Master had initiated. But it lessened each minute I stayed near Beka. Like she was a cool drink of water. Bright stars sprinkled against the deep night sky blinked as if to welcome me back to the living. So many years had passed.

Jessica had morphed into Merus. When I'd almost touched her before I was taken, she could have banished my demon half had my skin connected with hers. The memory of that night was blurry at best. Fighting the consuming fire allowed me to focus on only one thing, Beka. The rest went to the wayside.

I got a peaceful, cool feeling when my thoughts dwelled on her. Jessica's touch had given Beka beautiful, bright angelic wings. She was already radiant, but the majestic wings amplified her beauty, including my draw to her.

I waded out of the stream and onto the shore. I dried off as much as possible with my shredded shirt, then slid on my frayed jeans. The meaty smell of rabbit cooking over the open fire triggered a rumble in my stomach. To eat food again after so long, even if plain and cooked on the run from demons, would taste heavenly.

I ran my hands through my wet hair. The grime had washed away. Floated downstream, but fatigue weighed heavy on my bones. Twigs crackling nearby sent prickles down my spine.

~ ☾ ~

"Hi." Beka emerged from the surrounding darkness.

I tossed my damp cloth to the side. I had to restrain myself from yanking her into my arms. She'd changed into a skintight cream tank top but still donned the body-hugging stretch pants and black combat boots. Her light, almost glowing, skin lured me in like nothing I'd ever experienced. Maybe because she was forbidden. Things we could not have always held more appeal.

Maybe that was why she wanted me. I was forbidden to her as well.

Regardless. I wanted her. More than anything.

She took two long strides and leapt. Her body collided with mine, and she wrapped her arms around my neck. I stumbled back at the surprise of her actions, but wove my hands around her waist, and hugged her close. She rested her elbows on my shoulders while her fingers combed through my hair.

"Finally alone." She took my mouth with hers.

Her tongue danced with mine with an urgency of lovers separated for years. But we were not lovers. We were not supposed to be together. My body didn't care. It perked to life with raw hunger. A need to unite with this woman. To protect her for always.

Her warm hands grazed over my shoulders to my neck, tilting my head for deeper access. I devoured her mouth, suckling her bottom lip. *More.* She leaned back and palpated her hands down my heaving chest.

"You're really here," she whispered.

"Beka, we—"

She silenced me with a kiss. I crushed her to me, her body molding to mine. I danced my fingers up her spine, and she ducked out of the kiss.

"Careful," she said with a husky voice. "Sensitive there."

"Where are they?"

Her chest swelled and pressed against me. "Your hands are like magic to me." She touched a kiss to my cheek. "I've dreamt about this for thirty-five years, David. I ache for you to touch me. Just down the back is very, *very* sensitive to me now."

~ ☾ ~

Her hands massaged my bare stomach. A current of blazing heat zipped through my veins.

She gasped when I did and out came her wings. The gust startled me, but she curled her feathers around us, blanketing our bodies. I swept my gaze over her shining eyes. The slight curve of her cheekbones to her chin. She raked her teeth over her lip, igniting another pleasurable wave of warmth. That taunting gesture plagued my dreams while in punishment.

Her neck begged to be nipped, but I kept sweeping my eyes downward. I trailed my finger to where the zipper met her tank top, smooth skin beckoning my touch.

"David," she sighed.

I cupped her breasts, and her wings went rigid.

She clasped her fingers behind my neck and pulled herself up to me. Her wings cooled me, but the beast within still pierced my heart with its molten claws.

Take her.

My hands navigated her hips and over her backside. I hoisted her up. Her legs cinched my waist, and she latched her feet behind me, kindling the inferno. Not the demonic flame, but one of lust. Desire.

"I've waited for you, David."

"Why? We cannot be together." I grazed on her jaw line down her neck.

"Not yet." She suckled my earlobe. "But soon."

"How? You're betrothed. I am de—"

"Shhh. Do not say that word ever again." She palmed my face. "You are my David. I do not want to ever hear that evil word come from your mouth again." She drew in her wings and slid down the front of my body to her feet.

Her thumb brushed my lips. I held her palm to my cheek. "How are you so cool to me?"

"The Light. It flows through my veins now. From Jessica." Her gentle kisses spanned my chest, to the collarbone. Her hands rested on my sides.

I lost my breath at her softness, and my body throbbed. "Please stop. I cannot bear it."

"I'm sorry. I just missed you so much." She hugged me and lay her cheek against my chest. "It took years to find you."

~ ☾ ~

"How did you?"

"Followed demon after demon. We recognized the big ones you called the Elite Guard. They still hunted Jessica, even though her conversion had been complete."

"What is Jessica?" I petted Beka's long, soft hair as she clung to me. Thankfully she'd stopped moving against me. The contrasting cold emanating from her, and the warmth of her body challenged my weakened resolve.

"Pure Light." Beka gazed into my eyes. "Able to convert evil to goodness just by her touch."

"Demons?"

"Those not fully converted."

"There are more half-demons like me?"

"No. There is no one like you, David. You're the first of your kind, but yes, there are people who choose evil, but before they do the act required of them, take an innocent's life, they are not fully demon."

"I've heard of that. Jessica can remove that evil from them with only her touch?"

Beka nodded into my chest.

"And she can do that for me? Remove my demon half and vanquish the contract?"

"We just need to get you to her. The loss of our vehicle has slowed us, but we'll get you there. If it's the last thing I do, David, we'll get you there. I pledge it."

I leaned back, forcing her to look me in the eye. This didn't make sense. She wasn't free to be with me. "Why are you doing all this? You're betrothed."

"Your majesties." Russell stepped through a split in the trees. "Come, the food is ready. Let's rest and be on our way."

My heart slammed against my chest. "Majesties?"

~ ☾ ~

CHAPTER 32

"Sit. Eat. You must get your strength back." Russell handed me a piece of bark fashioned into a plate overflowing with chunks of meat. "We are far from the city."

I peeked at Beka, and she nodded.

"Please, tell me everything," I said as I shoveled the first bite into my mouth, still stumbling over Russell calling me *Majesty*.

The raging campfire in front of me crackled, sending sparks up into the darkness. Trees towered over us, but I spied a flicker of the full moon through the foliage. Beka sat close to me, legs crossed, and Russell and Abraham sat on the leaf-padded ground across from us.

"Remember how precious a treasure Jessica was?" Russell said.

"Yes. I remember you sacrificing your Queen for her."

Russell coughed into his hand. "But you were there to save her. And you will soon see that Jessica was well worth it."

"Why is she not here?"

"We couldn't risk her safety to bring her to you for your rescue. She's back in Arizona under guard," Beka said.

I devoured the rest of my meal in three bites and handed Russell my wooden plate for more. "Go on."

"When Jessica received the pure Light, with it, she received inspired sight."

"Inspired sight?" I asked.

"She looks through eyes unlike anyone's. They see deep into people, their soul, their goodness, and their evil. She shared some of her insight with me when she touched me. She confirmed me as Queen. Turned me into what I am now. A Guardian Angel." She nestled closer to me as she picked up

~ ☾ ~

a piece of meat. "Part of that insight was a picture of my mate. The one who will rule with me."

I gulped a stray piece of meat lodged in my throat.

"I'd always known I would join with someone to rule, and I've saved myself for that person, but when I met you, I was willing to give it up just to have you by my side." She slid the back of her hand over her mouth. "But how could I mate with a demon? Evil could never rule over the Guardians."

"Exactly," I said.

"But Jessica sees through different eyes. When she looked at you, she saw the future. It was you by my side as my King. That's why she had to get to you. But your Master's Elite Guard stole you from our grasp before she could make contact."

"How? Why me?"

"She sees the full prophecy, not just the little part we knew of, about my being queen and joining with an angel to rule. Your mother made a contract with Lucifer. Sold the soul of her first born into servitude. But Michael, the Archangel, knew you were destined to be more than a demon, so he instituted a clause into your contract."

"Clause?"

Beka nodded at Russell. He sat up and the fire cast a dancing shadow over his face. "David," he said. "He gave you choice. If you were to choose the life of a demon, so be it, but you had to be presented with a pure choice. Lucifer knew the fleshly needs of man—meaning—he knew how tempting sex can be to men, so he made that the deciding factor. Should you choose to lay with a woman, you would be confirmed demon, and you would lose your humanity. But all these years, you didn't. You made it to Michael's final moment of choice."

"Jessica," I whispered.

Beka smiled. "Yes. When you chose to give up Jessica to us, to the Light, you chose humanity over darkness."

"Why did I not shed my demon at that moment?" I set my wooden plate on the ground before me and rested my elbows on my knees. "If it is just choice, why continue the punishment?"

~ ☾ ~

"Jessica needed to touch your skin in order for your demon to be banished." Tears welled in Beka's eyes. "But you were taken."

"Why would Master send me to retrieve Jessica, knowing all of this? I'd never wanted to be full demon. He's always known that. He must have known I would choose Jessica."

"Part of the agreement. By contract, your Master *had* to allow you to come here. He awoke you a few years early of your sentence, did he not?" Beka asked.

"He did. I never knew the reason."

"That is why. He knew the sensory deprivation would leave you hungry and thirsty for worldly pleasures, including finding comfort in a woman's arms. My guess is he'd hoped you would fall before you retrieved Jessica. Be too weak to face another sentence by turning her over to us, or letting her go. Therefore, your choice made, you wouldn't step into your destined role."

"He's known this all along." I kneaded the back of my neck. My limbs felt heavy, like iron rods, lead flowing through my veins. "The timing of my punishment, to leave me vulnerable. Sending me to that club hours after my release. *Everything.*"

"He's deceived you this entire time. If he would have gotten you to give in, chosen your demon side, making it to Michael's choice wouldn't have mattered. Lucifer would have mated you with Master's Queen and you would rule the demonic world instead of Master." Beka gripped my forearm.

"He never would have allowed that."

"Right," Russell said. "If you were demon, he would be able to kill you; therefore, remaining in his position."

"No wonder he wanted me to convert so badly. He would have killed me outright." So often he'd tempted me. Gage, too.

I bolted to my feet and ambled a distance away. I'd preserved my humanity, hoping for a way out of my contract. To become human. Never had I expected this. I could not be a King of the…I'd killed so many Guardians. Brought innocent people to Master. This couldn't be true.

The further I got from the camp, the more the burn settled

~ ☾ ~

in. I stopped. The blazing needles punctured my heart. I allowed some of my evil to surface and analyzed the ebony nails slicing through my fingertips.

Something like me could never become king of the Guardians. No being had the ability to purge four centuries of darkness coursing through my veins. The things I'd done.

Don't hope for redemption.

"I know it's a lot to take in, David," Beka said. "I've had thirty-five years for the truth to sink in, and sometimes I still can't believe."

"There has to be a mistake."

She stood shoulder to shoulder with me. "No. It's not a mistake. Can't you feel it?"

"What?"

"How did you feel the first time you saw me?"

"I thought you were an angel. Dancing on that floor. I joked that two hundred and fifty years of confinement would be worth a few minutes in your arms." I studied the ground. "And here you turn out to be an angel."

Fingers twined with mine. Her light skin sharply contrasted mine. She brought my hand close to her face and brushed her cheek against my knuckles.

I retracted my talons. "How can you stand to be so close to me when some of my demon is surfaced? How are you not repulsed?"

"Because I know it's not your true self. Something your mother cursed you into before you were even conceived." Her jaw muscles twitched. "She had no idea what she'd done when making that deal."

"I've hated her for centuries."

"But, despite what she'd done, she'd started the prophecy. Your prophecy, David." She closed her eyes and faced skyward. "Our destiny. As mates."

Light strokes of softness tickled my arm. I turned to find feathers massaging my skin, cooling the demon inside of me.

"Where do the wings go?"

She rested her head on my shoulder. "They fold behind me and dissolve into my skin when not needed. That is why I must have two slits in everything I wear, in case I need them

~ ☾ ~

quickly."

"Does it hurt?"

"Somewhat. But nothing like what you've endured for all those centuries in captivity." A single tear slid over her cheek and dripped off her jaw. "I can only imagine the agony, the—"

"Don't." I swallowed the bitter rage. "I am strong. I choose you, Beka. Take me to Jessica. If I am to be your mate, I would like very much for that to happen soon."

Her arm snaked around my waist, and her wing encircled my shoulders. "As would I, but you can hardly stand on your own volition. You need to rest, then we will move quickly."

"How far are we?"

"You slept many hours in the car, but we are still outside Arizona's borders. The Guardians are on the move toward us, with Jessica, to a blessed spot in the northern corner. We were to meet there tonight. I will take to the sky and scout ahead, looking for a town from which we can procure a car and get you more food. We need you strong."

"It is dark, how will you see?"

She turned into me. "My eyesight is quite good now."

I absorbed the sensation of her body formed to mine. A flicker of doubt fanned to life in my stomach. Everything I'd ever dreamt of in a female stood beside me. A precious woman to cherish and make love to. A chance to remove my demon rested in Jessica, a young girl hiding only hours from me. Waiting to help me.

Even though I was new to this century, disarrayed from thirty-five years of captivity and plagued with the constant twinge of Master's punishment, I was still aware of the phrase *too good to be true*.

~ ☾ ~

CHAPTER 33

"Hurry, my king, we're close," Russell said.

"Don't call me that." I stomped toward him.

He chuckled and pointed ahead. I peeked around the corner of the building. Beka's slight frame stood proud as she talked to a tall man, with dark hair. He leaned in over her.

A thundering rumble rolled in my chest.

"Going to be one of those possessive-type husbands I see," Russell said with a snicker and waved me to follow him. "Relax, she's just wooing him with her angelic charm. We need a car quickly. She said she saw a bunch of demons combing the woods and this small town, looking for you."

"*A bunch of*...your language has changed."

"Hanging around a teenager will do that." Russell smiled. "Jessica is a unique mixture of teenager, adult, and ancient. It's quite intriguing."

"Teenager? It's been thirty-five years."

"You'll understand when you see her. She may be the prophesied Merus and nearing fifty years old, but she looks no more than eighteen." Russell slapped my shoulder. "Don't worry about it. Just trust us. We'll get you to her."

"So, Master has known this entire time that should I choose Light, I would become something different?"

So much had changed while I was away. "Yes. Lucifer is his boss, after all. He's the one who made the deal with Michael and put you in his care."

"Care." I wouldn't have chosen that word to describe how Master treated me.

We came to a stop, and squatted behind a thick tree trunk fifty feet from the rental lot. Behind us, cars sped by. Sun sifted through the swaying branches sheltering us, and the

~ ☾ ~

breeze carried a fruity scent from nearby citrus trees.

"He's not winning any Daddy awards any time soon that's for sure."

"No wonder he always sought to punish me and to tempt me. Yet, had I given in, I would have dethroned him—if he couldn't kill me."

"I'm sure Master would have tried, yes, but I truly doubt Lucifer would have allowed you killed." Russell stared straight ahead. "Who is Master to argue with what Lucifer wants, right? You demons are sick creatures."

I dug my elbow into his ribs. "Careful, I have been away from my Beka's cooling touch for some time now. I could morph and end you in a second, you realize that, don't you?"

He faced me and crinkled his forehead. "It's nice to see you have your humor about you. The nap and three meals must have helped."

"Yes. I'm feeling better." I glanced at him. "The burn worsens when I'm separated from her, though."

"All the more reason to fully believe the prophecy to be true, is it not?"

But I'm evil.

"How can you doubt? You've loved Beka since the minute you saw her. I saw you in the bar that first night watching her."

I nodded.

"Your body has craved her touch as hers has for you since that meeting."

"She tells you such things?"

"We've been together for centuries, I know a little about her. I could tell. That was what frightened me so deeply. How could Light be attracted to darkness? But now I see it clearly, my *King*."

Another growl.

"Growl all you want, *Demon*. I've watched her agonize over being separated from you for thirty-five years. It's been agony witnessing her disappointment every time we thought we'd found you."

"I did notice the darkness beneath her usually bright eyes."

"Indeed. Many hours of sleep sacrificed thinking about

~ ☾ ~

WASTELAND

you, tracking you."

I sat on the dirt, back against the tree trunk. My knees ached as did the muscles in my back and neck. I needed several more meals to work through the knots in my human muscles from thirty-five years of punishment. I didn't dare stay in my demonic form long to speed the healing.

"Why couldn't Jessica just figure out where I was if she is so powerful?"

"Doesn't work that way. When she sees someone, she sees the truth. The only knowledge she came to supernaturally was that of the prophecy. Beka to unite with an angel. Jessica saw you as the angel."

I was hardly an angel.

"She looked into some of the demons we'd captured trying to find you, but they knew very little." Russell sat up. "Okay, I think we're getting close."

Beka eased away from the man and offered her hand. He plopped something into her palm and walked away.

"Come on." Russell stood. "We must hurry. Many demons in this town."

"Where is Abraham?" I asked as I followed Russell to my Beka.

"Here," he said from behind us. "Just checking the premises."

Beka's green eyes flared at me. "How are you?"

"Feeling better."

She stepped toward me, hand outstretched. "We will be to Jessica by nightfall. Come, let's go."

I slid my hand into hers and reveled in the cool feelings she sent up my arm. It chased the burn away, yet left me pleasantly warmed. She tossed Russell the keys. Gentle hands guided me to the back door and cranked it open. She waved me in.

The small car shook as Russell and Abraham filed into the front seats. "No SUVs available, My Lady?"

"Be thankful we got this one. Drive." She skimmed her knuckles down the side of my neck. "We'll get you more food and some clothes at the first gas station we stop at."

I patted my chest. I'd almost forgotten I was bareback and

~ ☾ ~

barefoot.

She gathered me close. "Rest until then."

Her cool arm coiled around my neck and coaxed me to her soft body. Her fingers combed through my hair. The car jostled over bumps and turns of the city. Distant horns blared. The air carried a hint of exhaust and gasoline, but the scent of lilac dominated them all, calming me. The gentle sensation of her fingers caressing my scalp lulled me into a state of hypnosis.

"How can you want someone like me?"

"Your soul is pure, just tainted by an evil contract. I see your soul. Jessica sees your soul."

I nestled closer to her neck. Her pulse thumped against my forehead. "You sound so sure."

"I am."

I didn't share her confidence. "How did you know that before Jessica said I was to be your mate?"

"I can't explain it. First saw you in the club, so stiff and tense, cringing every time someone touched you." She let out a chuckle. "But you were so beautiful. So innocent looking."

"Hardly."

"My heart, soul and body had never reacted so intensely to a man before. Well, to be honest, it never had."

"How can you care for someone who has killed your kind before?"

"You sound like Russell now." She kissed my hair. "That was the contract. You wouldn't have done that otherwise."

Fatigue tugged my eyelids closed, but I wanted to stay awake, to feel her close to me. "Tell me more about you."

"My family members were the Guardians in Bulgaria. We'd guarded the area for centuries. I was born to my parents already a Guardian. Usually we go through the transformation at puberty or shortly after, but from birth, I was magical." She settled in the seat and let out a long sigh. "My dad—I can still remember him even though so many centuries have passed since I last saw him."

She combed her fingers through my hair and nuzzled her cheek on the top of my head.

"He and my brother were called to the north. I stayed back

~ ☾ ~

to watch over our city. Demons had infiltrated the area, killing innocents frequently. I begged to go with them, but they said no. I was the younger Guardian, despite being fully developed. So, I honored their request."

She cleared her throat.

"Stayed with your mother?" I asked.

"No. Mother died nearly seventy years earlier doing battle with a legion of demons invading a nearby town. Anyway. My father and brother didn't return for many moons so I defied their orders and rode my steed toward where they were headed.

"I found the camp, burned to the ground. The remains of their bodies near a fire pit. I recognized the shoes and belts they'd worn amidst the dust. Many humans littered the ground as well."

I opened my eyes and tilted back. "Demons."

Her blond locks shifted forward as she dipped her head, and her hand guided my face back to her neck. "My father had been the oldest of our kind, my brother next in line, but since both were killed, that left me. A young Guardian, a handful of centuries old, but the eldest of our kind. Abraham and Russell found me less than a century later and have been with me ever since."

"We guard our Queen with our lives," Russell said. "The house of David lives on in Beka."

The name *House of David* sent me jolting upright.

"What is it?" Beka glanced out the windows.

"House of David?" I inched away from her.

"Yes. You know of it?"

Dread struck me like a sword to the chest. I knew something would happen to come between us. I knew I could never deserve a woman like Beka. I was demon to the core.

"What is it, David?"

"Nothing." I shook my head. "I—well—I have heard of that name from Master. I remembered the name so vividly because it was mine." Total lie.

"Yes. They had a long line of Guardians. I am the last, though, until I produce a child." Her thumb grazed my cheek. "Are you sure you're okay?"

~ ☾ ~

"Just hungry again." I faced forward, staring at the road approaching us as Russell sped on. My world fell into a blur.

I could never tell Beka that I, per contract, was the one who had murdered her father and brother that day in Constantinople.

~ ☾ ~

CHAPTER 34

I sat in the backseat of the car, watching Beka through the gas station store windows, as she navigated the aisles. She disappeared behind an aisle, then popped up, holding a bag. She glanced in my direction.

Always guarding.

She would no longer share those feelings when she learned I killed her brother and father. The last of her line. I remember the day like it happened yesterday and not so long ago. My second assignment. To bring young Alexander Malka—a demon to be—to Master. I'd tracked the young kid to this camp and within minutes of my arrival, two Guardians showed up.

Master's Seers had warned me about them. Even gave me their names. Now I understood why.

They fought gallantly, but when faced with a creature such as me, it didn't matter how gallant. They perished at my hands. I studied my fingers, and a tremor of regret and anger rattled through them. The burn intensified, and my nails darkened. I picked up the acidic scent of fear emanating from my body.

Beka will reject me.

I cranked on the handle and dashed out of the back seat. My knees creaked with stiffness from sitting. The thermal desert-air hit my bare skin, adding fuel to the invisible flame beneath the surface. I faced a single lane road that paralleled the gas station. Past that, only treetops. Probably another cliff. The sun hung in the bright sky, indicating late afternoon. Sweat popped from my forehead beneath the stifling heat.

One other car next to the pump beside ours sat empty. The

~ ☾ ~

woman and child who had occupied the vehicle were in the store. No houses or buildings within sight. Only trees on either side of the meager gas station and a deserted road behind me.

"We're almost there, David," Russell said over the top of our car. "Is it tough to fight the flame?"

"Getting tiresome."

"Hold Beka close, she'll ease the pain."

I nodded. My heart cracked at the thought. She wouldn't want to touch me ever again once she found out I nearly obliterated her bloodline. *How will she ever forgive that? How will she ever accept me?*

"What is it, my King?" Russell said.

"I told you to quit calling me that." I glanced around.

"No one is nearby."

"It is not that. I am nobody's King." I tunneled my hand through my hair and stomped toward the road. Three cars zoomed past. The wake of wind flapped my hair back and sent sand and rock pinging off my skin.

"Not yet you aren't, but you will be. We're only an hour from Jessica."

"It is just weird to hear of Kings and Queens in the twenty-first century, isn't it?"

"Indeed. But, who are we to fight destiny, *my King*?"

I growled but a scream thwarted my attempt to intimidate Russell. We whirled.

"Look, mommy." A little girl pointed to the sky. "Wings."

Beka's bright wings flapped, holding her fifteen feet above the gas station while Abraham rolled on the ground with two large figures.

"They found us?" Russell sprinted toward Abraham.

Beka darted in my direction, then veered right. A high-pitched squeak rang in my ears. A demon grabbed the little girl. The mom lay on her back unconscious next to the car. Beka drew a dagger from her pant leg.

I dashed to the car. Each step I neared, the more my demon took over.

"Let her go," I yelled, stopping five feet from the monster. The tiny girl kicked her legs against the demon's body.

~ ☾ ~

"Lemme go. Lemme go." Her young voice cracked. She looked at me. Her mouth opened, and a screech rolled off her tongue.

"She sees you for what you truly are, David." The demon clutched the girl against his chest.

"Yet, you hide behind a human face," I said.

He morphed into a demon. Elite Guard of course. "I have come to take you back."

"No."

A gust of wind signaled Beka landing beside me.

"You side with the Guardians?" he said.

"Yes." I edged closer.

The monster snaked his fingers around the girl's neck. "I will kill her."

"That is the price I will pay for my freedom from the contract." *Lie.*

Beka gasped.

"This child's life. You would sacrifice it?"

I inched closer, hoping to get a better position with the lies I spewed. "Wouldn't you, *Demon*? Have you not sacrificed hundreds of children and adults for the sake of your Master?"

He lifted his chin in Beka's direction. "You think she'll want you after she finds out you killed her --"

A woman screamed. The demon turned his head. The mother stabbed something into the beast's calf. He howled. I leapt, and I slashed. The girl, and the hand that had been holding her, fell to the ground. The mother snatched her into her arms and rolled beneath her car.

I squeezed the demon's neck.

"If you make it to the Merus and become human, you are fair game." His smoky breath plowed into me. "You will die. Master already has this planned.

"Then I will die a human." I raked my nails across his neck, and he melted into a pile of ash and tar.

I turned. Beka stood, wings out wide regarding me with narrowed eyes.

"What did he mean?" she asked.

I hurdled over the shaking mother and daughter, past Beka. My pulse hammered my eardrum. I wanted so much to

~ ☾ ~

take Beka into my arms and have her cool this fire for me, but I had better get used to the feeling, because she would surely reject me as her mate.

Master was behind this. No end to his wickedness. He knew he'd lost me to the Guardians. Turning them against me to ruin my chance to be with Beka—perfect revenge. Until he tracked me down and killed me.

"David?"

Russell and Abraham came to her side. "We should leave," Russell said.

"Yes, Abraham, ready the car," Beka said, still staring at me. "David, tell me. What did that demon mean?"

My focus bounced from Russell to Beka. "Maybe we should talk after we get to Jessica?" I could get rid of my demon half, live a human life without Beka. She wouldn't want me for a mate any longer, but at least I'd be free from my demon.

"Tell me now." She pressed on, her smooth forehead creased.

"He's a demon. He spews lies. He—"

Beka gasped. "House of David."

I grimaced and studied my feet. I willed my demon away, but he remained. I would need his strength to accept what I knew would come next.

Rejection.

"House of . . . ." Beka coughed. "It wasn't because of Master you knew that name, was it?"

My chest tightened. *She knows.*

"My true Guardian name, Rebeka David. Daughter to—"

"Samuel David and sister to Jonathon David," I said, my voice scarcely above a whisper. Finally I faced Beka. "I—"

"How do you know those names?" Russell asked.

I didn't divert my gaze from Beka, but I saw the realization creep in and darken her eyes. Muscles twitched in her forearm.

"Four hundred," she said. "You're four hundred years old. You said—" She coughed. "You said you'd killed Guardians before."

I tried to morph down to human form but the demon

~ ☾ ~

inside refused to let his hold loose. "Beka, I'm—"

"You killed them. Didn't you?"

"I—"

She pounced, planting her palms against my chest with such force I flew back several feet. The gravel pierced my back as I skidded across the ground. I hopped to my feet, crouched, ready to defend.

"You killed my father. It was you. You!" Tears streamed. "My brother."

She bent her knees, and I thought it was to fall to the ground. Instead, she leapt into the air with one powerful movement of her radiant wings. She hovered inches from my reach.

"Beka—"

"Russell. Get him in the car and to Jessica." She pinned me with a glare. "I will not ride with the demon."

~ ☾ ~

CHAPTER 35

I curled into myself in the back seat as Russell drove. Without Beka near, the inferno seared through me like a raging fire. I deserved it. I wasn't worthy of Beka's love or Jessica's redemption. Russell and Abraham talked up front, but the pulse drumming in my ear drowned out their words.

I heard Beka's name a few times and prophecy once. Master had planned this, too. I knew it to my core. Predicted to join with Beka, he assigned me the task of getting the demon he knew was under Samuel and Jonathan's protection.

Beka's family. The hurt in her eyes sliced my heart worse than the demon.

"David?" Russell asked. "Just hold on. We're nearly there."

"It no longer matters," I said through clenched teeth. "She will not have me now."

"She does not get to choose, my friend."

I ordered my clamped eyelids open and saw the back of Russell's head. "What?"

"Can't change prophecy. It's a done deal. We just need to get you there."

"I will not do it."

Russell craned his neck and looked into the backseat. "What?"

"Will. Not. Force. Her." I sucked in a breath. Talons mangled my intestines. "To marry me." I bit back the bile. "I killed her family."

Gravity tugged me along the seat, but the leather clung to my skin, holding me in place.

"There. See it?" Abraham said.

"Yeah," Russell said. "Hurry."

~ ☾ ~

Squealing tires. Burning rubber. Sizzling pain. My senses overloaded.

The car jolted to a stop and pitched me onto the floorboard. Doors clicking open and slamming shut rang in my ears. A hand clamped my arm, I lashed out with my nails and hissed through my fangs.

"David. Hold on." Russell dodged my assault. "Come on, buddy. Hang in there."

Two strong hands gripped me by the arms and lugged me out of the back seat.

"I haven't gotten you this far for you to give up. You are my King, David, whether you accept that or not. I am to deliver you to Jessica and I will or die trying."

I chomped my mouth in his direction.

"Your long teeth do not scare me," Abraham said.

Russell laughed. "Abraham run ahead. Scout the area and check in with the other Guardians. Make sure we're safe out here."

"You saw her, Russell. She no longer wants me. She called me demon."

"The contract made you do it."

"Still."

"She knows that. She was just hurt. The flight to this place surely cleared her mind." Russell tugged. "Come on. This is what you've always wanted, isn't it? Humanity is only one hundred feet away. Man up."

Despite my fear I straightened. Maybe Jessica would still expunge my demon. And maybe someday, Beka could learn to forgive me. Yes. I would work to win her favor again.

Abraham approached the door of a quaint log cabin. Tall pine trees surrounded the structure, shading it from the penetrating sun. It resembled an old oil painting, hanging in the Louvre with a stream of smoke coming from a stone chimney.

The door whipped open and a hulking man filled the space, dagger drawn. He bowed and stepped to the side. Through the open door, I saw Beka kneeling before Jessica. Her hands rested on Beka's shoulders, and she leaned forward.

~ ☾ ~

Beka sagged to the ground, hands over her face, shoulders shaking. Her head shook side-to-side. Beka's sobs cut through my soul.

I'd caused the woman I loved such sorrow.

Fire stung my eyes. I had my answer. A roar thundered through my stomach so fierce I was sure it diced my intestines. I twisted from Russell's grasp and burst to my feet. He reached for me. I batted him away, spun and kicked my foot against his chest, sending him through the air.

"David," Russell yelled.

My demon burst forth, and I darted to the trees. I had no idea where I was, but I wouldn't stand by and witness Beka cry over the fact that she had to marry me. I would rather be demon. I refused to sentence her to anything. Not after I'd been forced to do horrible things against my will for so long.

I busted through the first line of trees, shredding anything I could scrape my talons against. Twigs snapped, tree trunks cracked. The branches carved into my bare chest, but I welcomed the pain.

Tears ruined my vision, and my shoulder clashed with a tree, twisting me off balance. I stumbled back. Something cold pierced me between my shoulder blades. The silver tip of a sword stuck out from my chest.

Strong fingers clamped my neck. "Demon."

The hand shoved me forward, the sword retracting from my chest cavity. I clasped my skin, working to slow the blood pouring out onto the ground. I faced the man.

He swung his massive weapon at my face, probably aiming for my neck to behead me. I put up my hand, shielding me from the metal. It clanked off my wrists. The Guardian stopped, eyeing me with elevated brows.

He reared back and swung the weapon again. I ducked and rolled, concentrating on the gaping hole in my chest so it could heal. The heat emerged, cauterizing the wound.

"Wait." I showed him my palms.

He surged, swinging, his eyes wide. "Demon." His booming voice reverberated off the trees surrounding us. Shuffling nearby alerted me to more Guardians approaching. My demon surged within me. He wanted to kill them all.

~ ☾ ~

Violently.

I refused to hurt Beka and Russell that way, though. *I must stay in control.*

"Let me by. I am friend to the Queen."

"Lies." The Guardian huffed. "No demon is the friend of the Queen."

Two more Guardians barreled through the woods. I rolled and darted to the side, deeper into the thicket, they followed. They wouldn't stop until they had my head.

My demon demanded I kill these Guardians. That would hurt Beka. But the demon overpowered me. Separated from Beka so long weakened my control.

My toe caught a root and pitched me forward. I rolled down the side of the hill. So steep. Branches, rocks, thorns ribboned my skin like a thousand razors.

The Guardians still pursued. They didn't roll down, they slid, coordinated on their feet. A boulder larger than the cabin broke my descent. Ribs cracked like dried twigs. I flopped onto my back, gasping.

Three cool blades pricked my skin. One in each bicep and one to the chest. Three mountainous Guardians loomed over me.

"Go on, try it. Take my head." *Please.* If only they could.

The one on the left withdrew his blade and swung. The metal clashed with my neck, sending sparks showering over me.

"What kind of magic is this?"

Pricks to my shoulders followed. "He bleeds, yet he cannot be beheaded?"

I lay on my back listening to my ribs crack into place. Another clank to my neck from the other side rolled me onto my stomach. I pushed to my feet. "It does not detach my head, but it does hurt," I said. "Just stand down, and I will leave this place."

Three swords pointed at me, unwavering.

"Please. I do not want to hurt anyone, but I am having difficulty controlling the beast. Right now." A growl ripped through my stomach. "I am friend to the Queen, Russell, and Abraham. Seek them out, you shall have your answers."

~ ☾ ~

"Lies." The tallest of the three guards marched forward, weapon drawn. "Demon."

Flapping above me drew my gaze. Beka descended between the tall trees with the grace of a swan, eyeing the Guardians poised to skewer me. "You dare point swords at your future King?"

"King?" Their eyes snapped wide. She landed softly next to me. The Guardians lowered their weapons. They didn't go as far as to sheath them, but they backed off nonetheless.

She turned and regarded me with blood shot eyes. "David. What are you doing?" She inched forward, her cooling mist tingling against my skin. A slight breeze ruffled her expanded wings.

"I am nobody's King, Beka."

"I beg to differ, as does Jessica." Beka eyed the Guardians. "Please, go secure the area. We still have Jessica to protect. I will walk David back to the cabin to Jessica."

"My Queen, I—"

She showed them her palm. "It's okay. His appearance is a bit distracting." She turned toward me and nodded.

My human side resurfaced. The Guardians emitted a collective sigh. They must be new ones, not aware of demons and their human masks.

"Now you know him in both skins. Do not forget it, because soon, he will take his rightful place by my side."

They bowed their heads and backed away. Once out of earshot, I turned to Beka. "But—"

She pressed a finger over my lips. "Please, allow me to speak first." She grabbed my hand and guided me back the way I had come. "I am sorry, David."

"You have nothing to be—"

"I called you demon." She hung her head low. "I was wrong to do that."

"No you weren't. I am demon."

"Not for long."

"But—"

"I was hurt. To learn I have given my heart to the one who killed my family was quite a shock." She cleared her throat. "I overreacted."

~ ☾ ~

"No, you didn't." I sucked in a deep breath of the pine-scented air. "I understand. You can't be with the one who killed your family. I was trying to leave when these guys attacked me."

"Thank you for not killing them."

I flinched. "It did take some restraint, my demon is angry."

"Because he knows he is about to die."

We neared the clearing surrounding the cabin. I stopped and Beka faced me. Despite her cool hand in mine, my body flamed and fiery teeth chewed at my chest. "Let me leave, Beka."

"I cannot do that."

"Because of the Prophecy. I will not let you be forced into-"

"It's not because of the prophecy." A shade of pink dusted her cheeks. She pulled her shoulders back and stood straight. "I cannot let you go because I love you, David."

"You couldn't possibly..."

"I love you with my entire soul." She skimmed her knuckles down my cheek. "I'm incomplete, half a person, without you by my side."

"How are you okay with this? With me? You were crying at Jessica's feet."

"You saw that?" Her gaze deviated to the ground, but she drifted closer. "That's why you ran?"

I paced. *Did I dare hope?*

"I'm sorry you witnessed that. I went to her with my anger and hurt, she helped me see through it." The grip on my hand tightened. Her gaze captured mine. "And all I saw was you. I respect you, David. All you've endured to make it to this point. Your strength is enviable." Tears welled. "And I love you with my entire being. Please, join me and be my King."

I secured a lock of hair behind her ear, and she leaned into my touch. No disgust. No hesitation. I nudged her chin with my finger and tilted her head back. A solitary tear streaked her face. My heart pounded, stuttering my breath.

I touched a kiss to her lips, and she held me close to her cool body by my shoulders. Her sweet, lilac scent washed over me. With her wings extended, I didn't know how to hug her, and I wanted to feel her against me. I wove my arms around

~ ☾ ~

her waist, where I hoped was safe.

"I do not know what kind of king I will make, but I will love and protect you for as long as I have breath." Her body shuddered against mine.

"Hurry. Let's get you to Jessica."

~ ☾ ~

CHAPTER 36

Jessica's slight frame stood in the open doorway as we approached the cabin. Russell and Abraham paced the room behind her. Her diamond-like eyes flickered, and a smile split her face. She bolted out the door and down the two steps.

"Go." Beka released my hand. "No interruptions this time, please."

I turned and ran toward Jessica. Long flowing red hair, slight figure, but she had the glow I remembered seeing the first time we tried to connect before I was taken into solitary. She'd grown into a radiant young woman.

Three feet left. The light in her chest intensified. My heart throbbed.

One foot left. I took one last stride and she leapt into my arms. Much like a child would a parent. Not that I would ever know the joy of having children, but I imagined it would feel this peaceful.

Her flaming hands flattened against my back as we twirled.

"David," she sighed. "You finally made it."

Her voice sounded like bells. Coolness washed over me, like it did with Beka. But Jessica's chill was more intense, icy. A feral rumbling deep inside me quaked the walls of my stomach. I let go of her, fearful I would morph and hurt her. She was my contracted Mark, after all.

"Wait. Careful," I said. "I am not in control."

She slid from me but snatched my hand.

The ground yanked me to my knees with unseen ropes. Rocks slashed through my frayed jeans, piercing my skin. Jessica's eyes flashed, and her skin brightened, rivaling the sun. She let go of my hand and placed hers on my chest, over

~ ☾ ~

my heart where the hideous mark of my Master was.

Her eyebrows puckered, and her jaw clamped shut. Her nails dug deep but never punctured my skin. Instead, her fingers dissolved into me. Every muscle in my body contracted, and I flopped onto my back, spasms rocketing up my spine. Jessica's hand never left my chest.

Needles stabbed my heart like a pincushion. Black soot spewed from my mouth. The air expelled from my lungs until they blazed with a fire I thought was straight from Lucifer himself.

Shattering glass lured my focus back to Jessica. The glass surrounding my contract sprayed over my body. She palmed the scroll, and a milky flame erupted. Its intensity toppled over me like a tidal wave.

A biting pain sliced my chest as Jessica retracted her hand. Her creased forehead smoothed, her jaw muscles relaxed, and her lips quirked into a grin. Finally, her hand was completely out from my chest, and I felt only the thudding of my heart.

No more burning.

No more prickling needles.

She helped me to a sitting position and knelt beside me.

"Human," I whispered.

"Dear, David, you are more than *just* human." Jessica's gaze veered from my eyes.

I followed her line of sight. On my chest, over my heart, the mark of the Guardian glowed a ferocious white. No more was Master's brand inked in my skin. New, peaceful, warmth coursed through my veins.

"Locien is no longer master over you."

"Locien?"

Jessica grinned. "Master's real name."

"I never knew."

"Of course not. There's power in knowing a name. He wants everyone to view him as master of them to dominate. To control."

"What have I become?"

"The Angel you were meant to be." Jessica glanced over her shoulder, then back to me. "With a mate who loves you,

~ ☾ ~

WASTELAND

King."

"King." Doubt seeped in.

"I have bound you two." She tapped her forefinger over my new crest. "She, too, wears this mark, showing your marriage covenant. You are only hers and she is only yours. A pure union."

Tears stung at my eyes. "Wife."

Beka's wings unfolded from behind her, and she leapt into the air.

"Go to her." Jessica grabbed my hand.

She lifted me with the strength of someone three times her size. Once to my feet, searing pain ripped down my back. Had a sword penetrated me?

I reached for Jessica to shield her.

"Just breathe, David. Breathe." She smiled. "It hurts the first time, but it'll get easier."

"What hurts?" Bones crackled, snapping, like a zipper unhitching down either side of my spine. "What's happening?"

Jessica captured my face between her hands. "Relax your muscles. Don't fight it."

Her touch calmed me, and I breathed, filling my lungs with the cool air they craved.

Ebony feathers expanded from behind me. A tremor rocked my body, bringing with it a burst of sweat. It seemed like an eternity before the agony stopped.

"Stand tall, King." Jessica smiled.

Russell and Abraham filed out from the cabin, eyes wide. Wings spanned out at least nine feet on each side of my body. The wind tugged me back as it met the mass of feathers.

"Black?"

"To resemble what you came from. What you survived. You are both of the Light and darkness. Able to relate to both—but compelled by Light because you chose it over darkness."

"Why?"

"To fight against the evil seeping into this world." She jutted her chin skyward. "Go."

Beka fluttered a distance away from me.

~ ☾ ~

I bent my knees, drew in a deep breath and jumped. On instinct, my wings flapped. I'd never flown, but how to shift my weight, hold my hands, and flex my stomach muscles flooded my brain.

"Yeah, David." Russell pumped his fist in the air.

I jerked to the right, and with one thrust, I streaked toward Beka. She powered away. I gave chase, my blood racing. My wings spanned at least five feet wider than hers, so I caught her in seconds.

She tilted her head back and met my gaze. "You're beautiful."

I dove down until I fluttered inches above her. Her body heat enveloped me, despite the wind whipping by us. I skimmed her back with my fingertips, between where her wings came out. She gasped and dropped altitude. She zoomed ahead, shot up and came in above me.

Her soft fingers trailed my spine. A shudder rocked my body. My vision tilted, and my body sprang to life.

"Sensitive, remember?" Beka teased. "Only for us to touch, Mate." Her soft fingertips danced across my skin until I feared I would plummet to the ground from the ecstasy.

She buzzed ahead, then turned over, showing me the length of her body.

"How?"

"Thirty-five years of practice, waiting for you."

I slowed to a stop and hovered. She did the same. My body pulsed with adrenaline and need. Hunger for my wife.

Mine.

We hung suspended fifty feet above the trees. Foothills surrounded us, but the silence, besides my thumping heart, was refreshing. No inner battles. No pain. Serenity.

Beka fluttered near me. The mark on my chest ignited, and hers pulsed, visible through the fabric. Her finger outlined my new symbol. Her touch branded the skin almost as much as the sizzling mark.

She gently pinched my chin between her thumb and forefinger and urged me close. Her soft lips brushed against mine. Our wings found a rhythm that kept us steady. I threaded my fingers through the belt loop of her jeans and

~ ☾ ~

jerked her close. She palmed my chest and moaned.

My tongue beckoned entrance. She opened and drew me in deep. My mark flared.

She trailed to my ear. "Follow me."

She darted away, and I zoomed after her. The wind clipped through my hair, and in two powerful pushes, I flew above her, but close. Our wings flapped in time, and she veered to the right. A grassy meadow, past the last grove of trees.

She slowed the pace and dove. Before her feet touched the grass, she gave a last push of her wings and landed gracefully. I stumbled, but stayed upright.

I left my wings extended, not sure I wanted to experience retracting them so soon. Beka's soft hand traced my spine, and for the second time, the gesture forced the wind from my lungs. She ducked beneath my wing to face me.

"My king." Her voice was low, soft as a feather to my cheek. "I give myself to you."

She covered my mark with her mouth, and her tongue flicked. Her wings retracted. I had to sample her mouth again. Needed to. I pulled her flush against my body. My wings encapsulated us like a dark blanket.

Her fingers grazed my feathers. She may as well have been touching my skin. I half expected the burn of the demon to seize my heart in response to the passion gripping my body, but it didn't. Only peace and comfort at the touch of my wife.

My mate.

Her mouth found mine, and she filled me with her warmth. The scent of lilac and sweet flowers from the meadow swirled. The heat of her body wrapped around me urging me on. I traced the grooves of her spine, over the curve of her backside and up her hips. She arched her back, opening herself to me.

I worked down the side of her neck to her chest where the fabric began. I eased the zipper down, grazing on her sweet skin inch by inch until the zipper was all the way down, and I knelt before her.

I captured her gaze. Her pupils swallowed her sea-green irises. "I love you."

"David," she whispered. "I need you."

~ ☾ ~

My hands grazed up her body, indulging in every dip and valley offered. "Beautiful."

"Yours."

I nipped at her shoulder and slid her garment off. I covered the glowing mark with my mouth.

Her slender fingers unbuttoned my jeans. "I've waited a thousand years for you, David."

Freed from our clothing, I lowered my wife to the plush grass bedding. Our flesh met, and my mark sent a shudder of electricity down my spine. Her skin slid like silk against mine. In four hundred years I'd never felt anything so soft. So tender. Never allowed to for fear of eternal damnation.

But no longer.

Beka was my wife, my mate for the rest of our immortal lives. I was free to make love to her, to protect her, to cherish her without fear of my demonic curse.

Her mouth found mine again. Her fingers feathered against my spine as she cradled me between her legs.

"My Queen."

My wings tightened behind me, a dark shelter hiding us from the universe as I explored my wife's body, becoming her husband in every way possible.

~ ☾ ~

CHAPTER 37

"I've never known such love." Beka's breath skimmed my ear.

"Nor have I." I combed her hair with my fingers as we lay on the grass, cuddled together under the cover of my wings. "I dreamed of it, but never believed I would actually have it."

I leaned into her again, outlining the soft contours of her naked body, memorizing every freckle. Such beauty lay beside me, and she was my mate for life.

"Thirty-five years I searched for you. I knew I would find you." A single tear rolled down the side of her face and onto my bicep. "I had only the nightmare of your pained face as the guards yanked you from Jessica's grasp."

"I, too, replayed that memory, coupled with the agony of the fire beneath my skin." I pressed my lips against her cheek, absorbing the trail of salt. "No more tears, my Queen."

"Only those of joy." She took my mouth with hers as if she'd been doing so for a lifetime.

"There is much joy to be had. I will never tire of the feel of your body." I rolled her beneath me.

A scorching pain pierced my heart, robbing me of my breath. *Oh, God.* Was this a horrible, torturous nightmare?

Beka's body tensing beneath mine alerted me that she, too, felt the pain.

"It's Jessica." She clutched her chest.

"How?"

"We're connected to her."

I pushed myself from Beka, spreading my wings. "What's happening?"

"We must hurry, she's in danger." Beka reached for her clothes.

~ ☾ ~

"We are very far from her."

"But we are quick." She snatched her jeans from the grass.

Within minutes we donned our clothes again and took to the sky. "Which way?"

"Close your eyes, David. Sense her," Beka said as her eyes closed. Her chest expanded with a deep breath while we hovered above the trees surrounding our special spot.

I pulled in a lungful of fresh air and focused on Jessica's illuminated face. It flashed before my eyes, and her mouth moved, calling out my name. *David, hurry,* she whispered yet it pounded my chest. I knew her to be east, I wasn't sure how, but I knew.

I opened my eyes. "East."

"That's what I felt as well. Come, we must hurry." She turned, and vaulted upward.

"You felt it, too?" I asked as I flew above her.

"Yes."

"Is that how it is with your charges?'

"*Our* charges." She smiled. "But no, it's not like that with everyone we're charged with protecting. Jessica is different. A treasure to be protected, but you and I are linked to her in a unique way. Always able to sense if she is in trouble."

The wind whipped through my long hair. The descending sun's golden rays baked my skin and sent my long shadow over Beka flying below me.

"Why do they want her still? She's broken my contract and changed me, what more could they want?"

"Other than revenge for your conversion and to kill her?" Beka's pace increased. "They want to end her so she does not save those who are undecided."

"Are there others with contracts such as mine?"

"Not exactly like yours, because yours had the Archangel's bond on it as well, but contracts in general, yes. Lucifer and his minions tempt many souls with worldly goods. Jessica can expunge those contracts with only her touch. She wouldn't need to touch the actual paper like she did for yours."

"But before I was taken, she said she needed to touch me, my contract was not with me at that time."

~ ☾ ~

"Right. She could have made you human at that time, but with the contract, she could fulfill the prophecy that gave you wings."

"Amazing."

"Indeed." She pointed to the left. "There."

Flames engulfed the cabin. Black smoke spewed into the darkening sky. Russell, Abraham and two others battled several demons on the ground. Their swords sprayed sparks as they met strike for strike.

"I don't see Jessica," I said.

I dove toward Russell and flapped out my wings at the last second before colliding with the demon battling my Guardian friend. I palmed the red-skinned monster's head and soared up into the air. Too bad I no longer had my lethal nails. The second I thought that, the black weapons extended.

My breath hitched. I swiped. The demon was dust.

Light and dark. Jessica's words rang in my head.

Beka charged the demon advancing on Abraham and buried her blade in his back, then dodged his sword. Abraham finished by detaching his head.

"Where is Jessica?" Beka yelled.

"She ran into the trees," Abraham bellowed.

Beka waved me to follow her. I banked left and circled, squinting my eyes. Every leaf and branch was detailed to the point I made out the individual veins on the leaves.

A break in the treetops revealed two demons darting through the woods. I dove and gathered my wings close to avoid the pine needles. I dropped to the forest floor with a thud in front of the demons.

The bald one struck. I bent backward. His sword whooshed over my head, leaving a wake of wind against my skin. I kicked his wrist, and the blade scattered into the dead leaves littering the ground. I swiped my nails at his face, and he ducked, landing a punch to my ribs.

He plucked a dagger from his boot. I jumped, my wings vaulting me high. I flipped my legs over my head and landed behind the attacker. One slice and he melted. The other demon had continued running. He must have Jessica in his sights.

~ ☾ ~

I ordered my wings close to my body and ran. The earthy scents of wood, fresh wild flowers and pine cones swarmed my senses. Knobby roots, jagged branches and sharp briars shredded my feet. Finally an opening. I took to the air and popped above the trees. Beka zoomed toward me.

"South." She pointed. "Cliff edge."

Oh no. Would Jessica see the edge in time to stop? I zoomed south and within seconds the treetops ended. I scanned the ground. A fleck of light followed by two dark figures darted between trees.

"There." I pointed. "Two in pursuit."

Beka plunged into the woods. I surged forward. The trees ended. The bottom was so far away, the river looked like a thread of blue yarn. I hovered fifty feet from the edge scanning for Jessica.

"David," Beka screamed.

A streak of light burst out from the trees and over the edge. Jessica put her arms out to her sides as if doing a swan dive into a pool. I bolted to her. Two dark figures leapt after her. Their flailing arms did nothing to prevent them from descending to the ground.

One demon fastened onto Jessica's ankle. Her graceful dive vanished as she plummeted with the added weight of the beast.

I curled my wings in and fell toward her like a rocket. She reached for me, her face radiating confidence. No fear, no screaming, only peace.

Our fingers connected, and she smiled. The skin prickled on my arm. I grabbed her wrist and let my wings out slowly as to not jerk her too much. Beka zipped by and with a flick of her blade, the demon's head rolled. The fingers clasped around Jessica's ankle turned to ash and sifted away.

The sudden loss of weight slung us up higher, and I hefted her into my arms. She kicked her legs up and over my outstretched arm. We soared upward.

"That was close," Beka said.

"I knew you'd find me." Jessica winked in Beka's direction. "Let's go down to the bottom."

Beka drifted closer. "To the river?"

~ ☾ ~

Jessica nodded. "I need time to regenerate. And we are no longer safe in this area. Well, and the house went up in flames."

"You are injured?" I asked.

She nodded and rested her head against my shoulder.

Beka fluttered to me, hand outstretched toward the treasure lying in my arms. Her fingers brushed Jessica's forehead. "What of Russell?"

"I didn't see," Jessica whispered. "Can't see much now. So tired."

Beka pinned me with a worried gaze. "Time to regroup."

~ ☾ ~

CHAPTER 38

"She is not immortal?" I asked as I lay the unconscious Jessica on the sandy shore next to the river.

"Not like you and me. She is not meant to live eternally so she still ages," Beka said.

I brushed my fingers over her forehead, pushing strands of hair to the side. A tint of darkness dusted the corners of her mouth. "I noticed she was older than the last time I saw her."

"Her aging is slower. Thirty-five years have passed since you last saw her. Her sister, Elizabeth, has moved on, married and has children, living a human's life." Beka peeled up Jessica's shirt, revealing a gash across her side below the bottom rib. "But Jessica has only aged a few years."

"Yes. The young looking fifteen-year-old I remember is gone. She is taller, has longer hair, and her face slimmer." I brushed her hair off her forehead.

"She's got quite a wound here." Beka lowered the shirt. "We have no supplies here to clean this."

"I will scout for some aloe vera. Clean it best you can with the stream water, then tear some of her shirt to make a bandage."

Beka's jaw gaped. "You know this?"

I cradled the nape of Beka's neck. "I will hurry and see what I can discover."

"It will be deep darkness soon, be quick." Beka clasped her hand over mine while keeping the other on Jessica's shoulder.

I pointed to my eyes. "Excellent sight, remember?"

She grinned. "But no more protection over your neck is what I'm more worried about."

I dipped my head, conceding to her logic.

~ ☾ ~

With one push, I was airborne. The cool wind rustled through my hair and tickled my bare chest. Centuries of restriction and control, the freedom my new wings allowed sent my blood soaring.

I hugged the riverbank, hoping the water would allow for the vegetation I needed. A handful of Aloe Vera would help facilitate healing. Hiding a day or two while Jessica recovered would provide a chance to talk with her, be with my wife, and learn more about what I'd become.

Lethal demonic nails, long, *black* wings and the mark of the Guardian. Connected to both worlds. But how did I function as part Light and part darkness? Let alone as a king?

The moon rose, filtering its rays through the trees. Like a beacon, its illumination revealed a patch of the treasure I sought. In aplenty. I banked right and swooped a circle, scanning the area. All clear.

I landed on steady feet, each time becoming more graceful and easier to navigate. Despite how natural flying had come, I still stumbled.

Two long strides brought me to the treasure. I squatted and plucked two handfuls of the healing leaves. Perched on the heel of my foot, I tilted my head back, took in the fresh air, and closed my eyes as the breeze cooled my face and ruffled my feathers.

Quiet, save the stream flowing behind me. Peaceful. No demon rioting with my human side deep within my chest. Nothing scratching at my heart. My entire existence I'd wanted to be rid of the demon within me, and it had finally happened.

Rustling beside me disturbed the calm that had settled over me and sent me to a crouch, ready to fight. Hairs prickled along my forearms and neck. My nails surfaced as I scanned the area. Tips of bushes and shrubbery swayed in the wind before me.

I squeezed the treasured aloe vera and inched toward the water. Probably an animal rustling for a midnight snack.

A cough resonated from the bushes to my left.

I froze. "Hello?"

"Here," a weak voice I recognized as Russell's trickled out

~ ☾ ~

of the darkness.

A hand reached through the weeds and flopped to the ground.

I hauled him to the stream. The moonlight exposed deep lacerations on his shoulder, arms, and face. None to the neck, he must have protected that fiercely. I waded into the water, holding him to my chest.

"Russell."

He moaned. I splashed water onto his face. He cringed. I scooped some to his mouth, and he lapped it up.

"Russell, say something."

His eyes went wide, then the lids hung heavy. "My King."

"What happened?"

Russell's hand navigated to his throat. "I saved my head, but lost my footing." He coughed. "That is a long fall."

I scooped a handful of liquid over his wounds. "You fell from the ledge?"

"I saw Jessica dive off. Two demons followed, one grabbed her. There was one more about to leap and take her from your grasp." Another cough rocked his body. "I got him, but we tumbled, fighting for a bit." He sat up, and I stood in knee-high water. "Those Elite Warriors you call them, they are very strong."

"This I know."

Russell, on his own volition, wiped his wounds clean and drank more water. "Another came. I dodged a sword to the neck, but fell over." He winced. "I've never fallen so far and hope to never again. Are Jessica and the Queen safe?"

"Yes. I'm out gathering what I can to help Jessica's wounds heal."

"She was struck by the Venefir blade. I saw it happen."

"Venefir blade? I do not know of this."

Russell stood, water dripping from his tattered shirt and jeans. "It will kill her."

My heart thundered within my chest. "But Beka said she can heal, just a little slower than us."

"Us." Russell smiled. "I still can't believe you're one of us. But no. I mean, yes, usually she would heal, this weapon is different."

~ ☾ ~

I waved him to me, then reached down and snatched my pile of aloe vera. "Come, we must get back. Explain to me on the way."

"You can't carry me, I'm too heavy. You go ahead. I must heal."

"I am stronger than you think, *friend*." I gripped his shoulder. "Unless you are ashamed to have me carry you to your Queen."

"Give it your best shot, *King*."

"Oh, and I do wish you to stop calling me King."

"But that's what you are."

"Regardless, I wish you to call me David, and if I am your King, you should listen to what I ask, right?"

Russell nodded. I hopped into the air and hovered above him, hitched my arms beneath his armpits and lifted. He was heavy, but I gained enough altitude to move forward.

"Now, tell me of this blade."

"Jessica is human, for the most part. She ages slower than humans, but she is still fragile, in need of great protection, hence the strong link you and Beka have with her."

"Yes. I felt her pain."

"She is vulnerable to magiked weapons."

"Magiked?"

"Yes, you know magic? Spells?" Russell rolled his eyes. "It's all just a mess. People get involved in it, some are brought to a dark place and Lucifer uses them as his personal magicians. They can throw hexes on things. Much like that hell they kept you in during confinement or solitary, whatever you called it."

"Yes. I remember it all too well." I didn't mention the illusion Locien had played on me with the girl in his office to make her look like Beka. "Dark magic is very powerful. *And* seductive."

"You can tell when the weapon is hexed because it gives off a soot-like aura. Only agents of Light, like us, can see it." Russell coughed, and I lost some altitude with his movement. "Abraham called it out when he saw it. But I got the wonderful pleasure of witnessing it plunge into Jessica's stomach."

~ ☾ ~

"She did not say anything."

"I'm not surprised."

The wind whistled through me, despite its warmth, it made me shiver. So young, yet so strong, Jessica had made me into what I was. Now it was up to me to save her. And no matter what, I would.

"How can we heal her?" I asked, scared to hear the answer.

"Find the demon who cursed the blade, kill him or her, and the magic dies with the demon."

The glow of a campfire came into view. Beka sat next to Jessica, combing her hair with her fingers. Her radiant, white wing draped over Jessica like a blanket.

"Let me guess. The demon is with Locien."

"Probably. No way to tell, really."

"So you're saying she is doomed to die?"

"Well…we could go back to Locien's location, kill them all and hope we get the one who hexed the blade."

"Not real fond of the shotgun approach."

"I'm sure they'd love to get their hands back on you." Russell peered at me. "Want to trade?"

~ ☾ ~

CHAPTER 39

"Russell." Beka darted from Jessica's side. "What happened?"

"Fell off a cliff. Luckily I can't die, right?" He coughed as I sat him down on a rock near Jessica. "But it sure hurts like hell."

I knew what hell felt like, literally, and he got off easily, but I said nothing. "Russell, are you well enough to get these leaves packed onto Jessica's wound?"

Beka tilted her head to the side, eyeing me.

"Yes, my K—David, I can do that." A smile tugged at the corner of his mouth but quickly cupped his cheek. "Okay. No smiling yet."

"Beka, come with me." I offered her my hand.

She glanced from Jessica, to Russell, to me, jaw muscles twitching.

"I will take care of Jessica," Russell said. "Go with your mate."

She hurried toward me with wide eyes. "Is everything okay?"

I twined my fingers with hers and mustered a smile, knowing she'd never accept the idea of me going to Locien. But maybe she had a better plan. Something involving less pain on my part.

"Yes. Everything is fine. First, can you tell me how to pull my wings in as you do, so they do not show?"

We strolled along the riverbank. "Just bring them close and will them inside. It's a bit uncomfortable at first, but you will get used to it."

I stopped, sucked in a breath and with only a thought, my wings obeyed. Like they were extensions of my hand. They

~ ☾ ~

tucked close to my body, the tickling feathers flicking against my bare back. The dreaded zipper unhitching on each side of my spine followed. Then, the feathers were gone.

"Amazing. I've never seen that." She ran her finger down my back. "The skin opens, slightly, and they dissolve into the slits. Unreal."

I tensed at her touch. "Still very sensitive, though."

"Always." Hot breath skimmed my skin. "Only for us to enjoy."

Her lips tickled along my spine, and it set me on fire more than her fingertips did. Her hands snaked around my waist from behind. One palmed my stomach the other massaged my pectorals. I was going to tell her something....

"Beka," I whispered.

She ducked beneath my arm and appeared before me, her body pressed against mine. She stared up into my eyes. "Yes."

"Did you notice anything different about Jessica's wound?"

"Very deep, bleeds dark." She brought her fingers to her lips. "Magic."

I touched her cheek. "Venifer Blade."

Her hands rested on my hips, and she propped her forehead against my chest. "No. No. Not Jessica. I've seen Magiked blades before. I...I just thought her blood ran darker because of what she was."

"I don't know much about this, but Russell says if we kill the demon who cursed it, Jessica would survive."

"How to find the one in such a vast sea of demons, though?" She lifted her head and met my eyes.

I pressed my thumb on her cheekbone, and grazed it to her temple. She closed her eyelids, and a tear escaped.

"Your heart pounds. What are you thinking?" she asked.

"Russell says they might be interested in me for a trade. The demon that cursed the blade for me," I whispered.

"Russell has no right to say that of his King. How dare he?" She pushed off my chest. Rocks crackled beneath her. "Where is his loyalty?"

"To Jessica." I stepped in front of her. "She can convert people close to damnation. I cannot do such a thing. She is

~ ☾ ~

more valuable than I."

"No." Beka shook her head. "No. I won't let you. I only just found you."

"Beka—"

"We need our King. You can't be taken from me just after becoming the prophecy. It can't happen. I—" She showed me her palms. "There has to be another way."

"I am completely open to finding alternative means of getting the demon. Believe me. I do not want to be near Locien again." I palmed her neck and cradled her to me. "Not after I just found you. My mate."

I covered her mouth with mine, and she eased her hands around me. Ripples of pleasure pulsed through me as her fingers grazed my spine. The spot only her touch could elicit such emotion.

"Either we figure out another way, or I'm going with you."

"No."

"I live with you, or I die with you, it's that simple. I won't go through time without you again. Thirty-five years was enough. It nearly drove me into madness, and you were still demon at the time. Now that we're united, I won't stand to be apart from you." She nipped at the mark on my chest.

Its light pulsed, as did hers.

I toyed with strands of her silky hair. Slowly, I trailed her soft curves. "I should like to see your mark again," I whispered.

She offered a sexy smile and tugged at her zipper. My heart stampeded harder within my chest each notch she lowered. When the last hitch of the zipper clicked, I ducked my fingers beneath the fabric and pushed it from her shoulders. Her skin sizzled beneath my touch.

Her mark glowed a ferocious white, cutting through the darkness surrounding us. A silver cloud slid over the moon as if to give us privacy.

I feathered my hands over her flesh. "You are majestic, my Queen."

"As are you, husband. I've thought of little else than being close to you again." Her mouth latched onto my throat.

"Me as well."

~ ☾ ~

"I guess that happens when you do not lie with someone for a thousand years," she said, her breath steaming against my neck. "As it was meant to be. Completely yours, shared with no one."

"I only abstained four centuries, you have had much more time to be tormented. How ever did you restrain yourself?"

"I didn't do so well in the alley, do you not remember?"

Her hands found my spine again. Her touch robbed my strength, and my knees nearly buckled. "I remember. I had never been so tempted before then." I took her mouth with mine. I couldn't get enough of her sweet flavor, despite how deep my tongue plundered.

She moaned softly against my mouth. She pulled herself close and moved her core against me. "I knew my faithfulness would be rewarded, as the prophecy foretold." She reached for the button on my jeans, peering at me through the shadows of her long eyelashes.

"Why did you have to abstain?"

"Our offspring." She nipped my neck. "Will be." She suckled my earlobe. "Strongest Guardians ever."

I sucked in a breath. "You are more than I ever could have hoped for, Beka." I skimmed my hands over her hips, urging her closer.

Her legs entrapped my waist, wrapping me in warmth. She pulsed against me, and my heart vaulted against my chest.

"I found a place while hunting for aloe," I said with a ragged breath. "I would like to take you there."

She gazed at me with heavy-lidded eyes. "I hope it's not far." Her hand slid down between her and massaged the front of my jeans.

Even through the denim, her touch blazed. "I will fly fast."

She grasped my neck and tightened her legs, bringing her core to me.

I called my wings to the surface, and Beka was right, not so uncomfortable this time. She buried her face in my neck, gently grazing. I bent my knees and launched us into the air. I held my precious wife close to me as I flew to the cave I'd discovered. I would love her like never before, because soon

~ ☾ ~

we may face my former master to save Jessica, and I was not optimistic about my chance of survival.

~ ☾ ~

CHAPTER 40

"I am so glad there is another way. I wasn't keen on us storming Locien's lair," Beka said as her wings flapped near mine.

"Me as well. I'm glad Jessica will be able to see who cursed the blade if we can recover it."

She bolted forward. "Let's just hope it's near where she was stabbed. Abraham was able to kill the demon that stabbed her before he met his end."

"I'm sorry for Abraham," I said.

"The leather around his neck didn't work like your bonds once did. He will be greatly missed."

The morning sun peeked above the trees. Streaks of orange split the blue sky. My wing brushed Beka's. Jessica's worsening condition propelled us into quick action. Her already pale face resembled a sickly green when we had returned earlier that morning.

"We'll start at the cabin, sift through the remains, and work her path to the ledge," I said.

"Agreed," Beka said. "Let's do a fly over quick to make sure none of your former brothers linger." She winked.

"They would be your brothers-in-law then, is that not true?"

She laughed. "Thank the Light they are not. I would hate to know that I'm killing my relatives when I slide my blade across their necks."

What was left of the cabin came into view. Soot covered the remaining wood, and it still smoldered. We did a lap and detected no activity, so we landed in the center of the clearing in front of the cabin.

"On the porch," Beka said as she slid a dagger from her

~ ☾ ~

ankle holster.

I hurried to the front door. A mild heat from the glowing embers wafted over me. Not much left of the front porch. It had caved in on itself. I stuck my hand in the smoking coals searching for the cool metallic blade. Nothing.

Beka scoured the grass with her angelic eyes, scanning each inch for the precious weapon. Worry churned my gut. If we were unable to find the dagger the original plan of raiding the lair would be our only option, other than letting Jessica die.

"Let's follow her trail. She said she went left once out the door, right?"

"Right." Jessica had only been conscious long enough to take in a bite of food and tell us of the new plan. She must have sensed my suicidal plan of attacking Locien.

We made our way to the trees, keeping five feet between us to scan a wider area. Just patches of dried grass amongst the green. We entered the thicket through an opening in the trees. Our weight crunched dead pine needles covering the ground, igniting a crisp scent of wood and pine.

"What happens if she dies?" I asked.

"Let's hope it doesn't come to that," Beka said with a sigh.

"But if it happens? We are connected to her, do we die as well?"

"No. We'd feel her void, of course, but we would survive."

"Survive, but?"

Beka rolled her shoulders. "It would hurt for some time, I would imagine. There isn't a manual that describes our connection with the Merus. But we would survive. We can't die unless beheaded."

"Then why do they want to kill her so badly?"

"She could live more than a couple of centuries at the rate she's aging. Think of all the lost souls she would reach over that span of time." Beka glanced in my direction. "I'm sure that angers your former master. Evil thrives on chaos and destruction. Those souls would be lost to the Light without Jessica. He would like to prevent their salvation."

"Indeed. And cause me misery. He would get much pleasure from that."

~ ☾ ~

My toe met something cold and smooth. "Wait." I knelt and sifted through the brittle foliage. A small dagger, golden handle with a silver blade, maybe eight inches long, etched with vines.

"What have you found?" Beka's voice was close.

I seized the weapon. "Is this it?"

"No black aura."

"Damn it." I whipped the knife at a tree trunk. "I am familiar with the phrase, 'needle in a haystack' and I think I understand its meaning more than I wish to."

Beka chuckled. "Who knew a demon could have a sense of humor."

"Ex-demon, thank you, *wife*."

Beka's harp-like laughter ricocheted off the trees surrounding us. "I'll never tire of hearing that word from your lips, *husband*."

"Good."

Beka stutter-stepped. "Wait. Let me see something." She bent over. Just as she did, a knife splintered the tree where her head had been.

"Beka." I turned. Two Elite Guards barreled toward us. "Up."

She grasped a handful of the dead leaves and let her wings unfold. Mine fired out of my back with a burst, and knocked me forward. I jumped. Beka lunged, but didn't gain altitude.

"Beka."

A dagger fastened her wing to the tree. She leaned over and plucked the blade tacking her radiant feathers to the trunk. Another one sunk into her shoulder.

"David, catch." She threw the contents of her hand in my direction.

A shiny object surged toward me while leaves and clutter flittered down. A subtle black glow encased the weapon rushing my direction. I darted to it, but something collided with it with a clank, and both fell to the forest floor.

"No," Beka yelled. "David, get it." She reached for the dagger in her shoulder.

The demons had come with many weapons. Hovering fifteen feet above ground, I did a full circle. They'd crept up

~ ☾ ~

on us from behind. *Only two?*

Beka grunted. Her wing was free. Blood starkly contrasted her snow-white feathers. She hurled the weapon in the direction of one of the demons, but he ducked and it drove into the trunk of another tree.

She jumped, but faltered, her right wing doing most of the work. I darted toward the two demons, nails extended. They would pay for hurting my wife.

I hurled the dagger I'd extracted from my stomach, and it speared his chest. He reached to his forearm holster, which held many weapons, and pulled two out. He launched one after another. I jutted left, then right, dodging both, and rammed into him.

I clapped hands on his ears and rushed upward. I cranked his head and slid a talon across his throat. I banked toward the other one still pursuing my wife.

She moved to where the daggers had fallen and stumbled. Her legs bent, and she launched into a summersault. She flopped over and crawled on the ground, her hands sifting through the forest debris.

Mere feet separated her from the demon. Too close for her to dodge any weapon thrown at her quickly. Sure, she would heal, but I didn't want her bleeding more than she already was.

I folded my wings close to my back and dove at the demon. A quick glance around me showed no others approached. Strange to have only two forge an attack. Maybe they were scouts or survivors of yesterday's battle.

But if some remained, they would have seen where we had gone. My heart cramped at the thought. What if demons found Jessica and Russell?

"Beka." The demon wound his arm back, ready to throw the dagger. She dove behind a rock and crouched. The blade clanked off the rock.

I sunk my nails into the back of the demon and lifted him off the ground. "Are there more of you coming?"

"Traitor." He reached back and raked his wicked claws across my forearms. "Master will kill you and your white-winged Angel."

~ ☾ ~

"Who cursed the dagger?"

He snarled.

I approached a hundred year old oak tree and slammed the body into the trunk, sending bark raining onto the cluttered ground. I soared up and flipped my feet over my head and landed next to the demon.

He stood and grabbed my neck. His asphalt eyes bulged, and his fangs descended. "I can kill you now, traitor."

"You can try." I flashed my hand. His eyes widened. I stuck my forefinger in his jugular and tar-black blood spurted. He flinched but kept his hold. I would buy my sweet wife time to locate the dagger. "Who cursed the dagger?"

"I'll never tell. I hope your girl dies a slow, agonizing death from the darkness consuming her organs." Rancid, sulfur-tainted breath spewed from his mouth.

Rage jolted through my body. I swiped my nails across his jaw. Must have been deep enough, because he released his grip.

"Got it." Beka's voice rang out.

The demon looked to his left. I, however, did not. I yanked him close, my nose nearly touching his. "It is *Master* who will die."

~ ☾ ~

CHAPTER 41

We broke through the trees and dove off the cliff. I'd never experienced anything so liberating as a free-fall. The cliff rocks blurred into hues of copper and tan as I plummeted to the ground.

We got the dagger. Jessica would soon identify the one who cursed it. We would save her. Had to.

Streams of heated wind whipped through my hair. Finally, I eased out my wings. They caught my weight with a tug across my ab muscles.

"What are you doing?" Beka smiled, hovering near me.

"Tell me you didn't do that once or twice after you got your wings." My chest heaved as I gulped air. Such a rush.

Beka's cheeks flushed. "I've had my wings thirty-five years and still do it."

"Besides making love to you, jumping off a cliff is the biggest rush I've known."

She toyed her wing against mine. "Boy, you know all the right things to say, don't you?"

I darted in front of her and pointed down. "There we are."

She tucked her wings in and dropped. Hair flapped behind her like a blond cape. She flipped her body and faced me as I torpedoed toward her. She brought the cursed dagger to her chest and winked, then rolled over and dove.

The ground rushed us. My nerves fired into overdrive. My skin prickled. Beka opened her wings and darted up. I followed, and we flew next to one another.

"Amazing," she whispered.

I glanced to the riverbed, where the campfire burned but didn't see anyone. "Where is Jessica?"

Beka slowed her wing cadence and glided. I scanned the

~ ☾ ~

area and saw no sign of her or Russell. No evidence of a struggle either.

I closed my eyes and zeroed in on Jessica, asking myself where she was. I didn't sense much other than a weak blip to the north. Beka nodded to her right, and we veered together.

"I do not sense her pain," I said.

"Me neither. But I don't feel her very intensely like I normally do."

"She must be fading."

I caught the tremor in Beka's lips. "We'll find her, figure out who cursed the blade and go rip their throats out. Okay?"

Her body trembled.

"What?"

"You *were* just a demon, weren't you?" She smiled. "I forget that."

"Sorry?"

"Rip their throats out?"

I grinned. "Four hundred years. . . hard to wash away in just a couple of days."

She grinned. "Let's go find our charge, then go rip some throats out."

"Not quite as vicious coming from your sweet lips, though."

"Good, because to say it makes my mouth taste like ash."

So pure. I do not deserve her.

We veered around the bend, a quarter mile from the campsite and hit the ground lightly beside the water.

"Nice landing," Beka said.

"Finally."

She chuckled and crept toward a cave. "Russell?"

A glimmer of silver sliced the darkened entrance. I snatched Beka's arm. "Hello?"

Russell's image formed as he emerged from the entrance, sword drawn.

Beka ran forward. "Russell. What's wrong?"

"It seems some demons may have fallen off the ledge as I did, because three came up on us."

"Jessica?" I asked.

"She's in there, but she's not looking well, David."

~ ☾ ~

Beka flashed the dagger. "We found it. Is she awake?"

"No." He stepped toward me. "David, let's go get some wood. We need to warm the cave."

"I'll stay with her, cover her with my wings. They are warm."

"Good idea." I offered her my open hand.

She slid her fingers into my grip and smiled. I followed Russell toward a patch of trees before us. The stream flowed nearby but was out of sight.

"Why do we seek out wood? It is warm."

"She's cold. It's the poison. When night draws near, she'll be even more chilled." He bent over and grabbed a handful of twigs.

"She must survive . . . ."

"What will you do if she can't see who cursed the dagger?" Russell asked.

"Original plan, I guess." I commanded my wings inside me. Not quite used to skin ripping in such a manner yet.

"Suicide." He clutched a bundle of branches to his chest and kicked at a trio of stones.

"It was your idea, remember? What alternative would you suggest? Let Jessica die?"

Russell stopped. "I suggest you send me, instead. We can't lose our leaders."

"Alone, you could do nothing."

"You and Beka could fly to a phone and call for reinforcements. They're in Utah. They'd be here within hours via airplane. In the meantime, I would go ahead."

"Go where? You think they are still in the building in California where they kept me?"

"Yes. No time to leave yet. Plus, I believe this has been the plan for them all along. If you converted to the Light, they would come and get you and Jessica. That old master of yours has probably wanted you dead for centuries. Just could never do it with the contract hanging over his head."

"But now my contract is gone, of course he wants me dead. And why not lure me to him with the being who converted me."

"David." Russell grabbed my shoulder. "You know it's not

~ ☾ ~

her who converted you, don't you?"

"I do not understand."

"You made a choice when you didn't kill her. When you refused to turn her over to your former master. That's where your conversion started. That's when you stepped into the prophecy." He released his grip on me.

I snatched some twigs. He had a point, yet it was still difficult to believe.

"You doubt that, but it's true. Search your heart, David. You may have been part demon for all those years, forced to kill all those people, including your wife's family, but it was never you. You never wanted that." He toed a rock embedded in the sand. "Anyone else, a bit weaker than you, would have given up. Would have given into the temptation and converted. You gutted it out for centuries."

"Thank you, Russell."

"I say all that for two reasons, *King*."

I sent a glare at him, then resumed snapping brittle twigs from a dying bush for kindling.

"One, you are an inspiration to all Guardians. Look what you endured. It gives us all hope. And two, you deserve to live with and love your mate for a long, long time for all that you've endured. Let us other Guardians handle this."

"Jessica needs action now. Other Guardians will not be to you in time. You, yourself, said she fades quickly." I shook my head. "No. Once she wakes and identifies who cursed the blade, we go after them."

"At least let Beka stop by a phone, since our cell phones have been destroyed, and call headquarters so they can send help anyway."

"Of course."

With my arms full of kindling, I turned toward the camp. Russell hurried after me.

"Where do you think this demon or witch is?" he asked.

"If it's not one of Locien's, then I have no idea. I just hope Jessica can tell us something helpful. Our time runs short." The cave came into view. "I fear the demons we found near the remains of the cabin, have relayed our location. But with only three after you, I can't imagine it was because they know

~ ☾ ~

where we are. I'm sure what you said was true, that they fell over the ledge and stumbled across you."

"Let's hope. Because when you guys leave, we're sitting ducks here."

I stopped. "You are right. We should fly you out of here and get you to a secure place. Can you bless another location, like a hotel room?"

"Sure. I can bless the cave as well."

"But your Guardian friends will have difficulty getting to you. I can carry you out of here and Beka can carry Jessica."

"*Our* Guardian friends. And you're, my k— yes, right. We should do that."

Panic seized my gut, cramping it into boulder-sized knots. The kindling scattered to the ground, and I darted into the dark cave. Beka lay sleeping beside Jessica. But Jessica's eyes were wide, her hand resting on the weapon lying between Beka and her.

"Jessica?" I whispered.

Beka jerked awake.

"What is it, honey?" Beka petted the girl's wild hair.

Her face glistened with sweat, and her chest heaved with each labored breath. Beka retracted her wing, and Jessica pushed herself up, gripping the dagger to her chest.

"You see who cursed it," I said. "Tell us. We will go kill them to save you."

She moved her head from side-to-side.

"Please. That's the only way we can save you," Beka said.

Jessica fixed her stare on me. "I'm not worth the risk you will face."

"Yes, you are." I fell to my knees beside her. "You will help many people as you helped me. I will not allow you to sacrifice that. What is it you see?"

Her gaze danced between me and Beka. Her eyes narrowed and dropped to her fingers. In that instant, I knew she'd seen Locien. Of course he would curse it himself. He knew I would challenge him. It would be his chance to kill me.

I leapt to my feet.

"What, David?" Beka stood.

~ ☾ ~

My hand navigated to my throat. "Looks like we are charging the compound after all."

~ ☾ ~

CHAPTER 42

Beka's hand tugged at mine as I stormed to the stream. "David."

My heart cracked at my ribs. I'd finally rid myself of the collar yet Locien still cinched a leash by harming Jessica. He lost me, so he went after her.

I peeled my hand from Beka's grip. It wasn't her I was mad at, but I was angry. Rage bubbled within my heart. Reminded me of the demon swirling.

My wings blasted out of my back, and I rocketed into the air. The sun hung high above me, and I aimed right for the light. The brightness seared my eyes, but I stared until I could no longer bear the pain.

I slammed my eyelids shut and neon dots spotted the darkness. My blood pulsed, strumming my inner ear like a drum. I slammed my hand against my thigh.

I knew having to face the demon who raised me was a likely possibility, but the look in Jessica's eyes when she told me, not to mention her hesitation to, made it worse. Like she worried for me. Her fear confirmed the sense of dread I wouldn't survive this encounter.

Locien was too strong for me to kill. He hid behind a vast wall of elite guards I would never penetrate.

"David." Beka's soothing voice serenaded my ears. "Not so high."

I opened my eyes and slowed my ascent.

"You'll show up on radars soon." She grabbed my toes, then my pockets, guiding herself up my body. Her wings flapped in time with mine until she reached my chest. Her feathersmot retracted, and she clung to me.

"He planned this," I said.

~ ☾ ~

"I'm sure. Locien lost you, now he wants you dead, along with Jessica. The one responsible for your Angel status."

My heart sunk. *I am no angel.*

Beka's soft fingers traced my jaw, urging me to face her. "Come on. Free fall with me so we're not so high." Her wide eyes pleaded, the skin around them crinkling.

I dipped my head. She touched a kiss to my chin and pushed away, her intense gaze fixed on me.

Her face got smaller and smaller as she dropped. Locien's building was to the west. I should go there now. On my own. They'd see me coming alone. Locien would meet me. As much as I hated him, I knew his sick mind. He would want to kill me himself. Would need the pleasure of staring into my eyes as his cold blade or black nails detached my head.

He'd done it countless times when I was under contract, but only sparks resulted. His loud, frustrated howl echoed in my brain.

He was ancient and strong, rich with magic. Tough to kill. Maybe I was created for that reason. Part Light, part dark, but stronger than both.

A gust of wind stirred my feathers. I snuck a peek at Beka. If I left, she would follow, but my speed exceeded hers. She couldn't catch me, but she would give chase, nonetheless. I couldn't allow that. Harm would come to her if she did.

I brought my wings to my body and fell. My stomach plunged from the sudden altitude change.

Beka and I should go together. I might have a chance if we fight as a team.

Locien could not survive my nails. But he would have many Elites surrounding him. I could feign offering myself back into his servitude.

A bluff would never work. He'd see through it.

The wind from the free fall howled in my ears, jerking me back to the moment. Beka's blanched wings expanded, and I approached her like a rocket. I spread my wings, stopping three feet above her.

"I'm glad you didn't go, David. I didn't want to chase you down."

"You knew?"

~ ☾ ~

"Our connection is deep, Mate." She pressed her palm over her heart. "Your struggles are my own."

I fluttered to a dead tree with thick branches below us. It supported my full weight without cracking. Beka joined me, standing only inches from me.

"You are no longer alone, David. We will fight him together. We are strong."

"He is stronger. We cannot beat him."

"Alone, no." She pawed at my mark. "Together, yes."

"He is Lucifer's right hand man. You cannot saunter up and kill him. Even an Elite Guard demon is no match for him." I shook my head. "I cannot get to him."

"You must. Or Jessica dies."

My body tensed at the thought.

"He has many who could have cursed that dagger, does he not?" she asked.

"Yes. Many dabble in the dark magiks. He surrounds himself with mystics yet knows more than most."

"He wants you to come to him. That's the only explanation as to why he, himself, cursed the dagger. You're meant to fight him. Defeat him."

"He knew I would go after whoever did it to save Jessica, you're right. Jealousy, rage and the inability to kill me has driven him mad." I clasped my hand to Beka's. "But it has also strengthened his resolve, making him more dangerous and vicious."

"He's probably relieved you didn't fully turn, you would have taken his place," Beka said. "He can kill you with blessing from Lucifer since you're an Angel now."

"Russell suggested we carry him and Jessica to a hotel. He will bless it, notify the Guardians at headquarters, then hide there until they arrive."

"Logical. There are many Guardians, possibly near us to help. We have been out of contact for a few days now since our phones were destroyed. I would guess they'd started sending some our way anyway."

"We do not have time to wait."

"I agree." She took a seat and dangled her legs over the edge of the branch. "Jessica says the cursed dagger will help

~ ☾ ~

in killing Locien."

"How do I do it?" I sat next to her and scanned the sea of treetops before us. The blue sky went on forever without a cloud anywhere.

"If the dagger is jabbed in the heart of the one who cursed it, its evil intent will take him tenfold."

"So, behead or stab him with the cursed dagger. But stabbing means a more torturous death."

She rested her hand on my thigh. "I could be the one with the dagger. You attempt to behead or expose his chest, and I'll throw it. I'm a crack shot with those things."

"Indeed you are."

"He would expect you to carry the weapon, he knows your anger, does he not? And your will."

"Yes. I think he would expect I show up on impulse, like I almost just did." I covered her hand with mine. "You want to know something demented?"

"What?"

"He is the only father I've ever known. He raised me."

"That *is* sick." She patted my thigh. "You are not his kin, David. You are a Light in this dark world. You are my husband, my mate for our entire existence."

"I am both dark and Light. Jessica said as much."

"You have a touch of darkness, held only in your wings and nails. Your heart is pure, that is what makes you the Dark Angel."

"Dark Angel." I straightened my back. "Then you are my White Angel."

"Indeed." She hopped to her feet. "Come, let's hurry and *rip some throats out* as you would say."

"Leave that kind of talk to me, okay?" I spread my wings. "Let's go."

~ ☾ ~

CHAPTER 43

"She hasn't moved in a while," Beka said as she flew next to me.

I regarded the girl in Beka's arms. She seemed to have shrunk five inches in the last day. When she'd held me during my transformation, she stood tall, filling her small five-foot-two frame with such confidence.

Now, she curled up in a ball close to Beka's chest as we flew toward town. We followed the winding road down the side of the mountain. The last sign indicated only seven miles left to a town.

Russell shifted in my grasp. "I feel like such a girl being carried like this."

"I do not particularly enjoy carrying you like this either," I said with a snicker. "We are almost there."

"It's amazing flying, though," Russell said.

"You could say that." I stared ahead, nerves on end. "I cannot go very fast holding you, though, and Beka and I need to speed to California. Jessica fades quickly."

"I'll call in the troops, they'll be here quickly." He craned his head toward Jessica. "She does not look well."

"Has she indicated how long she thinks she has?"

"No. The aloe slows the poison, I think. I will continue to take care of her. I just wish Abraham would have made it, he knew the healing arts very well."

"I am sorry."

Russell's body stiffened, and his arm straightened. "There. Motel 6. See it?"

A structure, resembling a small strip mall sat shrouded by trees. Two stories, ten navy doors on each level, and only four cars parked in the gravel lot. Perfect.

~ ☾ ~

We banked right and set down near the timber across the street. A road sign showed amenities one quarter of a mile down. "Should we move more toward the city? It is isolated out here."

"We'd have to walk. Russell will bless the room and bless the perimeter. Should work fine," Beka said. She pulled Jessica close.

"I'll go get a room." Russell scooted across the road.

"David," Jessica whispered.

I moved toward the girl. "I'm here."

"Don't listen to his lies." Her weak voice cracked. "He is a deceiver." She smacked her lips. "You are an Angel. *The* Angel."

"Dark Angel."

The corners of her pale, cracked lips flicked upward. "Dark Angel. But you fight for Light."

I brushed my hand over her sweat-dampened forehead. "I fight for you, sweet one."

My heart cracked at how frail she had become in the last few hours. She slumped against Beka's chest again. She touched her cheek to Jessica's forehead. "Hold on, honey."

"Here. Let me carry her." Beka placed her in my arms. A bag of feathers would have felt heavier. "Let's go."

We hurried across the street and Russell came out of the lobby. He held up a key, and we followed him upstairs to the room on the opposite end. He dodged into the room and to the phone. "They have some clothes in the lobby. Tourist t-shirts and stuff. Go grab some, and I'll call in the troops. Let me know when you leave." Russell turned his attention to the phone again.

I set Jessica on the bed. It dwarfed her as Beka draped the flowered covers over the girl's frail body, to her pale chin. The dark walls made for a dimly lit room, a perfect place for her to rest.

Beka blinked, her eyes moist. "Let's go."

I turned to Russell who typed in numbers on the phone keypad. "Russell, start your blessing of the room right away, we will leave for California directly from the hotel lobby after I get some clothes."

~ ☾ ~

He offered me his hand, and I grabbed it. "Return safely, my King."

Despite my dislike for the title I knew he meant it out of respect. No time to argue. "Keep Jessica safe."

He bowed his head and hung up the phone.

Beka stood by the open door. I plowed through and stomped downstairs. "You remember how to get to the building where you rescued me?"

"Yes."

"How long?"

"Few hours. We fly quickly."

We rounded the corner into the lobby. A turn-rack of folded shirts sat near the end of a tall, shiny oak desk. I snagged the first black t-shirt I saw. "This will do."

"Slide it on while I find some scissors."

I poked my head through the neck and eyed her. My face must have matched my confusion because she smiled and peeked over the front of the counter. "Hello?"

No one answered.

She held up a pair of scissors. "Wings, remember?" She flashed her back to me. Two long, tailored slits in her second-skin top paralleled her spine.

What I liked most was how the fabric clung to her body. *Focus, David.* I showed her my back. "Have at it."

Her fingers trailed my spine, sending a ripple of energy through me.

"Sorry, have to feel where to make the cuts."

"Torture." Despite the danger we prepared to face, her touch still brought forth a feverish desire.

The fabric went taught over my chest, and snipping followed. Seconds later, Beka nipped my neck. "Don't worry, husband, once this is all over, we will have a proper honeymoon back at our home in Utah."

I faced her. "We have a home?"

"It's more like a castle. We live in the twenty-first century, David, but some of the old ways still exist."

"That is why Russell always calls me King or Majesty, right?"

"You'll fit right in with your old speech."

~ ☾ ~

"I have much to learn."

"It's difficult for me sometimes, too. We'll do it together." She smiled as she dropped the scissors onto the top of the chest-high desk. "Hello?"

"Just leave some cash." I wiggled my toes. "No shoes, but at least I am no longer bareback."

Beka threw a twenty-dollar bill on the counter and faced me. "We need to get you boots. I know you heal quickly, but it'll be tough on your feet and for you to blend in when we get to the city."

"Let us hurry. We are short on time."

"Okay." She tugged my hand. "Here, out the back. It faces the trees, we can take off from there."

We hurried around the desk, and into a sitting room with orange-clad couches facing a dark TV. A cup of steaming liquid, and an open magazine sat on the side table and another cup on the table in front.

I skidded to a stop, heart hammering. "Something is not right."

A towering demon busted through the maintenance door behind Beka. A silver sword skewered her chest. Her eyes went wide, and she stumbled forward.

I roared, sounding like my old demon self, and attacked, nails out. The red monster grabbed my shoulders and turned my body. The wall met my back with such a force, the wind rushed from my lungs. Drywall rained.

Two more demons filed in from the back door and toward Beka. She groped for the sword in her back, unable to reach it. Pinned against the wall, I couldn't get to her to pull it out. I slashed at the demon, but my nails only met air.

I cranked my fists down against the crook of his elbows. His grip weakened. A quick thrust forward, and I cracked his nose with my forehead. He stumbled, his heel catching the hem of the thick rug. I swung my hand but met his forearm. On his back, he whipped his legs over him into a backward summersault and bounced to his feet.

Beka's scream rent the air. The tower in front of me blocked my view. He wore his master's mark on his forehead. Two more demons turned the corner and sprung at me,

~ ☾ ~

swords drawn.

A table propped against the wall wobbled as I inched sideways, staring at the demon, but trying to get a glimpse of Beka and her situation. Her whimpers ripped my heart to shreds. I crouched down, nails bared and out of habit I curled my lips back. No more fangs, but still...

"No," Beka yelped.

A wall of three demons blocked me from Beka. I glanced up. Cathedral ceilings. I squatted. One upsurge, and I was airborne. My wings shot out to give me height. I flipped over the demons, out of their reach and landed behind them and swung, slicing their necks from behind.

Two demon heads rolled, but one stumbled forward, grasping his neck to stop the bleeding. I pounced on the two assaulting my wife. A short demon held the sword in her back, but her flailing arms kept them from getting her hands. They didn't seem to want to kill her, neither impaled a dagger into her neck.

I buried my lethal nails in the back of the sword-holder and tore him away. I eased the blade from her body. She slumped forward. The second demon leapt into the air and came down, swinging. I spun and dropped. My heel cracked against his knee. He collapsed.

The leather surrounding his neck was no match for my claws.

"Beka."

Doors crashed open from either side of us. Demons poured in the front and from the back like steady streams of tar. I picked up a chair and vaulted it to the ceiling, aiming for the highest window.

"Beka." I leapt. "Up."

Her wings unfolded, and she sprung. A demon advanced, grabbing her right wing and jerked her down. She tossed me the sheathed dagger.

Beka thumped her other wing, banking her body around, and she planted her shoe in a demon's face. She pulled a small knife from her ankle holster and whipped it at the demon holding her wing. It spliced his throat.

Finally free, she fluttered to the ceiling, but unsteadily.

~ ☾ ~

The tip of her wing bent in an unnatural direction, but she made it to me. A quick burst sent me through the window. The glass zinged my wing, sending a sting up my shoulder.

Beka blasted out of the window and plummeted. Three daggers stuck out from her back. Two quick flaps brought me to her. Her weight altered my trajectory, and I spun.

I hit the ground, ribs crackling. Bursts of white light dusted the corners of my sight. Beka's body trembled against me as she coughed, spewing crimson-stained saliva from her mouth. I reached behind her and eased the daggers from her back. Rings of bright red blood soaked the feathers near her spine. "Beka."

Too much blood. Too much pain for my wife. I had to protect her.

Shuffling behind us propelled me to my feet, holding Beka close. "I'm okay."

I took hold of her waist and hurled her into the air. Her magnificent wings spread out in all their glory. A heavy hand anchored to my shoulder. A blunt object cracked my skull.

"David. Fly," Beka yelled.

Cold steel plunged into my side, shattering ribs, slicing through muscle and tendon. My lung seized, filling with sizzling, metallic fluid. I staggered, stars biting at my vision, but kept the dagger sheathed. It would only be used on Locien.

I dropped to my knee, holding myself steady with a palm to the ground and kicked one demon. I severed the ankles of two more standing over me. They fell back. I dove over them into a summersault. The gravel scored my skin through the fabric.

"David, up," Beka yelled.

A dagger whizzed past my face, and into the forehead of a demon lunging. I sliced through the air and banked left. "Tree tops," I said.

Beka joined my side. We rounded the corner to behind the hotel. Three men lay on the dirt ground, facedown and motionless, arms sprawled to their sides. Probably the front desk attendant, and the customers from the lobby.

With an unsteady rhythm, our wings limped us skyward.

~ ☾ ~

WASTELAND

My side throbbed in time with my racing pulse. The intensity of the attack surprised me. We passed the door to our room, and it was undisturbed. Russell must have blessed the room already, keeping the beasts out.

Twenty demons milled behind the hotel, noses to the air as if searching for something. Jessica and Russell were safe for now.

Too broken to launch an attack on those beasts, I veered right to a thick branch atop a tree beside the hotel.

Beka settled beside me. "Now *that* was most unexpected." She covered my bleeding side with her hand.

"I hope none of those daggers are cursed."

"Dark magiks don't work on us."

"Only Jessica?"

"She's an anomaly, vulnerable to age-old sorcery. We can withstand anything, but she is not immortal like us. Only thing to end us is—"

"Don't say it." The ruby line across her throat had not faded over the years. I still remember her near decapitation as if it happened five minutes ago.

Her crimson-stained fingers grazed her throat. "Sorry."

The tension in my side eased as the wound healed. "How are you, Beka?"

"Healing. Fine in a few minutes. They were Elite Guards."

"Vicious."

"What are we going to do?"

"Seems Russell blessed the room, the demons aren't going near it, so they are safe until reinforcements arrive." I stretched my hands skyward, testing the healing. A slight twinge still, but the wound was closing quickly. "We must get to Locien."

"I'm positive Russell will enlist Durk to lead the Guardians here. He is strong. Between him and Russell, Jessica will be safe. So, you're right, we must leave."

"Rushing off so quickly?" A familiar, raspy voice breached the air behind us.

My body tensed. Beka bolted to her feet. "You heard that, did you not?" I asked, my chest heaving, and my mind brimming with doubt.

~ ☾ ~

"Yes."

A blur of darkness approached from my left. It zoomed at us like a rocket and left a trail of black mist behind its base.

"What is that?" Beka asked.

The dark mass was upon us in the next breath. I shoved Beka off the branch. An unyielding force rammed my chest. I planted my hand on the branch, bark spearing my palm, but the impact knocked me from the tall tree. Surrounding twigs encroached, razoring my wings. No chance to gain altitude.

I tucked them close to my body and groped for tree limbs to slow my descent. The dried, pointy branches shredded my side, ripping my shirt with acid-laced twigs. I twisted at the waist and reached for the next branch. More scrapes, up the chest that time. The fabric snagged, slowing my descent. Another pivot, and I hugged another limb. The branch broke, and I slammed against one as big as the trunk. The jolt knocked the dagger from my grasp.

"No." I reached for it but caught only air. The coveted weapon ricocheted off the branches below me and fell toward the ground, out of sight.

"David?" Beka yelled from above. She manually climbed down the tree.

"The dagger fell." I hugged the branch close, fighting to find some air for my aching lungs.

"What was that thing?" Beka asked as she neared me.

"Seems Locien has grown a pair of wings of his own."

~ ☾ ~

CHAPTER 44

"We have to get that dagger," I said as I sat perched on a branch. I plucked three more twigs embedded beneath my skin. I raked my dark nails up and down my shirt until the wasted fabric slid off my body. More of a hindrance than anything.

"I will find it, and bring it to you. Go locate Locien." Beka flashed her bright eyes at me.

Blood splattered her forehead and her cream shirt, but still, she smiled. Such confidence. She had no doubt this would work.

That was okay. I had enough for the both of us.

I cradled her neck and tugged her to me. My lips met hers hard and fast. She returned my kiss with equal vigor. I disconnected but kept her close. "Be careful."

Her gaze dipped. "Always."

I claimed her mouth one more time, then sat straight. Time to face Locien. Beka breezed her fingers across my hand as she dove off the side. Her wings crept out a little to glide down.

I catapulted into the air to the neighboring tree and hugged its base. The bark bit into my cheek, but I held fast. There had to be an opening in this thicket for me to spread my wings.

"Come out, come out, wherever you are, little demon," Locien sang out.

I checked the sky. Overhead, a dark figure followed by a trail of mist circled. I leapt to the next tree. This one was shorter, giving me more space to expand my wings. I crouched on the highest branch that would support my weight and filled my lungs with the crisp, woodsy-scented air.

~ ☾ ~

One more check showed the blue sky. I leapt, soaring above the trees and scanned the entire area with one spin.

All clear.

My heart hammered. "Show yourself, *Demon*." My voice echoed.

"Master to you, son." He darted from the trees behind me.

I dodged his reach, spinning around. The stench of smoky sulfur smothered my senses. Anger and power. Combined, they often proved lethal.

Locien approached again, his eyes flaming red, but his once-chalky skin was coal black. Long, wings protruded from his back and flapped with a misting fury.

I hugged my wings to me and lost altitude, while holding up my hand to slash through him. I met only dark mist and came back covered in soot.

Dark magiks.

A wicked laugh ripped through the open sky. He veered left and circled back to me. I couldn't fight something that wasn't solid. I darted ahead, full speed, and he followed. I dipped, he dipped. I soared to the heavens, he mimicked.

Think, David.

He must have worked a jet engine into his demonic spell, because Locien veered below me and rocketed up. His body might be mist, but his head felt like a cannon ramming into my ribs.

Black nails lacerated my chest. He swiped at my neck. I bent my knee into his stomach and caught a solid piece. A quick flick of my wrist and my nails went through his neck.

Mist, like his body.

Only parts of him were solid?

Another guttural laugh rolled out from his fanged mouth. "I'm not called *Master* for no reason, son."

"I am not your son, *Locien*." I pushed my hand against his face, and he disconnected.

"I raised you. You're my son."

"By contract only, and if you haven't noticed my wings, the contract is gone."

"It's so much more than a contract. You have no idea." He swiped his long-nailed hand at me.

~ ☾ ~

WASTELAND

A sharp jerk of my wings, and I darted out of his range.

"I warned Lucifer you would betray us."

I hovered a safe distance away. Crimson mist sifted from his beady, red eyes as they flamed, focused on me.

"Somehow, your human side dominated, despite having demon blood in your veins."

I lunged. One swipe at his chest and one at his neck. He solidified his foot and planted it against my chest. The force sent me soaring across the sky.

I kicked my feet over my head and flipped, then sped toward the hotel, hoping Beka found the dagger. The blade to the heart must be the only way to kill him. His neck never solidified for me to sever his head.

"Can't you feel it, son? The darkness in your blood coursing through your veins."

I thrust harder, distancing myself from his pursuit. Beka's bright wings appeared in a distant treetop.

I veered toward her. Please let her have found the dagger. I glanced back, but Locien was gone. I slowed and did a revelation, scanning the skies. How did I fight that which I could not see or touch?

Keeping a keen eye on the trees below, I approached Beka. She hopped to her feet and launched into the sky. A long, dark cloud trailed her.

She fluttered to the side with the speed of a hummingbird, dodging his advance. She bolted toward me. The dark mist approached her quickly.

"Beka. Behind you."

She tucked her wings and did a free fall. The mist zoomed over her toward me. I advanced. I would meet him head on, if he solidified his head to hit me, I would snap his neck.

We collided like two Mack trucks, but when I reached for his neck, it was mist. Yet two arms encompassed my chest from behind.

"David," Beka yelled.

Locien sunk his fangs into my neck. The pain was instant and intense. The sting seared up to the base of my skull. Tendons and bones popped and crackled beneath the pressure of his jaw. It was as if he was trying to detach my

~ ☾ ~

head with his teeth.

I clawed at his stomach, but his grip limited me. His body crushed my wings to my back. No room to fly.

Suddenly, his fangs retracted. He let out a howl that burst my eardrums. Black blood spurted from his neck. He released me and swung. His palm met Beka's chin. She flipped backward.

Darkness nipped at my vision as I fell through the air, my wings cramped and bent close to my body. Locien aimed for Beka. Her scream sliced the foggy daze the blood loss and wound had caused.

She darted side-to-side, dodging Locien's vicious nails. The sun reflected something falling from Beka on that last dodge.

The dagger!

I raced toward the weapon. Locien turned and sped at the falling object. He was faster, but I was closer. I pumped my wings with a strength I didn't know I had. In seconds I was upon the weapon. I snatched it to my chest, inches from the treetops. A whoosh of cool air sifted by me as Locien zoomed past. He crashed into the trees, and another spine-tingling howl ripped through the air.

"Beka. Cave." I took off in the direction of the river, toward our special spot. I knew my former master would follow.

Beka joined me, flying close below. "He's nothing but mist."

"I know. Solidifies parts he needs. I have slid my nails over his neck, but it is never solid. I think only the knife can end him."

A dark mist wove between the trees beneath us. "Take this." I lowered to Beka and passed the dagger to her. "Come to the cave from a different direction. Use your stellar knife throwing skills when you can."

"But he's mist."

"His heart must still beat. Pierce it with the dagger. Like Jessica said."

I lowered myself to her and traced my hand against her spine. "Be careful, Mate."

"You, too." She winked. "See you soon."

~ ☾ ~

WASTELAND

She veered left, then straight up. I turned my focus to the shadowy figure in the trees below me. I only wished it was my shadow from the beaming sun overhead. Sweat trickled down my temple, stinging a cut that had yet to heal. My pulse hammered.

The trees ended, and I zoomed over the deep valley. The trees expelled a black figure. Locien flapped his wings and gained altitude.

"Sending your wife away?"

"This is between you and me. And will end with me killing you."

"You'd kill your own father?"

"You are not."

"But I am. And not just because of the contract." He groaned. "I still remember the supple breast I suckled while having my way with dear, sweet, mother, Margaret."

~ ☾ ~

CHAPTER 45

My stomach cramped, and my wings went limp, sending me plummeting to the ground. My distraction was rewarded with an iron-hard blow to my face. I jetted into the air.

"No."

"Didn't read about that in your little prophecy, did you? Did your precious Jessica share that bit of information with you?"

I aimed for the sun. He followed, keeping his distance but staying within earshot.

"Your little mother-to-be made the deal with Lucifer. After she signed, he let me loose on her, and I enjoyed every inch of her." A wicked growl spewed out from Locien's thin, black lips. "*Every* inch."

"Lies." Jessica warned me about his deception.

I tucked my wings in and dove at the demon. I stretched for his neck, but my hands went through him. His palm connected with my chin, and a burst of iron-tainted liquid gushed in my mouth. Tears ruined my vision.

The cliffs whizzed by me as I fell hard and fast to the river. *My father?*

No wonder Beka's blood blazed when it merged with mine while I held her neck together. Darkness *literally* tainted my blood. Even now, after Jessica converted me. Hence the dark wings and nails.

No. Jessica said to not be deceived. He is lying.

I flapped my wings and darted left. A screech demanded my focus. Locien approached me like a torpedo, holding a shiny dagger. My hands met his. I knew they'd have to be solid for him to hold the metal object.

I squeezed, his bones grinding beneath my grip. He

~ ☾ ~

pushed all his weight into me and put his other hand on the hilt of the dagger for added pressure. The tip neared my neck. I flapped my wings but was on my back. I couldn't maneuver well. Hadn't practiced like Beka.

The riverbed rushed toward me, specifically the massive bolder aimed to collide with my back in seconds.

"It saddens me to have to kill my offspring." Locien's rancid breath churned my gut.

"You lie."

"True. But not about this, son."

I pushed against his hand, trying to get the blade farther from my flesh.

"You are demon, no matter what kind of feathers shoot out from your back."

"No."

"Yes. No matter how often you bed your white angel, you will always be demon. You are not worthy. You will never be pure. You are *my* son. Flesh and blood demon."

"I chose the Light. No longer demon."

A roar erupted from Locien's mouth, and his strength intensified. "You've made your bed, time to lay in it. Isn't that what they say these days?"

"You're a little outdated, *Locien*." Beka's white wings came into focus like a laser beam. Her pale-skinned hand cuffed Locien's, and ripped it from me. Most of her body went through his mist, but she held onto the solid portion so he tumbled off me.

He backhanded Beka's cheek but she was relentless. He flicked his hand up, nails extended.

"Beka," I yelled.

He slashed at her neck. She ducked. His nails grated her cheek instead. She grimaced, but held on. He swiped again and nicked her neck. Her wings spread, she fluttered up and over Locien as he oriented himself to flap his wings.

"Here." Beka tossed me the dagger.

I snatched the treasure from the air and ripped off the sheath. Locien darted at me. Our weapons met with a spark. He swiped. I poked at his chest. He dodged backward, the edge grazing his stomach.

~ ☾ ~

His blade nicked my shoulder, stinging like acid on my skin. We faced one another again, hovering barely ten feet from the rocky riverbed. Beka fluttered above, her eyes shifting from me to Locien, probably searching for a time to swoop in and help.

He'd raped my mother. That image fueled my fury. I charged. I'd never known what Mother looked like, her name, or anything about her. But I'd imagined.

Not much else to do in confinement.

I'd envisioned long raven hair, height matching Beka's, but her eyes were Mediterranean blue. Her actions condemned me to over four hundred years of servitude to Locien. All the killing I'd done. All the demons I helped convert. Anger fueled my power, and I torpedoed toward Locien.

His dagger, pointed forward, rush toward me. I rolled, swiped my weapon at his neck, but it caught air. I circled around the other side of him, and jabbed my dagger into his chest.

His red eyes flamed, and he swung his knife. I bent back, evading the weapon, but kept my arm straight, my blade buried in his chest. He laughed and cracked his knuckles against my nose.

I'd missed his heart.

I pushed off him and flipped away. He was on me in the next breath, the blade cold against my throat, splicing my skin. But he stilled the weapon.

I stopped my wings. He slowed his cadence.

"I've waited four hundred years for this moment, David." He bared his fangs. "Lucifer's favorite, protected, half-breed."

I locked my fingers around the boney hand holding the knife. "Outlasted your temptations, though, didn't I?" I said while I snuck my other hand toward his chest, dagger held tight. If I was going to die, he was too. At least Jessica would live.

"David," Beka yelled.

My eyes stung. Locien's gaze flicked upward.

I stabbed.

He sliced.

Warm liquid spewed from my neck, splattering against his

~ ☾ ~

hand, and my world tilted. Stabbing rocks dug into my back. Bones crunched. Probably my wings snapping, ribs shattering. Breath rushed from my lungs, and a sharp pain ripped through my spine. Locien's face hardened, fangs bared. His mouth opened, but his tongue turned ash gray.

Soot and smoky ash streamed onto my face, scratching my eyes, stealing the air my lungs so desperately needed. My arms fell limp by my side and Locien's ashes settled over me.

"David." Beka's voice was frantic, but it sounded so far away. Muffled, like cotton filled my ears.

Streams of icy air whipped through my neck. Like wind blew right through me. I told my hand to move to my throat to cover the wound I knew gushed, but it didn't obey. Nothing did. Not even my lungs. They burned, screaming for air. I gasped, but only liquid oozed in, choking me. Gurgles bubbled in my throat.

Rocks pinged off my cheek and forehead. Beka fell to her knees beside me.

Her mouth moved but static drowned out her sweet voice. I wanted to hear it. Needed to. One last time. I knew she said my name, though. I could tell by how her mouth moved, and her teeth touched her bottom lip. Tears streamed, leaving flesh-colored streaks down her red-stained cheeks.

I felt the tugging as she clamped her hand around my neck. Her other hand slid beneath the back of my skull. I wanted to reach out and touch her silky skin, but my arms were dead weight. A chill seeped into my bones, starting at my toes, like I was being immersed in ice water.

Her mouth moved so fast, talking to me, but no sound filtered in through the thickness. Darkness curved the corners of my vision until I looked through a small hole of light. But it was Beka's face at the end of that dark tunnel. The last thing I would see would be Beka.

I could die with that.

~ ☾ ~

CHAPTER 46

I stood in the middle of an unending sea of sand. Bleached, like granules found in an hourglass. I patted my bare stomach. Warm, like the sun had baked my skin for hours. I touched my neck and found it intact. My massive, ebony wings extended from either side of me. A slight breeze ruffled the feathers, cooling them from the penetrating sun perched in the orange-tinted sky.

"Beka?" My voice echoed, yet I was in the open. Nothing surrounded me but an ocean of sand. It went as far as the skyline, making it difficult to determine where the sand ended and the sky began. "Jessica?"

Had I been banished to the wastelands? Not worthy of hell because of my wings, yet not worthy of heaven because of the demon blood tainting my veins.

No matter where I was, if it was apart from Beka, I would consider it hell.

"You are not in hell, David," a man's voice said from behind me.

I whipped around.

"Do not be afraid. I am nothing you should fear." The man smiled.

He stepped toward me, hands clasped behind his back. Brilliant pearlescent wings, with a span of twenty feet, stuck out from behind him. His towering presence threw a long shadow over me.

"Where am I?"

A breeze gusted over us. His russet hair flittered back, off his shoulders. A deep scar spanning the right side of his face glimmered beneath the sunshine. A belt around his flowing, white shirt cinched the fabric to his narrow waist and housed

~ ☾ ~

a dagger.

I couldn't get a sense of him. Friend or foe? I inched back. Grains of sand whispered over my bare feet. I readied my wings for flight.

"Where do you think you are?" he asked.

I faced the cobalt sky, then focused on the stranger. My nose tickled at the faint hint of lilac. My heart tumbled as the scent triggered images of Beka in my mind. My eyes burned.

"If I must smell Beka, yet can never touch her sweet face again, then I would assume I am in hell."

The stranger's leathery face creased as the corner of his mouth shifted into a crooked smile. "I forget, you were demon for so many years, new to the life of an Angel."

"Who are you?"

"I am Michael."

"The Archangel?"

He nodded.

"You know my mother." I scanned the never ending dunes. "Is she here?"

"No. I'm sorry, David. She sold her soul, along with yours, to Lucifer. She suffers along with the other souls he's captured."

"But you saw her. You know—" Emotion stole my voice.

"Your imagination of what she looked like was not far off, yet, her hair was red. She often wore a subtle smile, as if she knew a secret no one else did." The man studied the ground. "But she was not content with her station in life."

"Station?"

"Slave. She longed for a life of luxury, as many mortals do." He shook his head, sending his shiny hair into the air around his face. "It brought her to darkness."

"But not me."

Michael inched toward me. I retreated. He reached out his hand, but I waved him off. "Your mother did not know of your importance, otherwise, she would not have sold your soul into bondage so easily." Michael's chest puffed out, and he speared me with a stare. "You have been the prophesied Angel all along, young one. Lucifer knew this and tricked your mother into possession of your soul."

~ ☾ ~

But now I was dead. It didn't seem fair.

"We intervened to the extent we were allowed."

"Allowed?"

"We cannot impose our will among the humans. We can only present choices. Options. You had to be given a choice. So, I demanded a clause to allow you that same choice between good and evil your mother's actions stripped from you." Michael's hand went to his side.

The long, white sleeves covered his arms, to his knuckles. His loose cream-colored pants waved in the subtle breeze. My pounding heart robbed me of the breath my empty lungs craved.

"Had Lucifer not imposed his will by tricking your mother into selling your soul, you would have been born and fallen into the role as Guardian Angel. The one prophesied to join with the Guardian Queen, Rebeka David."

"Instead, Locien raped my mother, made her pregnant, then she died while birthing me." My knees buckled beneath my weight, and I slouched to the ground. I fisted palms full of sand. "The things he made me do."

Anger and hatred constricted my lungs. Acidic tears streamed down my face.

"Yet, you refused to turn your heart to darkness. You've battled every temptation thrown at you for centuries. Well, not the two and a half you spent in confinement, but for one hundred and fifty years of your contract, you resisted."

"Only to experience love, become an Angel, then die at the hands of the very being who created me." I scanned the barren, tan, surroundings. "Now, meant to spent eternity, without my Beka, here in this wasteland. I'd rather have darkness."

"You rid the earth of a strong evil presence."

"There will be another. Many *Masters* out there, are there not?" But there will never be another Beka. *My Beka*. I clenched my hands until my knuckles ached.

Michael kneeled before me. Tears streamed from his eyes as if he felt the pain ripping through my heart as his own.

"I only had Beka for a short time. Now we are apart. She is alone."

~ ☾ ~

"But Jessica is safe and Locien is dead. You have done what no other creature could have."

I gestured to my surroundings. "This is how I am repaid? I am not sure it was worth the sacrifice."

"You got to love a beautiful woman, however short of a time."

I buried my hands in the sand. Despite its heated, silky feel, I would much rather touch Beka. My chest constricted.

"You never thought of yourself as a King, able to lead anyone anyway."

My shoulders sagged. "How can I lead such good when I am the seed of such evil? Locien's blood runs through me." I peeked at Michael again. "Is that why I have dark wings and dark nails and am stuck here, between heaven and hell?"

He grinned. "The Light flowing through your veins is stronger. Light is always stronger than darkness. Even before you found it, you chose it by saving Jessica and Beka. Then, after accepting the Light, you sacrificed yourself for Jessica. Why?"

"She's worth more. She will save many people. Beka and Russell will keep her safe. She will keep many souls from this place." Tears stung at the mention of Beka's name.

"You think like a leader, yet you do not trust it."

Fountains of soft, warm sand sifted through my fingers, floating in the gentle breeze. "What is this place?"

"Somewhere your mind has created."

"My demon blood keeps me from heaven, doesn't it? Is this my afterlife? A desert, alone?"

"No." Michael stood. "You are much too precious to exil earth so quickly after coming to the Light. There are many things for you to do for us on Earth before your time expires. Yet, you sit here, in no man's land, because you do not believe yourself worthy."

"I am not worthy. I killed Beka's family. I have killed hundreds of people. I have demon blood running in my veins, I—" Tears choked my throat. "I am evil. Will always be demon."

"That is your father talking, David."

Anger skewered my gut. A heavy hand landed on my

~ ☾ ~

shoulder. I met Michael's brilliant, sapphire eyes. They welled with moisture.

"Do you not want to be with Beka?" Michael faced skyward.

The wind breathed my name. *Beka's voice.*

"Do you not want to love her? To take care of her? To protect her?" Michael released his grip on my shoulder.

"I do. I want all of that."

"Have you not already done so for her when you held her neck together? Protected her with the ferocity of a lion? And Jessica, too."

I stood. "I have. That is all I want to do for eternity if allowed."

A gust of wind sent grains of sand prickling my back. Beka's voice whispered louder. Frantic. "David," she said. "Please, David. I need you."

"She lies on the riverbed waiting for you, David. Are you willing?" Michael drifted back. His image began to fade. "You are worthy, Dark Angel. You must only believe it to be true."

I reached out for him, but my hand met air. I faced the sky. The blowing sand muted the sun's rays. Dust bit at my eyes. The wind gusted over me, lurching me forward, but I remained upright. Beka would help me lead the Guardians. She was my Queen. If I had her by my side, I could do anything. She was my mate.

I focused my thoughts on her face. "Beka. Where are you?"

Flaming sand filled my lungs, searing my throat. "Beka. I want to be with you. You're mine."

My lungs seized, and I tipped forward, face smacking the sand. Unconsciousness battled for supremacy and won. The howling wind stopped. The sand biting at my skin stopped. Then there was silence.

I must not have been worthy after all.

~ ☾ ~

CHAPTER 47

Warmth encompassed me like a blanket. Tickles on my chest lured me from the peaceful darkness. I opened my eyes, expecting the tan, dune-like place I'd been. Instead, twinkling lights on a canvas of darkness greeted me.

The air carried a hint of smoke. A crackling fire nearby. More tickles against my chest. Brilliant white feathers danced across my skin beneath the sway of a gentle breeze. *Lilacs.*

I tilted my head. Beka's sweet, ivory-skinned face lay inches from mine, her cheek resting on my shoulder. My skin prickled along my throat. Realization dawned on me, sending my heart cracking against my chest. I lay on the riverbed with my wife. Not in a barren wasteland. Not dead but alive.

I craned my neck so my lips met Beka's forehead. She jerked, her wing tightening across my stomach, and opened her eyes.

"David."

It reminded me of the voice the wind carried while talking with Michael in my wasteland. The sweetest voice I would ever hear. The only voice I ever wanted to hear. She turned onto her side, her arm snaking around my waist and pulled herself close.

"My David." Her eyes scanned my face. "You live." Tears streamed, following the contours of her cheekbones, to the crease of her lips. Her body trembled against mine.

I reached for her, thankful my arms moved at command, unlike before, and traced my thumb beneath her eye. "I heard you calling to me."

She nestled her forehead against my cheek, her body shook. The warmth of her tears flowed onto my shoulder, pooling near my collarbone. "You didn't respond for so long."

~ ☾ ~

Her voice cracked. "But you didn't turn to dust from your wound."

I nudged her with my mouth, kissing her nose, her cheek, finally reaching her sweet, soft lips. They trembled. Her hand grazed up my chest, beneath my hair to my neck. She peppered kisses along my chin, on my cheek, my eyes and my forehead.

"You're alive. You're really alive." She eased away, allowing a stream of coolness between us.

"Stay close." Felt like the desert sand coated my throat for how much it stung to speak.

She combed her fingers through my hair, pushing it off my forehead. "Are you okay?"

"I am now." I nodded. My stiff neck muscles knotted. No nodding for a while. "Locien is gone?"

"You killed him. And I thought he'd killed you." Two tears slid down her cheeks. "We now share two matching marks."

I gripped my neck. My fingers met a patch of smooth skin. A red line split Beka's ivory skin like a purple choker.

Matching marks on our chest *and* throat.

"Can you sit up?" she asked.

"As comfortable as I am with you against me, beneath the shelter of your wing, I should try."

"You've been lying here nearly two days." She shuffled back, retracting her wing.

"No wonder everything feels stiff."

She offered me her hand. "Go slow." She glanced to the side, and shook her head.

She guided me into a sitting position. My stomach cramped, and my abdominal muscles stretched until they twitched. Several people huddled a campfire ten feet from us. Russell, I recognized, but no one else felt familiar. The group watched with wide eyes.

"How does that feel?" Beka asked.

My wife knelt beside me, a hand gripping my shoulder. Dark stains spotted her shirt. Probably my blood. Her long, blond hair cascaded over her shoulders, matted and straggly. She still managed to look radiant as the pink sky spotlighted her smooth skin. My breath snagged at the view.

~ ☾ ~

"David?" She lifted my chin with her forefinger. "Are you okay?"

"Who are those people?"

"Guardians. In from Utah. Russell guessed, very well I might add, that we were here and brought them down." She let out a long sigh. "They got here late last night."

I reached for her hand. "Let's see if my legs work."

Her strong grip around my forearm, she guided me to my feet. She kept me steady by the shoulders as my equilibrium caught up with the movement.

"My wings?"

"They were mangled but retracted at impact, they've healed inside you by now."

I drew in a deep breath of the crisp, evening air. My nose twitched at the soothing scent of smoldering embers and lilac. Beka stood tall beside me, her hand resting on my shoulder. I gathered her into my arms. Her body felt like home.

No, it *was* home.

I called to my wings. Needles prickled my spine, bones repositioned, crackling beneath contracted muscles. The groan burst from my mouth before I could keep it in check.

"Breathe." Beka's warm breath swept over my neck. "Relax your muscles."

White-hot pain spliced either side of my spine. Razor blades carved their way through my insides. Popping and grinding, my feathered limbs hacked their way out.

Soft lips touched kisses down my chest. The ache lessened. Then stopped.

Wings fully extended my body sagged forward. They stirred and lifted. Beating forward softly, they enfolded my wife in a protective embrace that was warm as fever.

Beka nuzzled her forehead against my neck, and I hugged her close.

"Care to take a flight with me? Help me stretch my wings?" I nipped at her earlobe. "I have much to tell you."

She lifted her head from my neck and smiled. I unfurled my wings and eased her back. One thrust, and I was airborne. Gasps trailed behind me. I scanned the area. Seven people,

~ ☾ ~

six males and one female, stood from the ground and watched me.

Russell waved and gave me a thumbs up. Beka jumped up into the air, but circled toward the female. The girl with long charcoal hair, tossed her a package, then Beka flew toward me.

"Where is Jessica?" I asked.

"She sleeps in a tent near the fire, behind the Guardians."

"She healed okay?"

"Yes. Slowly, like you. She's still weak. Was near death."

We veered south, following the river. The moonlight reflected off the flowing water and I reveled in the earthy scent of moisture. My desert wasteland smelled only of dust and despair. My stiff wings loosened and within minutes the kinks worked themselves out, leaving the sense of freedom I'd grown to love in the short time I'd been flying.

Beka pointed to her right. "There, see the water?"

A line of trees hemmed a glass-smooth pool near the river. "Yes."

"Let's land there and clean up." She winked. "And you said you have much to tell me?"

My rubber legs sent me stumbling, but with the coordination of a newborn, I stayed upright.

"I will have the Guardians cook you much food. You must be weak."

"Feeling better by the minute, knowing I am here with you and not alone in a wasteland." I pulled her close.

She covered my mouth with hers. "I was so scared I would be alone," she said between kisses. "The cut was so deep."

"I will never leave you."

"I know now what you went through when holding me together. I hope to never go through that again."

I went to kiss her neck, but she ducked out from my embrace. "Wait, where—"

She unzipped the bag and pulled out a small, square object. She stood, staring at me and backed up to the water's edge. Her fingers went to the zipper on her shirt and tugged. Water rippled around her ankles as she stepped into the pool.

She peeled her shirt off and let it fall. My heart spiked into

~ ☾ ~

overdrive. Long, slender fingers slid over her hips, taking her stretch pants with them. The moonlight offered a silver outline of her naked body.

She waved me to her and dove into the water.

I drew in my wings, desire chasing away the fatigue gnawing at my bones. She was all I needed. All I would ever need.

I made haste shedding my ratted, blood splattered jeans and dove in. The cool, refreshing water revived my sore limbs. I surfaced and found Beka three feet away. The water lapped against her bare shoulders. Long, bright hair slicked back against her head, and her green gaze swung my direction.

"Come here." She rubbed something between her hands, barely above the water's surface. Suds bubbled in front of her.

"Turn around." She winked.

I obeyed. Her strong fingers wove through my hair, massaging my scalp. The smell of soap mingled with a hint of lilac poured over me. Her hands kneaded the knotted muscles in my neck.

"This feel okay?" Her lips feathered a kiss to my shoulder.

Thoughts scrambled. Words scattered, unable to form sentences to describe what her touch did to me. So I let out a moan.

Her body flattened against my back, and her hands grazed my chest, washing the soot away. A firestorm of heat engulfed my stomach. She paused at my neck, and I turned, rustling up gritty sand between my toes.

"I thought I'd lost you." She kneaded my chest with her soapy palms, keeping her gaze locked on my throat.

"I am sorry. I didn't mean to leave you."

Her fingers combed through my hair again, massaging. "Rinse."

I tipped back, dipping beneath the cool water, and resurfaced, free of the cleansing suds.

I reached for the bar of soap. "Let me."

I lathered and ran my hands through her hair, washing the grime and blood from the golden locks. My sudsy fingers massaged her neck, shoulders, following the slick skin to her

~ ☾ ~

breasts. She leaned back.

The moonlight reflected her smooth skin casting a glow about her. "You are so beautiful."

She turned and disappeared beneath the water. She resurfaced free of soap, and I palmed her back guiding her to me.

"This is what Michael meant about loving you." I trailed my fingers the length of her. "I know that now."

"Michael?" Beka paused, hands resting on my chest.

I wove my arms around her narrow waist. "I met him."

"The Archangel?"

I touched a kiss to her nose. "He asked me..." A kiss to her chin. "if I wanted..." A kiss to her chest. "...to stay with you." A kiss to her Mark. "To protect you and love you."

Beka clasped her hands around my neck and pulled her body flush to mine, stealing my breath more than the cool water. Heat coursed through my veins, coiling my spine.

"He sent you from heaven's door back to me?"

"I am not sure it was heaven, but it was somewhere without you, so it was hell." I tilted closer to her mouth. "He also told me of my mother." I teased my lips against hers. "And my father."

"Father?" she said, her breath ragged. Her moist tongue fanned the flames flickering beneath my skin. I chased her tongue into her mouth, and it felt like returning home. All the doubt and fear of my ability to be king dissolved beneath her feverish body.

I guided her up, and her bare legs encircled my waist. "I shall tell you everything."

We both moaned with our union.

"But first, I'd like to get back to the love part."

She tightened around me, and crushed her mouth to mine with a hunger matching my own. Fingers danced up my spine. The water rippled as I shuddered from her smoldering touch.

"Then we'll introduce you to the Guardians. They are anxious to meet their king." She pulsed against me. "But later."

I leaned in for another kiss. "Much later."

~ ☾ ~

CHAPTER 48

"How did we get these fresh clothes?" I stepped into cool denim jeans. The damp sand from the river's bank sifted between my toes.

"Nala is my lady's maid. When the Guardians started for Arizona, they brought her with. She brought clothes for me." She combed out her hair with a brush. "And Durk, one of the Guardians, is about your size. You're wearing an extra pair of his jeans."

I fastened the button. "So, Nala travels with you, wherever you go?"

She nodded.

"Human?"

"Guardian. Just a different station." She smiled. "Remember, on the roof? When Russell interrupted us, my shirt was on the ground?"

"Too well, actually."

"I'm their Queen. No one is allowed to see me indecent. Only my Lady's Maid, Nala, can assist me in dressing should I need it."

"I remember you saying that you wanted me to see you in a way no man has. But what I also remember—" I gathered her to me. "Russell stabbed me and the blade went through me and into you."

"Yes. He won't stop apologizing, either. It's been over thirty-five years, too." Batting her dark lashes, she smiled and touched a kiss to my chin. "I also remember you sinking your teeth into his neck, defending my honor."

I would always defend her honor. No matter what.

"Don't worry. He's not mentioned anything else about seeing me like that. He's too embarrassed."

~ ☾ ~

I circled my thumb over the silky fabric hiding her breasts from my sight. "No one will see you in this way again, other than me."

"Nor would I want anyone else to." She threaded her arms through mine. "I am yours and yours alone until my breath leaves me."

I buried my face in her neck, inhaling the scent streaming from her long hair. "As I am only yours, wife." Nothing ever felt so right. So true.

"We should get you to camp so your people can meet their king." She handed me a silken t-shirt. Stretchy fabric, cool to the touch.

"I am not sure what kind of king I will make, Beka, but with you by my side, I will do my best." I poked my head through the material and slid it over my chest. "A little snug."

"Nala didn't have much time to make it exact. She used Durk as the model, but had to guess where to make the slits for the wings."

"This is a shirt like yours?"

"Indeed. Can't have you walking around bareback forever. I will not stand for the other women gawking at your beauty. That is for me alone to do." She winked. "And you will do fine as king."

We let our wings unfold and took to the sky. A refreshing bath, the love of my wife, and a fresh set of clothes made me feel back to normal, if I knew what normal was, because from today forward, I was a Guardian King.

Until four days ago, I knew only the life of a demon. Now I was a husband, an Angel, and a king.

The campfire came into view. People scurried from tent to tent. My heart slammed into my chest, fearing demons had attacked in our absence. I dove toward the camp.

"Russell?"

He appeared between two tall Guardians. "What's wrong?"

"Why is everyone scurrying around? I feared a demon had come."

Beka landed beside me with a slight breeze. Her wing grazed mine, and she winked, not worried in the slightest.

"Nothing's wrong. We just prepare for your arrival. Nala

~ ☾ ~

alerted us that you were to clean up and return for introductions."

I glanced at Beka, and she dipped her head.

My heart slowed a notch, and I tucked my wings close to me but left them out. "Oh. I'm sorry. I thought..."

"That's okay. You have every right to be jumpy after all that you've been through the last few days." Russell gripped my shoulders. "I'm glad you are well, majesty."

I huffed.

"David. Sorry."

I faced Beka. "I think that will be the first rule to change. No more calling me King or Majesty."

"That might be a hard one to change for the old ones like Russell and Durk," Beka said.

A tall, husky man with a scar running down the center of his face stepped forward. "Your majesty. I am Durk, at your service."

"Of the seven here, Durk is the oldest, besides me of course," Russell said. "Behind him are Saul, Isreal, and Abarim." He motioned them near. "Come, meet your King."

A short man, with hair as bleached as Beka's feathers, stepped forward and bowed. "Majesty. I am Saul. At your service."

"I am Isreal." A thick-necked, bald man clutched my hand.

"Nice to meet you, Israel."

He moved aside, revealing a meek, timid guy. "I am Abarim, Majesty."

How would I ever remember these names?

Russell pointed to the right. "And lurking near Jessica's tent are Joshua and Andrew. Joshua is the redhead and the short guy is Andrew. I think he stopped growing when he was twelve."

A chuckle resonated from my mouth. It surprised me, because I hadn't felt any reason to laugh in so long. I'd almost forgotten how.

Russell smirked, pointed to the female, and beckoned her to us.

"Nala," Beka said with a smile.

"Your majesty." Long, charcoal hair spilled over her

~ ☾ ~

shoulders. Her ice-blue gaze bounced from me to Beka. "I am the Queen's Lady's Maid, but will assist you both should you need anything."

"Thank you, Nala." Beka twined her fingers with mine. "I couldn't have gotten through the years without you had it not been for her."

I bowed. "Then I am most grateful to you, Nala."

A ring of darkness formed on Nala's pale cheeks, and she backed away, to the fire where the rest of the Guardians gathered.

I eyed each Guardian as Beka stood by my side. "Nice to meet you all."

"David?" A squeaky, but muffled voice, shouted from behind the wall of people staring. "David?"

The click of a zipper filled the air.

"Let me through," a high-pitched voice I recognized as Jessica's said. "David."

I released Beka's hand and moved around the fire. The last time I'd seen her, Jessica was a frail pile of bones, hidden beneath a thick blanket, withering away by the hour.

Durk and Saul moved aside, and Jessica burst through them, right into my embrace. Her dainty arms linked around my neck. I hugged her close enough to feel her heart thudding against my chest. A subtle scent of peaches and vanilla wafted from her shiny hair.

"I was so worried for you." She burrowed her face to my neck. "I couldn't see what would become of you after the fight with Locien."

"No need to worry. I am here. You are okay?" I petted her hair.

She eased down from me and stood next to Durk's towering frame. "Yeah, I'm fine. Slow to heal, but getting there."

"You look much better than the last time I saw you." I offered her my hand. "Come, sit with us."

I led her to Beka, and we sat on the gravel surrounding the fire pit. Russell handed me a bowl of food, then one to Beka. "Are you hungry, Jessica?"

"Starved."

~ ☾ ~

"I'll be back with another bowl. Eat up majesties. We leave at sunrise," Russell said.

"You killed Locien." A grin filled Jessica's face.

"With Beka's help."

"I knew you would, but I was scared."

"Scared he would die?" Beka asked.

Russell approached with another bowl. He settled near Jessica and completed our half circle around the fire.

"Taste good?" Russell asked.

I took a bite of the hearty stew. "Thank you. I am famished."

"Two days you were out of it. Rebeka wouldn't leave your side," Russell said. "She refused to give up on you."

I winked at my wife, then focused on Jessica. "Did you know he was my father?"

Russell gasped. A murmur rolled through those surrounding us. Besides Durk, I didn't remember any of the names. That would take time, and I didn't even know how many others there were at home.

"Yeah. I guess I did." Jessica studied her untouched food.

"Your father? Who? What?" Russell asked.

"Why did you not tell me?" I asked Jessica.

"Would that have made a difference?"

"No."

"You say that now. But had I told you up front he was your father, things might have turned out differently." She picked at her bowl of stew.

"How is he your father?" Russell asked. "That's impossible."

I studied my fork. Images of Locien raping my mother flashed before my eyes. I'd never seen her before, but the thought of someone violating my Beka in such a manner made my blood pulse with rage.

"His mother made the deal with Lucifer, then Locien raped her. It was one big, dirty, disgusting plan," Jessica said. "From day one."

"Plan?" Russell set his empty bowl on the sand.

Amber flecks deep within Jessica's chestnut eyes flickered. "Lucifer knew all along your mother was to give birth to the

~ ☾ ~

prophesied angel destined to unite with Rebeka. He tricked your mother, she sold your soul, and hers, then she died while giving birth to you. Locien figured that if his blood flowed through you, you'd give in to darkness immediately and embrace your demon nature. He tried to take your right to choose away."

"But you remained strong and resisted." Beka teased her hand up my spine, sucking the breath from my lungs. "For me."

"Locien thought it would bring favor for him in Lucifer's eyes to have fathered the angel, and to sway him to darkness. He didn't know about the Archangel clause." Jessica smiled. "And when you kept resisting, and he couldn't kill you, it drove him nuts."

"Nuts?" Russell asked.

I set my empty bowl on the sandy gravel in front of me. Within seconds, Durk retrieved it and replaced it with a full one. He bowed his head and resumed his place behind Jessica.

Having my every need met so readily would take getting used to. Centuries of deprivation of one sort or another left me used to being in want.

"Locien found out about the plan for David's ascension to King of the Underworld, so he needed David either human or demon, then he could kill him. No contract meant no protection over the wrists and neck." Jessica slurped up the rest of her stew but kept the bowl in her lap.

"I can't believe all of this." Beka twined her fingers with mine. "You told me about Locien being your father, your mother and your visit with Michael, but not all this other planning that has gone on for centuries."

"Wait. Michael?" Russell asked.

I glanced at Beka, then faced Russell and Jessica. "Michael told me some things."

"How?" Jessica asked.

"While I was dead. I banished myself to a wasteland. He came and talked me out of it." I scooped stew into my mouth. Its savory essence coated my tongue, and the warmth enveloped my stomach.

~ ☾ ~

Jessica tilted toward me. "You feel you're not worthy to be King."

I nodded.

"That's why you sent yourself to the wasteland. Not sure where you fit in because of your demon heritage." She slapped my shoulder. "I see how that can happen."

It was so strange to talk of things centuries old with a girl who appeared no older than seventeen. She spoke with such slang I was sure she was human. Yet ancient words sprinkled her modern language.

"I felt your pain." Jessica grabbed her neck. "I was scared you were lost to us." She shivered. "We need you."

I bowed my head. Such wise talk from a young person. I would learn much from her.

"You met Michael, huh? What'd you think of him?" Jessica turned on her charm like a flick of a switch.

"Have you met him as well?" I asked.

"How do you think I get my knowledge?" Jessica chuckled. "But I don't meet him in a wasteland."

"You see the Archangel?" Beka asked. "How?"

"Visions, dreams, mostly while I was unconscious those few days before my conversion. We talked a lot." The campfire shimmered in her eyes. "He downloaded a bunch of information into my brain. That's why I stumble with speech sometimes. I mean, I have my way of talking, then his weird, old words kick in sometimes. Makes my head hurt."

"Amazing," Beka said.

"Sometimes I feel like my brain is about to melt. But he hasn't visited me in a while, not since that darn dagger stuck me." She pinned me with a stare. "But I knew you'd save me. Never doubted you for a minute."

"I think you did. You almost didn't tell me who cursed the dagger," I said.

She put up her hands in surrender. "My *one* moment of weakness. But after that, I never doubted. I knew, once I saw that flicker of determination in your eyes, that you'd kill him for me." She smiled. "I'm just glad you didn't go after him by yourself."

"Trust me, he thought about it," Beka said. "But we're

~ ☾ ~

strongest together, aren't we, King?" She leaned toward me.

"Yes. I was tempted." I rested my hand on her knee and inched closer to her warmth.

"What did Michael look like to you?" Jessica asked.

"Pardon?"

"When I see him, he has long blond hair, down to his butt, sparkling green eyes and wears skinny jeans and a long sleeved shirt." The skin at the corner of her eyes crinkled with her smile.

"That is not how he looked to me, why is that?"

"He gets into our head, helps us see him in a form we'd appreciate. Some of the thoughts he puts in us are a little tough to handle. This way just makes it easier for us to see him. Hear what he has to say." She toed the sand. "That's my theory anyway. I'll have to ask him next time."

I turned to Beka. "Have you seen him?"

"No. I hear his whisperings, but never see him."

"So now what?" Russell said. "Locien's dead, the demons retreated."

"For now," I said.

Jessica sat straight and giggled.

"What?"

"Already thinking like a King." She punched my shoulder. "Go on, what were you going to say, *King?*"

I glanced at Beka. "I think I would like to see this new home of ours."

~ ☾ ~

EPILOGUE

"No moat?" I said as we flew toward our home.
Beka laughed.
"It is chilly up here." The cool air whipped past me as I coasted toward the massive, brick house. Clouds hovered high in the bright, blue sky, but the sun didn't warm me as I would have thought.
"Come on, I'm tired, it's been a long few days. I just want to sink into a toasty, comfortable bed with you." She winked. "I promised you a *real* honeymoon. No more making love in caves or on rocky riverbeds."
"Those places were nice, but I should like to try the comfort of a soft mattress to learn more about your body." I darted out in front of her, my body tensing in anticipation. "Hurry."
She chased after me. I banked left and came in above her. She led me toward the rooftop. It wasn't quite a castle, but close. Massive lawns surrounded the sprawling estate. Six pools of water, lakes maybe, spotted the property.
People milled around equal distance between them. Standing post. I assumed they were on guard the way they kept a careful eye on us, probably unsure of me and my dark wings. Such a contrast to Beka's fair feathers flapping gracefully next to me.
"So, you said thirty Guardians live here?"
"Not at all times. There are thirty Guardians housed here. But, they go to different cities, wherever the need arises."
"And how do you know where to send them?"
"Hold that thought." She pointed and slowed.
I veered right, watching her land on a sprawling roof patio that led to a set of ashen French doors. I folded my wings

~ ☾ ~

close to me and descended. The cold, tile patio sent a chill up my legs through my bare feet. The sun was definitely less potent here in Utah than in Arizona.

"We know where to send the Guardians the same way I knew how to locate Jessica. A gentle whisper, from the Archangel, only my connection to Michael is not like what he has with Jessica." She paused, regarding me while her hand rested on the door handle. "Although, I wonder if you might have an even closer connection. He did appear to you in the wastelands. You're at your rightful position as king now. Direction might come through you."

"I guess we will find out. But it felt like his appearance was a one-time thing, to get me out of that place I banished myself to and back to you."

Her hands found a home on my chest. "I know you doubt your ability to be a good leader for these Guardians, but I don't. All you've been through, all that you've endured, has made you into something very powerful, very good, and very desirable."

I smiled and combed my fingers through her silky hair.

"And the seven who were with us in Arizona immediately accepted you. Pledged their fealty to you." She brushed her lips against my cheek. "Just remember that, okay?"

"Do we have to meet everyone right away? Or might you have time to show me that bed you spoke of."

"See, we'll have no problem ruling the Guardians. We already think so much alike." She flashed her bright eyes at me. "I landed on the balcony connected to our bedroom, because that's the only place we will be for the next couple of days."

"I think I will enjoy being King." I pulled the door open. "Lead the way, my Queen."

~ ☾ ~

LYNN RUSH

Lynn Rush began her writing career in 2008 and is actively involved with Romance Writers of America (RWA) and its special interest chapter Fantasy, Futuristic and Paranormal (FF&P).

Lynn has both an undergraduate and graduate degree in the mental health field and has enjoyed applying that unique knowledge to developing interesting characters.

When Lynn's not writing, she spends time enjoying the Arizona sunshine by road biking with her husband of fifteen years and going on five-mile jogs with her loveable Shetland Sheep dogs.

She always makes time to read a good speculative fiction novel, her favorites being Frank Peretti, Vicki Pettersson, Charlaine Harris and Stephanie Meyer.

Catch the Rush online:
Website: www.LynnRush.com
Facebook: www.facebook.com/LynnRushWrites
Twitter: www.twitter.com/LynnRush